I0658028

WHAT TRICKERY IS THIS?

SAM CHEEVER

ELECTRIC PROSE PUBLICATIONS

ABOUT ROME

Crafting worlds is crazy good fun. Authors love to make stuff up. Sometimes locations that are created for books seem like real places, even though they're not. That's actually good, because it means the author has done her job well. My fictional town of Rome, Indiana is not based on a real place. I've created a location that lives in my mind—one that fits the stories I wanted to tell. Hopefully you have enjoyed the picturesque town of Rome with all its paranormal challenges. I'm thankful for the opportunity to share this fictional town and its inhabitants with you.

xo

Sam Cheever

PRAISE FOR SAM CHEEVER

"You have that essential Je ne sais quoi that it takes to tell a story so mesmerizing you cannot stop reading once started. You are not telling stories to your readers...you are taking them with you on your adventures so that the experience can be shared by all as it happens and not simply replayed like a memory on the page of a diary! You are indeed gifted and it is my pleasure to read your books!"

Valerie Irwin

One of the great things about midlife is having the experience and knowledge that comes from decades of navigating jerks and mansplainers. Unfortunately, I had nothing in my repertoire to help me deal with a true Trickster.

Amid magical mushrooms, ghosts popping up in unexpected places, dangerous predators, strange pregnancies, barking cats, meowing dogs, and an endless array of other weirdness, I'm facing a foe unlike any I've encountered before as Lares of Rome. My new enemy is determined to destroy my dominion, and he doesn't care who he takes out in the effort.

He probably doesn't realize it yet, but he's in for a shipload of a battle. It's going to take the combined effort of an entire town and all of my council and allies, but I have no intention of giving my people over to the type of madness the Trickster generates.

THE LARES MUST HER INSTINCTS TRUST

A Trickster's wiles for men are dire, the world they
know is under fire, should the guardian hope to rule
the day, the Prankster's game she must not play,
When up is down and down is up, the Lares must
her instincts trust,

The World Implodes, a Trickster's Aim
Reality a Sucker's Game
What's Up is Down and Down is Up
A Lares Must Her Dignity Shuck
When Demons Call to Offer Aid
The Price in Blood is Surely Paid
An Unplanned Trip, A Witch's Ploy
The Trickster's Jest Will Give No Joy
Through Weariness and Desperate Times
A Rabid Royal Will Cross the Line
The Jester's Evil at the Helm

A Human Cop is Overwhelmed
A Terrible Wrong, a Fairy's Plight
Friend or Foe? Trust doth Take Flight
A Child is Born? The Prankster's Will
Loss of Control A Bitter Pill
The Demon's Lair A Deadly Goal
Terror Digs The Deepest Hole
The Warden's Pow'r A Fool Doth Thwart
The Queen her Subjects' Lives Abort
A Worm A Worm A Worm For You
The Search Alas Has Spawned Anew
Come Fang, Come Claw, and Deadly Beak
The Lares' Future May Seem Bleak
All Things Are Right. All Things Are Good. Just
Give the Pixie a Little Blood.

STAY IN TOUCH

Sam doesn't give away a lot of books. But she values her readers and, to show it, she's gifting you a copy of a fun book just for signing up for her newsletter!

SIGN UP HERE!
https://samcheever.com/newsletter/

1

THE WORLD IMPLODES, A
TRICKSTER'S AIM

"If that bell rings one more time...."

Gong!

"Goddess in a girdle!" I yelled to no one in particular. "Please make it stop!"

Gong!

"Aggy?"

I spun on my heel, spearing the intruder with what had to be a slightly crazy look. My straight black hair was probably standing up on end from me constantly running my fingers through it. My clothes were rumpled and stained with a hurriedly consumed breakfast of coffee and a donut. My breath smelled like the back end of a goat.

Wanda, my sixteen-year-old ward and the magical historian on my council, stared at me through eyes that were so brown they looked black, her lips twitching. "Bad day?" she asked, her eyes sparkling with humor.

I closed my eyes and pulled air into my lungs, fighting for calm.

Gong!

Control flew away on gossamer wings, dumping me into the pits of despair. "I'm losing my mind. How can there be so many crises in one day?"

Wanda's humor softened a bit, her gaze skimming guiltily away.

I narrowed my eyes on her. "What?"

She skimmed a lock of shoulder-length dark hair off her cheek and stared at her shoes, which were black high-tops and looked really cute with the short black skirt and black blouse she was wearing. Since coming to live with me, the teen had upped her fashion game...reluctantly at first...and she was finally showing signs of enjoying the shopping thing. Though she still bought everything in black.

At my nosy insistence, the teen's shopping sprees were courtesy of her father the demon, who had more money than the goddess herself and owed Wanda at least that since leaving her trapped inside a Groundhog Day spell for years when he could have saved her.

Long story.

"Talk to me," I told Wanda. "Why are you having trouble meeting my gaze?"

Contrary to the end, the teen lifted her eyes and glared at me. "I am not."

I arched my brows, hands on hips, and she sighed.

"Why do you always assume I've done something wrong?"

I bit back an angry retort. I didn't assume...well... not always. It was just that she usually looked so guilty when she told me stuff.

Or maybe it was embarrassment. I wasn't very good at recognizing the difference. I could handle most adults, but teens were a whole other species. Like Wanda, I was working on finding a clear path through our new living situation. Unused to kids in general and a new roomie in particular, I knew I was messing up right and left. I walked over and tipped up her chin, looking into her cute and stormy face. "I'm sorry. You're right. I shouldn't assume things. I'm a little frazzled because the town has gone crazy, and this job is going to put me into an early grave."

The teen relented, her expression softening to regret. To my shock, she wrapped her skinny arms around my waist and let me hug her. "I'm sorry."

"Why are you sorry?" I asked, crushing her to me and feeling like the worst kind of monster for making her sad.

"Because I need to give you another problem."

I pulled back, trying to keep my expression neutral. "What's happened?"

She winced. "I think you need to see it to believe it."

We stared at each other for another beat and then I nodded, wishing I could flee to the woods for some feral screaming therapy. "Okay, then. Lead the way."

It took us an hour to get where we were going. It wasn't that the distance was far. It wasn't. But, along the way, I had to stop the car two times to deal with problems.

My neighbor across the street was screaming bloody murder as I pulled out of my drive. The woman was in her late seventies and I hadn't even known she could vocalize that loudly. Her shrieks had brought the neighbors from all around out of their houses, but nobody had gone near her.

From the flailing of pale limbs near the top of a big oak, I deduced that she had somehow climbed the tree. A small orange and black cat sat on the ground, looking up at the woman as if she'd lost her mind.

After watching my neighbor's hysterical antics in the tree, I couldn't disagree with the tiny feline.

I stopped my ancient Range Rover on the shoulder in front of her house and climbed out, hailing the first person I saw to explain what I was seeing.

The man, who claimed he lived in the small ranch next door, motioned toward the woman and shook his head. "Nobody knows what's going on with her. She's been caterwauling like that for twenty minutes. She's delusional."

Standing beside him, an attractive woman with long, light-brown hair and a jam-painted toddler on her hip nodded in agreement. "She's screaming at poor Rufus, throwing sticks at him."

"Rufus?" Wanda asked, joining the group.

The man nodded, running a calloused hand through a thick mop of dirty blond hair. "Her cat." The man pointed toward the tiny feline.

"She's afraid of that little cat?" I asked, surprise threading my voice.

"She thinks he's a tiger," the woman said, frowning slightly. "I'm afraid she'll hurt him."

"Does she have a history of mental illness?" I asked. I hadn't lived on the street long enough to know everybody's history, but I had spoken to the elderly woman a few times and she'd seemed perfectly fine to me.

The woman with the toddler shrugged. "I don't think so. She usually seems very normal."

I walked over to the tree and looked up through the densely leafed limbs. "Mrs. Twimblee, it's Aggy from across the street. I'm the one who's renovating the old church," I reminded her. "Can you tell me what's wrong?"

The woman pointed a bent finger toward the tiny

cat. "Get away from him!" she shrieked. "Tigers eat people."

I walked over and scooped up the little cat. Rufus rubbed his face under my chin, purring like a champ. "Look, Mrs. Twimblee, he's fine. He's just your sweet little cat."

A stick flew out of the tree and whacked me on the forehead. "Witch!"

I walked back to the young couple from next door, bringing poor Rufus with me. "I'll call the fire department to get Mrs. Twimblee out of the tree. She'll need to be admitted to the hospital for treatment. Maybe she has Meningitis or something that's affecting her thought processes."

"Somethin's surely messin' with her mind," the man agreed.

I nodded. "Do you know if she has family? Someone will need to take care of Rufus until she's back on her feet."

The young woman shook her head. "No family that I know of. But Gregory and I will keep him for her. He's a sweet little kitty."

"You wouldn't mind?" Relief slid through me.

"'Course not," Gregory said, taking the cat from me. "We'll keep him safe until Mrs. Twimblee's better."

"Thanks for helping. You're good neighbors." I walked back to the car, leaving Wanda to play in the grass with the toddler, an adorable little girl with blonde hair and bright blue eyes, and the kitten. I called Chief Davis Marshal, Rome's head cop, and told him the problem. He sounded harried but assured me he'd get someone to Mrs. Twimblee's house as soon as possible.

Wanda and I left once the fire truck arrived. We managed to make it two whole miles up the road before we had to stop again. A woman stood in the middle of the gravel road leading into Rome. She was staring down at her stomach, her hands flattened against a rounded belly. I climbed out of the car and walked over, calling out to her as I approached. "Is everything all right?"

The woman didn't seem to hear me.

"Miss?" I reached out and touched her arm. She slowly lifted her gaze to mine, a look of pure wonder in her expression. "Are you all right?"

She rubbed a hand over her belly as I'd seen many pregnant women do. "How did this happen?" she asked me.

Behind me, Wanda snorted. I flapped a hand to shush her.

"How did what happen?" I asked, wanting to make sure I understood what she was asking.

She looked back down to her belly, her hands sliding over the obvious bump. "I can't be pregnant."

Ah, denial. She was simply in shock. Though it looked as if she was at least four or five months along. It seemed kind of late to have just noticed. "Have you talked to the father about it?"

She shook her head. "I haven't even been..." she slid a glance toward Wanda and blushed. "I haven't been *with* a man." She whispered the word "with."

My hazel eyes went wide. "Are you sure?"

Her head lifted, and she gave me a look.

I flushed with embarrassment. "Sorry. But there's only one way to get...you know...that way."

"Maybe it's a huge tumor," Wanda said helpfully.

The woman jolted and paled, her eyes going round. "Tumor?"

I caught her as she nearly fainted. "I'm sure it's not a tumor," I said, throwing Wanda a look.

The teen shrugged, unconcerned. Wanda was a straightforward kind of person. She didn't mince words. That could be good. Or it could be very bad. "Have you been to see your doctor?"

"No." She glanced around, seemingly surprised to find herself in the middle of the road. "I was just going for a walk, and then I found this." She caressed the bump again. "I should go call her, huh? My doctor?"

"Yes," I said, relieved. "You should go inside right now and call. I'm sure it will be okay."

I watched until she entered her house and then climbed back into my car, bumping my forehead against the steering wheel.

Wanda was quiet. I appreciated that she gave me a minute to pull myself together.

"Okay," I said a minute later. "Where am I going?"

"Are you sure you're up for this?" she asked, fixing me with a doubtful look.

"I'm good," I said, knowing it was a lie. "Better than good. Whatever this new problem is you're about to show me, I'm going to knock it out of the park."

"Mm-hm," Wanda said. "I wouldn't be so sure about that."

I stood with my mouth hanging open, completely out of my league. The teen standing in front of me stared back, her brown eyes impossibly wide. "Can you get it off me?" she asked hopefully.

My heart broke because I was going to have to disappoint her. I glanced at Wanda. "Can I speak to you for a minute?"

Wanda nodded, gave the girl a supportive smile, and led me out of the room. Closing the bedroom door behind us, I pulled Wanda down the hall so the teen couldn't hear our conversation. "Before I try to fix this, I need to know if...."

"Becca," she supplied for me again.

The name had just flown right out of my head after casting eyes on her. "Becca, yes. I need to know if she's one of us."

Wanda lifted her brows. "One of us?"

"Magical."

"Ah," Wanda looked relieved. "Yes. She's Fae, but she hasn't come into her magic yet."

I nodded. "She knows about magic, though?"

"Yes. Do you think you can help her?"

I grimaced. "No. But I was thinking maybe I could send the coven over. They've surely got something..." I broke off, turning a doubtful look toward the girl's closed door. "How did this happen?" I asked Wanda.

She shrugged. "The park has erupted in wizrooms. Maybe it has something to do with that."

I scrunched my face. "What are wizrooms?"

"Magical mushrooms. They give off a powder at dawn and dusk that hexes anybody it touches. Nasty things. I'm surprised you didn't get a summons for them."

Guilt washed through me in a wave. I *had* gotten a summons. Late last night. I'd been running around dealing with dozens of small problems that I'd thought were unrelated, and I'd believed a bunch of mushrooms could wait.

I rubbed a hand over my face. "My bad. I pushed them to the bottom of a long, long list." A terrible realization hit me "All of this stuff we've been dealing with has probably been related to those stupid wizrooms."

Wanda nodded. "Maybe." She glanced toward Becca's door. "We need to tell her."

I sighed. "I'll do it. It's my fault she's in this predicament."

"You should know, if it's the wizrooms, the effects will last until they bloom again."

Gripping the door handle, I grimaced. "How long will that be?"

"A year."

"Curse, swear, curse, curse," I murmured. Then I pushed the door open and went inside to tell a sixteen-year-old girl that she might have to live with silver-dollar-sized pink and purple polka dots all over her body for a full year.

Fighting three deadly Leviathans at the bottom of an ocean suddenly sounded preferable.

2

REALITY A SUCKER'S GAME

Wanda and I were heading to the Rome Police station when I got another summons. I jerked as if I'd been stabbed with a live electric wire and slammed the brake pedal hard enough to leave rubber on the road.

Bracing herself on the dashboard with two hands, Wanda turned a questioning gaze my way.

"We're going to the OB/GYN," I said, by way of explanation.

Her dark brows lifted. "You're pregnant?" The brows danced above her dark gaze. "Have you and our favorite angel been doing the naughty?"

Despite a maturity that had been hard-won through forty-five years of living, I blushed. The thought of doing anything naughty with Lungren Maker made me sweat and tightened my belly in a very pleasant way. I decided it was best to just ignore her question. "Apparently, the doctor has something to show us."

Wanda chuckled softly but didn't tease me again.

To my vast relief.

My relationship with Gren was one of the best parts of my new life. He'd brought feelings and emotions to life that I thought had died years earlier. But it was a new thing, still timid and green, struggling for life, and I didn't want to overthink it for fear I'd kill it on its tender young vine.

I pulled up in front of the Rome Medical Center and parked.

Wanda hopped out of the car with the endless energy of youth. I climbed out on a groan, willing my sore muscles to stop trying to strangle my bones and allow me to walk alongside the teen without looking like Quasimodo.

I mostly achieved my goal.

It had been a while since I'd entered the office of Meredith Lawson, Obstetrician/Gynecologist and closet fertility goddess. I'd been going to Doc Lawson for a couple of decades and had only recently realized she was magical. Imagine my surprise when I found out what she was. I'd canceled my annual checkup with her the previous month, telling myself I didn't have time. It was *minutely* possible that I was afraid her fertility proficiencies might somehow infect me.

My logical brain knew that I'd need to actually

engage in activities that caused that type of infection. I wasn't in any danger on that front. Though, the thought made me wince, realizing I really had no excuse to continue avoiding my yearly checkup and stirrup party.

Curse!

Wanda's eyes went wide as she looked around the busy waiting area. She leaned close and whispered into my ear. "Looks like Rome is about to have a population explosion."

She wasn't wrong. I'd never seen so many pregnant women gathered together in one spot before. One of the women even had graying hair and looked to be in her late fifties.

I strode up to the check-in counter. The woman behind the glass smiled at me, tucking a strand of graying brown hair behind her ear. "Hey, Aggy. What do you need?"

"Doctor Lawson wanted to see me," I told her.

The woman nodded. "Let me see if she's available...." Her voice trailed off as the door to the exam rooms opened, and Dr. Lawson stuck her head out. Her round face was too pale, and her eyes looked a little wild. She motioned for us to come back.

As soon as the door closed behind her, Dr. Lawson grabbed my arm, her eyes so large I worried they'd pop out of her head. "You need to see this!" she said in a slightly hysterical tone. She all but dragged me down the hallway and into her office, closing and locking the door behind us.

I swung a look at Wanda, and the teen gave me a wide-eyed look that told me she thought the doctor was acting crazy. I agreed. My experiences with Meredith Lawson had been positive and comfortable. She'd always struck me as a calm, professional woman who, admittedly, didn't have much of a sense of humor but whose manner was soothing enough to make even a jaunt in the exam stirrups slightly less humiliating.

"What's wrong?" I asked her, reaching for her hand to soothe.

But the doc whipped around, striding quickly out of my reach, and pointed to several x-rays she'd clipped onto the lighted reader on the wall. "Look at these!"

I blinked. I was many things...some of which I was just learning about...but I was pretty sure I hadn't acquired a medical degree with my guardianship of Rome, Indiana. "Okay," I said, squinting at the hazy gray pictures. "I'm looking. But I have no idea what I'm looking at," I admitted.

"You're looking at ultrasounds of the wombs of several of my patients." She ran a finger over an area in each that seemed more storm-cloud colored than charcoal. "This area here is empty in all of them."

"Ookaay," I said, unsure what she was trying to tell me.

"There should be babies there!" she exclaimed in a voice that stepped over the border into hysteria.

I glanced at Wanda, only to find the teen staring intently at the x-rays.

"Aggy, do you understand what I'm telling you?" Doc Lawson screeched.

I didn't. But I had a feeling that if I admitted my cluelessness, the doc might launch into the ceiling tiles, and I'd have to yank her back out.

Fortunately, Wanda saved us both. "Those women out there, in the waiting room. They looked pregnant."

Doc Lawson nodded enthusiastically. "Exactly."

I thought of the young woman in the road, staring bug-eyed at her belly as if she'd never seen it before, and what the doc was telling me finally sank in. "They're not really pregnant, are they?"

"No!" she exclaimed. "They're not."

Swear, curse, swear, swear! What was going on in my beloved Rome?

Wanda and I were back in the Range Rover, heading to see Chief Davis Marshal. I had let Doc Lawson vent for a few minutes, then promised to look into what might be causing the faux pregnancies in Rome.

Aside from the obvious problem with the situation, there was the added fear of what it would do to some of those young women when they found out they weren't really carrying a child in their burgeoning bodies.

"Could the wizrooms have caused the fake pregnancies?" I asked Wanda.

The teen didn't even hesitate before shaking her head. "It could be, but I don't think so. I've never heard of this before."

That made two of us. Actually, three, counting the doc. "Maybe there is literally something in the water that's fooling women's bodies into thinking they're pregnant?" I suggested.

"It would have to be magical, whatever it is. That woman in the street said her stomach just appeared, from one minute to the next."

I fought the urge to touch my belly to make sure it wasn't rounder than it had been that morning, only resisting because I'd had two bagels earlier. It would be embarrassing for Doc Lawson to ultrasound my round belly and pronounce me the proud parent of bagel twins.

I parked on the street in front of the Rome Police Station and linked my arm through Wanda's, giving her a smile as we headed into the narrow alley that hid the entrance to Chief Marshal's domain.

We pushed open the scarred, wooden door and

stepped into pure chaos. Wanda and I stood at the bottom of three wide steps that led to the station's lobby area. We didn't move forward because we couldn't. The place was wall-to-wall people, the room throbbing with voices and taut with an array of negative emotions.

Two of the town's uniformed cops were trying to make their way toward the door, but the crowd kept swarming them, at times aggressive and then frantic with need.

Above all the voices, I heard Chief Marshal's deep voice, trying to be heard above the roar.

"That's enough!" he finally bellowed. "We need to organize this, or nobody's going to get heard."

I glanced at Wanda. She made a face. "Can you do anything?" She had to shout to be heard above the noise. The people in front of us turned to glare at her as if she'd suggested shoving our way to the front.

I thought about my resources. Most of what I used was defensive. But I'd been practicing with my powers, and I thought I might be able to inject some calm into the room. I closed my eyes, opening my hands and feeling the warmth of my Lares energy spreading through my palms. I infused the energy with as much calm as I could gather, which, given the events of my morning, probably wasn't nearly enough. Then I instilled the calm with a gentle suggestion to return home and wait for someone to come to them to help. The sweet scent of lavender rose into the air around me, snapping my eyes open.

The magic was visible, like a soft purple mist that rose into the room and spread through the crowd. The chaos didn't change for a long moment, making me believe my attempt had failed. But then, slowly, the noise started to lessen. The erratic energy of the crowd slowed.

The two young officers moved through the becalmed people and pushed past Wanda and me, opening the doors and moving into the alley.

"Officers Wendt and Bristle will take down your names and contact information," Chief Marshal told the crowd, which was turning toward the door and moving calmly toward the stairs. "Someone will visit you at home and take your statements."

Wanda and I flattened ourselves against the wall and waited until everyone had filtered out of the room. Then we went upstairs, only to find the Marshal sitting behind his desk, his head in his hands and his broad shoulders drooping.

He looked impossibly tired, and when he lifted his gaze to mine, I saw more than weariness in their dark blue depths. "Aggy. Thank heaven. I wondered why they'd suddenly calmed down. I'll never be able to thank you enough for that."

I sat down in the chair in front of his desk.

Wanda drifted around the room, checking out the framed accolades and stories of the chief's good work in Rome. The space didn't hold much else. Aside from the chief's oversized desk and the two hard wooden chairs facing it, there was only a folding table with coffee fixings and two doors. One of which led to a small bathroom, and the other led to the cells, which had been spelled to contain magical as well as human prisoners.

"What's going on?" I asked the chief.

He rubbed the heels of his hands over his eyes. "I wish I knew. It's been like this since yesterday. The entire town has gone crazy." He jerked his head toward the door to the cells. "My jail is full. Every cell has at least five people in it. Magical folks as well as humans. This town hasn't seen so much crime since I've been a cop in Rome. And that's a long dang time."

I told him about some of the things I'd been dealing with.

The chief listened intently, and I got the feeling he was desperate for an explanation for the chaos. "Do you have any idea what might be causing this?" he asked when I was done.

"Maybe it's these wizrooms Wanda told me about," I suggested. I'd mostly just offered the possibility to take a little of the haunted look out of his tired eyes. "We need to eradicate those as quickly as possible."

He nodded. "Any chance your people can take care of that? My guys are going to have their hands full with all the interviews." He dropped back into his chair, looking as if he might cry. "I'm going to have to bring in a few temporary cops if this keeps up."

"I'll send Niele out to deal with them," I told him. The gnome was not only my groundskeeper and, therefore, an expert in all things green and growing, but he was also a member of my council and a trusted friend. "Is there anything else I can do?"

The chief leaned forward, placing his elbows on his desk. He looked me right in the eye. "If you took this knowledge of magic away from me, would all these magical problems go away too?"

I felt a grin tugging at my lips. "'Fraid not. But if you find a way to make that happen, you'll let me know, right? I could use a little vacation."

He nodded. "Done. Seriously though, did you have a reason for coming?"

"I just thought I should check in. I hadn't heard from you for a while. Maybe my people and I can take a few problems off your plate."

"I'd be forever in your debt." Chief Marshal stood and offered me his hand. "Thanks for your help, Aggy. You're good people."

I wasn't sure about that since I hadn't really fixed anything since waking up to the chaos. At least the summons gong had finally gone quiet. It had probably gotten overwhelmed and given up. "I'll keep you posted on the wizrooms and stuff."

"Thanks." He glanced at Wanda. "Young lady, how are you settlin' in at Aggy's place?"

Wanda shrugged. "Okay."

He raised a brow. "Problems?"

I waited, knowing what was coming and interested in how Chief Marshall would handle it. "I like it there. I love the dog and the bat...."

"Bat?" He looked at me. "You need an exterminator?"

I laughed. "Not unless you want to set off a whole new supernatural type war."

He lifted his hands in surrender and returned his attention to Wanda. "But...?" he prodded.

Wanda threw me a glare. "She makes me eat vegetables."

I nodded when the chief sent me a look. "It's true. All kinds. She's particularly fond of the brussels sprouts."

Wanda made a gagging sound.

The chief's lips twitched, and some of the weariness left his face. "A vegetable now and then never hurt anybody," he told the teen.

"Says a guy who probably lives on pizza and beer," she mumbled.

"Yes, but I get green peppers and onions on my pizza," he agreed.

I laughed, frowning at the teen. "Are you done

insulting Rome's top cop by pigeonholing him into the single man bracket?"

Wanda rolled her eyes.

"I'll be in touch," I told the chief. Wanda and I had descended the stairs and opened the door into the alley when the chief called my name. I stopped and looked back.

"How's your family doing?"

It might seem like an odd question for anyone who wasn't aware of the chief's "fondness" for my adopted mom, Mavis.

I knew what he was really asking, and I loved the idea of him being sweet on one of the kindest, most loving women I knew. "Bev's wonderful."

He lowered his chin and looked at me from beneath dense brows.

I laughed. "Mavis is great too. If you get tired of pizza and beer, you should stop by for dinner. She's an excellent cook." I turned away and left him with that thought. I was smiling when I walked outside and bumped into Wanda. She'd stopped dead in her tracks and was staring at the street, her mouth hanging open.

"What's wrong? You look like a fish out of water with your mouth hanging open like tha...." The words died as my gaze located the source of her attention.

"Goddess in a gilded girdle. What is going on around here?"

I was staring at my elderly Range Rover. Or, at least the underside of it. Like a dozen other cars I could see up and down Main Street, it had been flipped over onto its roof, like a turtle unable to right itself.

3

WHAT'S UP IS DOWN AND DOWN IS UP

"Hey, honey," Mavis called from the back of the house.

I followed Wanda to the kitchen, the teen zeroing in on something that smelled delicious.

"What's for dinner?" Wanda asked. "It smells amazing."

"Beef stew and butter biscuits," Mavis answered, pushing a strand of dark hair from the teen's pale face. "Why don't you wash your hands and set the table." Wanda hurried to do as requested. "How many people?" she asked.

"I'm not sure. Aggy?"

I was still staring in disbelief at the mother of my heart. At five feet seven, she was a couple of inches shorter than me and fifteen plus years older than my forty-five years. But her peaches and cream complexion was still smooth, and her new blonde pixie cut showed no sign of thinning. An intense gray gaze, so like her daughter's, skimmed over me, focusing on my face and darkening with concern. She frowned. "Are you okay, honey?"

"No, mom. I'm not okay. Is it possible you haven't noticed anything strange about the day? Anything at all?"

She gave me a smile. "You mean like that?" She pointed toward the mudroom door, and I nearly groaned. "I'm afraid to look."

"I know," Mavis said, "But you have to."

Sighing theatrically, I headed toward the door and went outside onto my cozy little patio. To my relief, the iron and glass table where I took my evening wine and my morning coffee were just where I expected them to be, undamaged.

Due to Niele's excellent work, the patio had been enclosed in a pretty little picket fence with climbing flowers and an archway as an entrance. In order to see the rest of the yard, I needed to go through the archway.

I didn't want to go through that archway.

"Look at the graveyard," Mavis called through the door. She came out as I started in that direction, drying her hands on a kitchen towel.

I jolted to a stop before I'd gone ten feet, my eyes widening in horror. "Where is it?" I turned to Mavis. "Mom? Is this some kind of joke?"

"More like a trick," she said, frowning.

The ancient graveyard that had occupied a picturesque spot surrounded by trees and infused with the pleasant scent of flowers was...gone.

I hurried across the yard, stepping through the gate in the freshly painted picket fence that had once enclosed the small square of hallowed ground filled with stone markers. I stared at the unbroken grass. There were no signs of anything. No tombstones. No flowers. No ghosts meandering around.

I spun on Mavis. "What about the ghosts? Where did they go? How will Reverend Dodson find his way back to us?"

The good Reverend, the only ghost on my council and a man I considered a friend, had gone missing after I'd sent him on a mission to find a ghost. I hadn't been overly worried since time passed differently on the spectral plane, and the Reverend had never kept regular hours anyway.

But the missing graveyard changed things. "He'll never be able to find his way back!"

Mavis hurried over and wrapped me in a hug. "It will be okay, honey. He's been around a long time. He'll figure something out."

I didn't really believe that, but I let her words soothe me. There were so many things to worry about I'd lose my mind if I didn't stay calm. "What's going on, Mom?"

Mavis absently rubbed her hands on the towel, her hazel gaze thoughtful. "I have some ideas, honey.

But I think you should call the council. If it's what I think it is, we're going to need everybody's help to get underneath it."

"Aggy?"

I spun on my heel to find Lungren Maker striding across the lawn toward me. His melted chocolate gaze was fixed on the empty graveyard, twin worry lines marring the space between his arresting eyes. "What's happened to the tombstones?"

I shook my head, my fingers twining frantically together. "Gone. Apparently caught up in the crazy that's taking over everything else in Rome."

He stopped beside me, his warmth and barely suppressed power making my belly tighten with interest, despite everything. He was still frowning. Without a word, he crouched down and placed a palm on the ground. The worry lines deepened and multiplied.

"What is it?" I asked.

"It's not just the markers that are missing, Aggy." He straightened, fixing me with a look filled with alarm. "The bodies are gone too."

"Swear, curse, swear," I muttered. "What is going on?"

The earth next to me geysered up and my gardener, the gnome, was suddenly standing there, dirt sifting off his completely naked self. Niele's heavy features were fixed into a worried frown, his frizzy silver hair like an aura around his head. Small, black eyes fixed on me like a portent of trouble to come.

Despite weeks to get used to seeing Niele's stick and berries bobbing around willy-nilly, I hadn't... gotten used to it. "It's a Trickster," Niele announced without prompting.

A trickster? I gave that one some thought. It certainly would explain the craziness of the last couple of days. "Explain," I said to the gnome.

Niele shook his head, sending a spray of dirt away from his frizzy gray head.

I closed my eyes as several clumps hit my face, blowing air through my lips to disperse a few that had stuck.

"I've seen this before," Niele told us. "Ancient Rome had a Trickster infestation. Three of the nasty things ganged up on the city and basically destroyed it."

"Wait," Mavis said, her gaze narrowing with skepticism. "You're saying ancient Rome was destroyed by Tricksters, not the Visigoths and the Arabs?"

Niele shrugged. "The constant wars and attacks didn't help, but the Tricksters pretty much finished the city off."

I shook my head. "Too many words." Rubbing my temples, I sighed. Glancing at Niele, I said, "I'm glad you're here. Apparently, we have wizrooms in the park. Can you take care of them?"

He grimaced. "Nasty things, wizrooms. The last time my people tackled a patch, half of us came out covered in polka dots and half in stripes." He shook his head. "I couldn't wear patterns for a whole year. Too clashy."

I raised my brows, eyeing his cloth-free state.

"I'm serious. I had to wear plain leaves for my ceremonial dress rather than my natty flower vest."

I snorted. "Well, you can thank Bev for your *plain* moss shorts, can't you. If you come out of this looking plaid, you'll still match your shorts."

He did not look amused.

"I'm sorry to dump this on you, Niele. But I have literally a hundred other problems to fix. The only way we can get this under control is to divide and conquer."

He nodded. "I get that. But you should put finding and killing the Trickster at the top of that list. Or your problems will just keep expanding."

"Aggy?"

I turned to find Wanda coming toward me across the grass.

"You have a visitor."

L ooking to be only a little over five feet tall, the woman standing in my living room was tiny. With a hundred and fifty pounds on my five-foot-six-inch frame, I felt like a giant standing next to her.

She smelled like sugar and had red-gold hair that hung straight down her back, with stick-straight bangs that brushed her lashes. Her lips were a pouty, naturally pale pink, and her nose was long, with delicate nostrils. But her most stunning feature was her eyes, which were large, with thick, dark red lashes that made her amber gaze stand out in her small face.

"Madam Lares," she said as I entered the sun-drenched sanctuary of my living room. "Thank the goddess. I desperately need your help!" She offered me a hand that was dusted with some kind of white powder.

I smiled in an attempt to soothe the obviously distraught woman. "Can I get you something to drink?"

She shook her head, the silken waves of red-gold hair shifting around her narrow shoulders like a shampoo commercial. I fingered the silver tips of my own straight black locks self-consciously. Maybe I should use a conditioner on it. It had been feeling a little dry lately.

"...this!" the woman said.

With a guilty start, I realized she'd been talking while I contemplated my hair. I looked at the object in her outstretched hand. It looked like some kind of vegetable from the fungus family. With a hooded top and a thick stem, the purple-fleshed object bore the faint shadows of...polka dots. "Is that...?"

"Don't touch that!" Wanda yelled from across the room. "Niele!"

The gnome moved quickly, his big hand clasping the object and carrying it away.

I looked at Wanda. "Wizroom." She narrowed her eyes on me. "Are you feeling okay?"

"I'm fi..."

"Please, Madam Lares," my visitor said. "This is a crisis."

I gave Wanda a narrow-eyed look and forced my attention back to my visitor. "I'm sorry, what was your name?"

"Tilly. And, before you ask, it's just Tilly. No last name."

I grinned. "Like Beyonce. Or Prince. Or..." My mind blanked out on me. Heat flared in my middle, and sweat suddenly broke out all over my body. My lungs struggled to fill. "I..." Rubbing my temples, I dropped onto the nearby couch. I fought to get a complete breath. "Just give me a minute..."

"Goddess in a garter!" Wanda rounded on our visitor. "What were you thinking, bringing a wizroom into this house. You know humans are very susceptible to them."

I realized the teen shouldn't be yelling at my visitor and tried to correct her, but neither of them seemed to hear me. In fact, I barely heard myself. My words got caught in a suddenly dry throat.

"I'm sorry," Tilly said. "I didn't think. When I saw them, I just panicked."

"So you picked one!" Wanda's voice was a shriek, and I tried to stand.

"Wanda!" I yelled, only it wasn't really a yell. It was really more like a gasp.

Again they ignored me. I fell back onto the couch again, unable to stand.

Wanda finally noticed me. "Mavis!" she yelled. "Water. Hurry!"

I heard footsteps running lightly down the hallway, and Mavis arrived, a glass of water in hand. She took one look at me and said, "Ohoh..." and stumbled backward, spilling some of the water.

Wanda's pretty young face squinched up, and she chewed her bottom lip. "Hey," she said, "Drink this water and you'll feel better." Without looking behind her, she motioned for Mavis to bring the water.

Tilly leaned over me, wringing her hands. "I'm really sorry. I didn't think. My whole pastry case was full of them and I panicked. All those pastries... gone." Tears swam in her eyes and the hand-wringing sped to double time.

"Here, honey." Mavis handed me the glass of water, her gray gaze not meeting mine.

I drank because if I didn't moisten my throat, the words would keep getting caught there, glued to my tonsils. A few minutes later, I started to feel better. "It's okay. I'm fine now," I told Tilly, giving her a smile to prove it. "Just a momentary wobbliness."

Tilly's face contorted into what I guessed was supposed to be a smile. It looked more like a grimace. A smimace. "Yes. You'll be fine." She waved a hand over me. "That will..." She spun on her heel. "I have to go see if I can salvage my product for the day. Take care of yourself."

She breezed out of there with nary a look back, moving as if a Hellhound was nipping at her stylish heels.

My gaze finally slid from her to Wanda and Mavis. They were both staring at me, their eyes wide. "What?"

Niele came back wearing his moss shorts. He had streaks of black on his cheeks. "I took care of it. Burned it good. I'm afraid I might have burned a ten-foot-wide circle in the grass th...." He jolted to a stop, his gaze finding me. "Oh!"

My heart shot into overdrive. I reached up to feel my face. It was still a bit damp but otherwise felt okay. "What's wrong with me? Why do you all look so shell-shocked?"

Wanda chewed a nail. Mavis fidgeted, still

unable to look my way. I looked at Niele. He started to turn around and leave. "Don't. You. Dare!"

The gnome skidded to a stop. He faced away from me for a full thirty seconds and then slowly turned. "Wizrooms are highly toxic."

I narrowed my gaze on him in warning. Sure, I could get up and walk into the bathroom to look in the mirror, but fear kept me rooted to the spot. If they were going to tell me I was polka-dotted, I needed a moment to get used to the idea before I saw it for myself.

"They do strange things to people." He gave a sad little laugh. "You never really know what..."

"Am I covered in polka dots?" I finally blurted, unable to stand it for another minute.

The three of them laughed. Cackled really. A really uncomfortable sound. "

"Don't be silly," Mavis said, still avoiding my gaze.

"That's ridiculous," Wanda added.

"Of course not," the gnome said, flipping a hand in dismissal of my question. "You're just kind of purple."

4

A LARES MUST HER DIGNITY SHUCK

"I'm purple?" I shrieked.

Mavis winced. "It's not that bad, honey. We can probably cover it with some makeup."

I pulled up the sleeves of my tee-shirt and looked at my ankles beneath my yoga pants. "Over my entire body?"

"On the plus side," Wanda offered. "It looks good with your hair."

It wasn't a light purple, like lilac. It was a dark, deep purple, which seemed to be spreading rapidly downward from my face. "This is terrible. I can't go out into public like this."

Mavis grabbed her cell phone. "I'll call a coven meeting. Maybe we can come up with a magical solution."

"Good," I called after her. "Because there are others with this problem. Not just me."

I dropped my head into my hands, my heart racing.

"I'll just go start getting rid of those wizrooms," Niele said, hurrying out of the room.

The couch cushion shifted under me, and I glanced at Wanda as she sat. Her lips twitched as I looked at her. "This isn't funny."

She fought to keep from smiling. "You look like Count von Count® from Sesame Street®."

I groaned. "What am I going to do?"

"You're going to do whatever you need to do. You'll rock the purple, just like you rock everything else."

Tears burned my eyes as her words touched my heart. "Your lips are still twitching."

She burst out laughing. "Purple People Eater? Grape Ape? Dizzy Devil?"

I smacked her arm. "You're grounded for life."

She snickered happily, dropping an arm around my shoulders. "I hope your winged boy toy likes purple girls."

Ugh!!! Gren! I turned a terrified gaze on her. "He can't see me like this."

As if my declaration had summoned him, my angel flew into my front yard. The light disappeared from the arched front windows as a large pair of wings got between the glass and the sun. A beat later, I heard the whisper of Gren's wings folding away. I envisioned him reaching for the front door handle.

"Too late," Wanda said, tugging me up from the couch and dragging me toward the door. "He's coming. Go to your room. I'll break it to him gently."

Nails clicked on the hardwood floor of the hallway as Monty ran toward the door, barking a greeting. He skidded to a stop with a yelp when he spotted me, his tail drooping. Then the horrendous happened. My sweet dog started to bark at me, his tail aggressively wagging.

I stood there, caught between Monty and Gren, and felt my world crumble out from underneath me.

The front door opened, and the most beautiful man I'd ever seen stood with the bright sun as his backdrop. The light gilded his mahogany hair, longer than when I'd first met him and with a bit of curl that somehow made him look even more masculine than before. Gren's smile found me and, for just a nanosecond, I thought my world was going to be okay.

But then his sexy brown eyes went wide, and his mouth opened in shock. "Aggy...What...?"

"Bark, bark, bark!!"

I gave Gren a strained smile. "A little altercation with some..."

"Wizrooms," he finished for me. "I heard." My dismay must have been apparent because he quickly cut the distance between us, wrapping his arms around me and pulling me in. A warm kiss found my lips. "Purple looks good on you."

I gave a watery laugh. "Just what I need right now. The whole town is in an uproar."

He nodded. "I stopped by Tilly's on my way here, thinking you could probably use some cupcakes about now." He grimaced. "The shop looks like it's been destroyed."

"I know. Tilly was here."

"That's why Aggy's purple," Wanda said, frowning. "She brought a wizroom into the house."

I looked at Wanda. "Why weren't you affected? Or Niele?"

"I don't know about the gnome, maybe he was far enough away, but demons aren't susceptible."

Ah yes. How could I forget? My ward was part demon. The realization had ceased to bother me. I'd feel good about that if I wasn't currently purple.

"Gnomes need prolonged exposure to be infected," Gren explained.

I nodded.

"There was a crowd outside the bakery, and they were close to rioting. Poor Tilly was beside herself," Gren said.

"Rioting? Over cupcakes and donuts?"

"Tilly's a Brownie," Gren said.

"Yeah, that doesn't help me at all," I admitted. I was really glad my judgmental advocate wasn't there to berate me over my ignorance. I would no doubt pay a steep price in critical looks and disillusioned glances.

"I'm guessing she puts a touch of magic in her delightful concoctions. Some people might be a tiny bit addicted," he clarified.

"Perfect," I said. That would certainly explain why I'd eaten myself into an extra five pounds over the last few weeks. "Would it be bad of me to say I'd kill for one of her cookies right now?"

Gren smiled. My knees wobbled from the sight.

"Then you'll be happy to hear I put some in the freezer for you last week," my most beautiful and treasured ward admitted.

I squealed happily, giving Wanda a hug. "You're my favorite person in the entire Universe."

Gren cleared his throat, and I gave him a wink. "Unless you have a box of cupcakes tucked beneath your shirt, you're just going to have to accept the demotion."

His melted chocolate eyes twinkled with amusement. "Demotion accepted."

"Okay, let's retire to the kitchen for a planning session." I mentally reached out to the others on my council. "We need to forge a plan to deal with all of this mess."

"Frogs in people's beds. Fish flopping around in trees. The buildings along one whole side of Randall Street are facing the wrong way, their front doors pointed toward the back walls of the buildings behind them..." Bev took a breath, shoved a medium-length strand of blonde hair off her cheek, and went on. "Cats are barking, dogs are meowing. The sky is brown above Peace Park and the ground is blue."

I held up a hand. "Stop. I can't take it. Clearly, we can't solve all of these problems magically or with my own personal favorite, brute force. So, what does that leave us?"

"I could get a bunch of gnomes together and we could just sink the whole town," Niele suggested. "We can all move somewhere else and start over."

Wanda snorted.

"Tempting," I told him. "But that won't fix everything. Besides, I personally wouldn't like it if Monty started meowing. I'd be confused over whether to feed him fish sticks or beef jerky."

"How about you feed him what dogs are supposed to eat," Ferral, the cranky advocate, suggested. He settled a judgmental silver gaze on me, and his square jaw tightened with pique. "As I've been saying for the last hour, we need to find the source of all this."

"How?" Trish wailed from above. We all glanced up as she whipped past.

The warrior fairy member of my council, Trish had arrived at my house in her fairy form rather than in her usual jeans and tee-shirt and hadn't come out of it yet. She'd been buzzing back and forth over our heads, mumbling to herself. I figured that meant something had gone wrong within the fairy community. But, since my list was already long and her problems promised to be particularly ugly given the nature of the fae, I didn't ask.

"You don't *find* Tricksters," Gren told the advocate. "They find you."

"Trap," Trish muttered as she flashed past my head. "Trap, trap, trap, trap."

I shared a look with Mavis, and she winced. "Trish, honey," the mom of my heart said. "Do you think you could land somewhere? You're giving me a stroke."

The fairy jerked to a halt and twitched, her ankle-length gown dancing around her legs like seaweed drifting on the bottom of the ocean. The gown had a vivid blue bustier and was cinched at the waist with a belt of knives. In her fairy form, Trish was only twelve inches tall. She held a knobby walking stick that was as tall as she was. A double strand of what looked like shimmering droplets of water encircled her blonde head. "We have to trap him."

I bit back a reference to her being Captain Obvious, knowing that to a warrior fairy, the term entrapment held a different meaning than it did to the rest of us. The fairies considered trapping an art form. And they were very good at it. "Do you have something in mind?"

She swayed as if she was jonesing to start flying again but managed to keep herself immobile. Just barely, if the juddering of her tiny foot on the air was any indication. "Not yet. I'm working on it."

I looked at Bev, the sister of my heart. Bev had been my sister in every way except blood since I was fifteen years old and lost my mom to a terrible disease. She and Mavis were my family as much as if we shared DNA. "Can the witches do something to draw him in so Trish's trap, when she comes up with it, can contain him?"

Bev grimaced. "Theoretically, yes. But historically, our containment spells have been unsuccessful with Tricksters."

"Why's that?" Luke asked. The shifter's golden eyes were an eerie bright yellow in his wolf form, and his white teeth were much larger. As a man, his "fur" consisted of a bristly jaw and longish dark hair. His voice was so deep he always sounded like he was an inch away from a growl.

"The Trickster is right in front of you yet impossible to see," Bev intoned as if reading prophecy. She ran her fingers through her blonde bob, making a mess of her straight bangs.

"What exactly does that mean?" I asked a titch impatiently. I'd never been a fan of prophecies. They always reminded me of fortune cookie messages... useless because nobody knew what they meant.

She fixed her gray gaze on me. "It means the Trickster is part of all this. He doesn't just create chaos from the background. He joins in the fun."

I narrowed my eyes and shook my head. "Okay. I still don't know what that means."

"He could be anyone or anything," Wanda clarified. "He can become one of his targets if he wants to."

Curse, swear, curse! If that was true, how in the name of the goddess's favorite goldfish were we going to find him? I shrugged. "I'm at a loss and open to suggestions."

Wanda got up from the table. "I'll go see what I can find in magical history about Tricksters. Maybe there's something that will help us get him."

"Surely someone somewhere has defeated a Trickster," I said.

They all stared at me, their expressions grim.

"Nobody?"

Ferral expelled a frustrated rush of air. "In every instance I can think of, the Trickster left after he'd completely destroyed his target. Nobody's ever figured out how to stop them."

"I have a suggestion," Bev said. "But you're not going to like it."

"I haven't liked anything since I woke up to polka-dotted teens and an upside-down graveyard," I said." Let's hear it."

"You can ask the crone for help."

The room became unnaturally quiet. Nobody moved. Expressions were perfectly neutral. I couldn't tell by looking at the members of my council what anybody thought.

"Am I to read the traumatized silence as disagreement?"

Mavis grimaced. "In my case, it's unhappy agreement. If anybody could help with this, it's the crone."

Ferral shook his head. For once, I was happy for his tendency to instantly resist any suggestion. "That's not a good idea."

"Of course it's not a good idea," Bev said, glaring at him. "There are no good ideas right now. But we need help from someone very powerful. She's the most powerful magic user I know."

We fell into a contemplative silence again. The quiet lasted until someone knocked on my kitchen door. I jumped at the sound, my cheeks heating with embarrassment because my first thought had been that I didn't want whoever it was to see me in all my purpleness.

I gave Trish a pleading look. She nodded and sent a wave of silvery sparkles in my direction. The glamour settled over me, returning my skin to its usual vampiric paleness. I sagged with relief. "Thank you."

Trish nodded and then returned to spinning frantically around the room.

Niele opened the door and glared at whoever stood outside. "What do you want, demon?"

Everyone tensed at the word. Everyone except Wanda. She glanced at me, a guilty look in her dark brown eyes, and went to join Niele. "Let him in, please."

Niele glanced at me and I nodded. After another moment's hesitation, the gnome stepped back, and Wanda reached a hand through the door. She gave someone a little tug, and the demon Bathos came inside. He settled eyes the color of midnight on me and smiled. "Hello, Madam Lares. You're looking well."

I inclined my head. "Bathos. I could say the same of you, but it wouldn't be true." I cocked my head at him. "To what do I owe the displeasure?"

5

WHEN DEMONS CALL TO OFFER AID

A long, low growl emerged from beneath the kitchen table, where Monty was having his nap. He emerged a moment later, eyes locked on Bathos and lip curled in a snarl. He was pressed against my leg. Whether for my protection or his, I wasn't sure.

As it had the last time I'd met Wanda's father, power rippled off him in waves that made gooseflesh rise along my arms. His silky black hair hung in soft waves to his jawline, perfectly coiffed yet somehow giving the impression of fashionable disorder. His too-handsome face looked pale against the darkness of his hair, and his usually pristine suit appeared slightly rumpled.

"Shall I kill you before or after tea?" I asked, lifting my brows in question.

His lips twitched upward at the corners. He

clearly recognized the threat he'd leveled on me when I'd dared to show up at his home the first time. "That depends," he said, playing my part in the game. "Will there be cookies?" His voice was a smooth baritone. It would have been pleasant to listen to if it weren't for the faint bass echo that distorted every word.

Wanda frowned with irritation. "Please don't kill each other."

Guilt swept through me at the look on her face. I should have known better than to tease her father in front of her.

Gren's warm hand found my arm, giving it a little squeeze. "Your father is perfectly safe," he told her, fixing Bathos with a hard look. "As long as he behaves."

Bathos shot a less-than-pristine cuff and smiled. "I have no intention of causing trouble. I've come to you to offer my help with the current...situation."

"Oh? I presume you're talking about the Trickster?" I said.

Bathos grimaced. "Yes. The fiend will destroy everything if not stopped."

"Do you know how to stop him?" Wanda asked, her expression hopeful.

Bathos settled a warm look on his daughter that surprised me. "The Trickster cannot be stopped."

The tiny hope I'd begun to nurture crashed and burned. "Then how are you proposing to help us?"

Bathos' black gaze returned to me, cold and full of evil promise. "The Trickster cannot be stopped. But he can be moved to another location."

"I can't in good conscience dump him on someone else," I argued.

Bathos shrugged. "It is not up to you. Tricksters will always exist. The best you can hope is that they don't settle their poisonous intent on you."

I shook my head. "My job is to protect, not shove danger off on some other unfortunate town to save Rome."

"Your job is to protect Rome," Bathos' voice sharpened. His black eyes flashed with irritation. "You are not responsible for the world, Madam Lares."

"How do you propose to encourage him to leave?" Ferral asked, stopping me from replying.

I glared at my advocate. It was like glowering at a noisy bird. He ignored me as if my opinion meant nothing.

Bathos didn't hesitate. "We must create an environment that is hostile to him."

"How do we do that?" Luke asked.

The demon glanced toward the shifter, a speculative glint in his eyes. "It will not be easy. It will require all of us working together to accomplish."

"We're listening," Trish said.

"No, we're not," I said. "I'm not going to shove

this problem onto someone else. There has to be another way."

Bathos responded as if I hadn't spoken. "We must become Tricksters ourselves. We must beat him at his own game. Turn Rome inside out and upside down. If we can do this, he will leave."

"What exactly do you mean by that?" Wanda asked. She glanced worriedly from me to her father.

I opened my mouth to interrupt again, but Gren's voice filled my mind. *Let him speak his piece, Aggy. There might be some part of his idea we can use.*

Something dangerous threaded through Bathos' black gaze. "We must engage the amalgamation spell."

Trish's wings stopped whirring, and she dropped several inches before she re-engaged them. Mavis gasped, her usually pink cheeks paling to chalk white. Bev surged out of her chair, her gaze narrowed with rage. Luke growled. Niele threw a chair aside to get to the demon, a snarl on his lips.

Gren moved so quickly he was a blur on the air. I blinked and my protector had a hand on Bathos' collar, twisting it to cut off the demon's air.

Wanda started to go to them, but I grabbed her hand, stopping her. "Hold right there," I said, directing my command to everyone in the room. "I don't know what this amalgamation spell is, but I'm guessing from your reactions that it isn't good."

"It's not good," said a familiar voice from the

doorway. I looked over to find Lost Princess Layla coming into the kitchen. "It's deadly bad. And that one should know better than to suggest it."

Bathos gave a cold laugh. "Desperate times, Princess." He cocked his head at her. "Not that I'd expect you to understand since you're hiding out here rather than facing your responsibilities in Hades."

Layla was suddenly at Bathos' throat with a long, curved blade, and Gren had stepped back, taking care to stay between me and the two demons. "What do you know about Hades, fool?" she growled. "You're earthbound. You've never had to live there. You've never felt the sting of its evil against your skin. Or lost those you cared about to its poisonous deceits."

Bathos looked perfectly relaxed despite the demon blade carving a thin line of blood in his throat. "Like you, *Princess*, I had a role to play. I've played it to its fullest extent and have been rewarded for my efforts. But you...you hide on earth, living in squalor and without the honor you threw away for reasons of the heart." His curled lip told everyone in the room how he felt about that. "You're the fool."

Blood, so red it was nearly black, ran in a rivulet down his muscled throat and into the starched collar of his shirt. Bathos didn't seem to care. His black eyes were locked on Layla and hers on him.

"Please, Layla," a small voice said.

The lost princess blinked as if coming out of a trance. She glanced at Wanda, her expression softening. She hesitated, her fondness for my ward seeming to finally win her over. With a moue of regret, Layla stepped away from Bathos. "Ironic, yes? You eschew love, yet it has saved your life yet again."

Bathos shook his head. "If you believe you could have killed me...."

"Enough!" I yelled, beyond sick of their antics. "We have ample problems already. We don't need you two acting like cranky toddlers while we're trying to find a solution. If you aren't here to help, then get lost."

Bathos' eyes turned hard, like black glass. His perfect mouth tightened, and his body went very still. I stared back at him, fear sizzling in my belly. But I couldn't show that fear, or I'd never be able to control the earthbound demon again.

Seeming to sense my thoughts, Gren shifted incrementally closer, giving me the support I needed to withstand Bathos' brimstone-laced temper.

Layla sighed. She shifted slightly and the demon blade disappeared from her hand, the movement too fast to follow. "Sorry, Aggy." She shoved long strands of curly blonde hair out of her face. Her copper-colored eyes were filled with apology. "I didn't come here to cause trouble. But I heard this one's proposal and lost it."

"I'd like to reassure you that we aren't going to

listen to him," I said, my gaze still locked on Bathos. "But I have no idea what this amalgamation spell is, so I can't speak to it. Why don't you tell me."

Layla glowered one last time at Bathos and dropped into a chair. She rubbed her hands over her pretty face and sighed. "It's demon magic," she told me. "Which should tell you all you need to know about using it."

"It's definitely a clue," I responded, feeling peevish. "But it really tells me nothing. What exactly does it do?"

"It pulls the demonic plane into this one," Ferral said, his silver gaze burning holes in Bathos. "And melds them together."

I sucked air and threw out a hand. My staff slammed into my palm and, with a single thought, magic sizzled from the orb on the end.

Bathos squared his shoulders and lifted his own hands. Flames emerged from his fingers, oily magic rising around him.

"No!" Wanda moved fast. Faster than I thought possible, and she was suddenly wrapped around her father like a monkey, riding him to the ground. He hadn't been expecting her to react against him, and that surprise was his undoing. He went down hard, slamming into the hardwood floor with a pain-filled grunt.

Wanda held her own flame in one hand, and it was formed into a small fist. I stared at her in shock.

I'd never seen her call physical magic before. "You will not summon magic against Aggy," she ground out through gritted teeth. "You will not hurt her."

The earthbound demon's expression was a mix of rage and pride. In the end, pride won out and he inclined his head. "You have my word, little fiend."

Wanda rolled her eyes and stood up, stepping away from him. "Don't call me that."

Bathos arched his body and sprang back to his feet.

I blinked at the acrobatic move. The man was likely hundreds of years old. How was he still so agile? I was only forty-five and I could barely navigate the hallway of my house without twisting a body part and falling over.

At Wanda's pointed glance, I let the magic die. But I didn't send my weapon away. Wanda might trust her father. But nobody else in the room did. "How dare you come in here after what we suffered from your people and try to trick us into giving demons a path to the earthly plane?"

"You've got it wrong, Madam Lares. That was not my intent."

"But it would be the result, yes?" Niele asked, his homely features formed into a mask of rage.

Smiling, Bathos held out his hands as if to say, "You caught me."

His smile turned my stomach sour. "You think this is funny?"

He sighed. "It is true the meld would temporarily pull Rome into the demonic plane. I can see why you might find that alarming."

Gren barked a laugh, the sound as far from mirth as it was possible to get. "Can you?"

Bathos shrugged. "Yes. I'm not as oblivious to human sensibilities as you seem to think. In my business, I must deal with humans and their emotions often."

"What exactly is your business?" Bev asked, her tone frigid.

"That isn't important here," Bathos said. "What is important is that the meld will disorient the Trickster. He will lose focus on his task and struggle to grasp the melded universe he suddenly finds himself in. He will be ripe for the plucking, as you humans say."

"At what cost?" Luke growled. "How many thousands of demons would be allowed into our world during this meld?"

Bathos' smile tightened. "That won't be a problem if we're prepared."

"We thought we were prepared the last time," Mavis told him. "Yet people lost their lives. And that was just one portal. What you're talking about would open the demonic plane wide. We couldn't possibly control that many demons. We'd be overrun and slaughtered."

Bathos didn't bother to deny it. He turned away.

"I've given you a possible solution. If you do not choose to utilize my excellent advice, you will get exactly what you deserve."

I waited until Bathos was at the door to call out. "And what about you?"

He turned back. "Pardon?"

"Will you get what you deserve? How much damage has the Trickster already done to your tidy little life, Bathos?"

The angry flush in his expression was all the answer I needed. "Maybe you should try a little harder to offer reasonable solutions," I told him. "If Rome goes down, you and your business will go down with it."

6

THE PRICE IN BLOOD IS SURELY PAID

I gave up trying to sleep around midnight. I'd fallen asleep briefly, only to have my dreams invaded by the sensation of running through the woods, wide green leaves splattering wetly against me as I ran.

In the dream, a soft rain gave the forest a glossy appearance, the moonlight painting everything in silver. The verdant scent of broken leaves and the rich, loamy scent of the earth burst into the air around me with each footfall, the concussive sound of large hooves dogging my every step. The adrenaline-fueled dash through the Mystical Wood was exhilarating...and terrifying.

My exhausted mind yanked me from sleep. I shot upright, blinking around at a room lit by slivers of silver moonlight. Beside me, Monty stirred, stretched his legs, and settled back into sleep.

I lay back on my pillow, my heart racing. As I calmed, my thoughts drifted to analyzing my mind's intrigues. It had felt more like an out-of-body experience than a dream. One where I wasn't me, but somebody...something...else.

Giving up on sleep, I climbed out of bed and padded down the hall to the kitchen. I grabbed a glass out of the cabinet and filled it at the sink, drinking it half down before the first summons arrived.

Come.

I sputtered, spraying water over the window above the sink. I coughed and spluttered for a minute, wiping my face on the dishtowel. I was imagining things. My mind was in rare form.

Come.

Half-turned from the sink, I stilled. A sudden awareness dragged my gaze back to the glass. A stunning white form galloped out of the woods at the distant edge of my property. I gasped, my heart picking up steam again as I watched the White Mare gallop toward me.

Come. She wishes to speak to you.

The crone was summoning me? *Curse!* The last thing I wanted was to go haring off after a deadly and irreverent super-witch in the middle of the night.

But the reality of her summons was galloping toward me across my yard. I didn't hear the cacophony of oversized hooves thundering toward me so much as feel them rumbling in my bones.

I lifted my gaze back to the window and sighed again. The White Mare waited for me just beyond the pretty, flower-covered archway. Fixing me with an expectant look, the horse clearly knew I was standing there, looking back at her.

Swear, curse, swear.

Resignation finally overwhelming my resistance, I opened the mudroom door and stepped outside. The mare shifted, snorting through flared nostrils, and rose up on her hind legs, silently pawing the air.

"I appreciate you not screaming your drama and waking up my neighbors," I told her.

The horse snorted, tossing her head. The moonlight sparked in her pale green gaze, and I got the impression she was laughing at me.

"What does she want?" I asked. I'd really hoped I'd never have to make the trip to the crone's hidey-hole ever again. The last time had been terrifying on many levels.

Another toss of the head, impatient prancing, and a swishing tail told me I had no choice but to answer the summons. "Okay, let me just go get dressed..."

The mare put her head down and trotted toward me. She nudged me with her velvety nose, then lowered herself to her front knees and snorted.

"But, I'm in my jammies."

She tossed her head impatiently.

"Okay," I said, grabbing a handful of mane and climbing onboard. "But I'm not taking any guff from her about my dancing pizza jammies."

Ignoring my embarrassment, the mare surged to her feet, nearly toppling me off, and spun around. I gave a short scream and grabbed a handful of mane as I was nearly unseated.

As we flew toward the intimidating darkness under the trees, I had just enough presence of mind to throw out a hand and call for my staff before the White Mare plunged into the wood, and my real nightmare started.

The mare eschewed the nice, wide paths and dove into the trees, dodging and weaving to avoid being stabbed by outstretched branches or tripped by random roots. The sounds and movement and colors of the wood flashed past fast enough to create a seizure-inducing kaleidoscope that made my head spin.

The familiar slap of wet leaves kept me alert and uncomfortable. Grasping limbs snagged in my hair and tugged on my dancing pizza pants. Echoing my restless dream, the mare's pounding hooves ripped into the forest floor and drove the scent of rich earth and torn leaves into the air.

I wanted to close my eyes...even went so far as to do it for a second...but the violence of our passage made them snap back open again.

I had no control over the journey. But at least I'd see what was going to kill me before it actually did.

That was why I saw the enormous, felled tree looming up ahead of us. The toppled trunk was four feet tall, even laying on its side. I clutched the mare's silky mane and felt my eyes go wide. "Um..."

She threw back her head, screaming a warning into the night as if the fallen tree would jump out of our way.

I pounded on her shoulder. "Watch out!"

Still, she sped on, fifteen feet from the tree. Ten feet. Eight feet. Four feet.

"Ahhhh!" I screamed as I prepared for impact. But as the mare's hooves reached for the tree, her back bowed, and a huge set of wings sprang free.

With a single, powerful pulse of the wings, we were airborne. And headed right for another tree, whose branches stretched high and wide, obscuring the way ahead with its prolific form.

I ducked then, finally realizing I didn't want to look death in the eye after all. Burying my face into the mare's powerful neck, I waited for impact.

It never came. Instead of slamming into the ginormous tree, we hit what felt like a wrinkle in the air. It snapped around us, tugging the mare to a brief stop and then ripping like human skin as she pulsed her wings and lowered her head. As the barrier broke, we shot forward, the magic biting my skin like a million fire ants.

Before I even had time to rub the feeling away, we were flying again, with a bright blue sky overhead and a panorama of black sand dunes rolling right up to the horizon below us.

I lifted my head and tossed my shoulder-length black hair off my face. A golden sun, looking twice as big as I was used to, bathed me in delicious warmth. The mare's stark white coat glistened under the light. Her wings shone with unnatural brightness.

"Nice," I said, stroking a hand down the horse's densely muscled neck. "If only I didn't need to battle leviathans when we got there."

The mare knickered softly, the sound like gentle laughter.

We flew for what felt like another couple of hours. Though I was enjoying the journey, my butt and legs were getting sore by the time my mount started her descent.

I frowned at the sight stretching below us. I'd been expecting the ocean, surrounded by a sandy landscape that was bounded by a low mountain ridge. I'd been dreading that ocean because of the multiple near-death experiences it had served up the last time we'd visited the crone.

What I saw couldn't have been more different from my expectation.

The ground flew up to meet us, and my stomach plummeted to my ankles as the mare surged toward her landing. Despite my fears, we landed smoothly in front of what could only be considered a tree-house town. The mare trotted to the base of the largest tree at the center and stopped, giving a violent shake as she tucked her wings away.

I slipped down her side and landed in an ungainly sprawl at her feet as my legs gave out.

"There you are!" said a familiar voice from above.

Shoving hair off my face, I looked up at the crone high above my head. She leaned over a rope barrier, two energetic dachshunds dancing at her feet. Both dogs were the longhaired variety. One was black and tan like Monty and the other was piebald, with a mostly white body and a black, brown, and white face.

"Woof!" the little dogs greeted in matching barks.

The ancient witch was dressed in her usual outfit of strategically torn jeans and tee-shirt with a cute saying on it. The current tee featured a picture of a black and tan dachshund and the words...Short legs, large attitude.

Truth in advertising.

About my height at five feet six, the ancient witch had stooped shoulders and a slightly rounded back. That, and the color of her thick mop of white hair, were the only things that gave away her age. She didn't move like an ancient crone, and her long face was smooth except for an array of wrinkles around her mouth. Her eyes were ocean blue, touched with green and silver specks that made them always seem to dance with humor. She had the brightest, most powerful aura I'd ever seen, and it was constantly changing to reflect the witch's hyperactive style.

"Why are you dawdling? Come. I have food." She turned on her heel, mumbling to the little dogs to follow as she disappeared into the treehouse. I blew air through my lips.

Something large and warm nudged me forward. I turned to find the mare's sleek head, her startling green eyes half-covered by the density of her forelock. "How am I supposed to get up there?" I asked.

The mare's wings snapped out in response.

I shoved to my feet, shaking my head. "No, thank you very much. My posterior is averse to more flight time. Nothing personal."

The horse stamped a hoof in irritation.

"Sorry," I told her as I looked around for stairs or an elevator. A few minutes later, I found a rope ladder that led upward.

"Ugh!" I'd never been good with rope ladders. My muscle-deprived arms weren't up to the task of wrenching me upward.

With a sigh, I grabbed the ladder and started to climb.

It swung violently under my efforts, nearly pitching me to the ground. When I'd managed to struggle my way halfway up, the thing went totally wild and I ended up twisted around with my back pressed to the inhospitable bark.

It took me several tries, flinging myself away from the tree to get turned back around. By the time I fell off the ladder onto the wooden walkway built around the tree, I was covered in sweat, and my muscles were shaking.

I lifted my tee-shirt and mopped at the sweat on my face, peering through the door that led inside.

The crone was sitting in the middle of a room that was way too big to fit inside a tree. I pulled my head back out and looked at the tree again. Nope. It hadn't gotten any bigger.

"Come, come. Heaven's sake. I've never met such a slow creature. You'd think you were part sloth." She gave me a thoughtful frown. "You're not?"

I stepped into the deliciously cool interior. "I'm not what?"

"Part sloth." The crone grimaced. "You're all sweaty."

I tugged sodden hair off my soggy neck. "If you had stairs or an elevator to get up here, I wouldn't be sweaty. And, I'd have gotten here ten minutes faster."

She narrowed her eyes at me.

I waved a dismissive hand. "Why did you summon me? I have a major crisis at home, and I need to get back."

The crone dropped a bony hand onto each of her dachshunds, who were snuggled up on either side of her in the familiar throne chair. I'd seen her sitting on the same throne in her kingdom below the sea. The witch's smile was tight. Her eyes flashed with anger. "How dare you speak to me so!"

The air in the room thickened and grew uncomfortably heavy. A wall of wind slammed into me, shoving me out the door before I had time to react. I hit the rope barrier, and my body toppled over it, plunging downward. I managed to grab the rope with one hand, my other hand snapping out to accept my staff.

The weapon smacked into my palm, and I screamed to be heard over the still-building wind. "Desist!"

The wind died, and my body wrenched downward, only my one-armed grip keeping me from plummeting. My hand ached as the rope tore at my palm, and my shoulder felt as if it would give way under my not insubstantial weight. I was realistic about my size. I wasn't skinny. Some might even call me slightly fluffy. But even slightly fluffy was a lot of dead weight for arms that were already wrung out from climbing the tree.

In sheer desperation, I pointed my staff at the ground and said, "Elevate." Golden-hued magic shot from the orb at the end of my staff and hit the ground below me, carving a perfect circle into the dirt. The magic built into a glistening gold tower that filled the circle and began to rise upward. I strained to hold on with only one hand, my arm feeling like it was going to rip in half.

Finally, I couldn't hold on any longer. My fingers slipped and I plunged downward, expecting to crash and break on the ground below. But my feet hit the golden column and sank into it, the power cushioning my fall and pushing me toward the walkway above.

The crone came through the door as I reached the top of the rope railing, her little dogs bouncing happily alongside.

The witch frowned as I hung in the air in front of her. "That's very flashy magic, Madam Lares. But it's an unnecessary use of power. Why didn't you just use the ramp?" As if to prove her point, the two dogs gave a little bark and ran down the walkway, stepping onto a ramp that rose from the level below, feeding a second ramp that led to the ground.

Curse, swear, swear!

7

AN UNPLANNED TRIP, A WITCH'S PLOY

"Please tell me why you summoned me," I said through gritted teeth. We were once again inside the treehouse. The crone sat in her throne chair, minus her small sidekicks. I stood near the door, intending to make a break for it if things got dicey again.

The crone turned sideways in the oversized chair, dangling her legs over one wide arm. It didn't look comfortable, but she seemed to like it. "It's a bit lonely out here, Madam Lares. I get bored."

My teeth ground together, at risk of being shattered from the pressure. "Please tell me you didn't call on me because you're bored." I forced my fingers to stretch open when they fisted.

"What?" The crone's age-worn face folded into a confused expression for a beat. A moment later, she shook her head. "Don't be silly. I'm not *that* bored."

My fingers clenched again. I wondered how fast I'd have to run to avoid death if I punched her. Likely faster than I was capable of running. "So, I'm here because...?"

The crone stood and started to pace. "I don't like to give in to the visions. Annoying things, visions. But when my mind isn't occupied, they come."

My ears perked. "You had a vision?"

Flipping a dismissive hand, she blew air through her lips. "I've had several. Dozens, actually. But only one that pertains to you." She turned a suddenly intense gaze on me, her magic aura thickening as she stood and extended both hands, palms up. When she spoke, the crone's voice didn't sound at all like her own. "The Trickster seems a random thing. But chance is rarely the author of happenstance. All revolves around the sylph. The corrupt one holds the world at her fingertips. Do not allow her perfidy, or all will cease to be as you know it."

The crone blinked, her expression clearing. "There you have it. Clear as mud." Flipping her fingers above her head, she turned her back on me and sat down.

A door opened behind the witch, and a woman came into the room. I recognized the kind server who'd helped Bev and me navigate the crone's underwater castle. "Hello again," I said.

Her pale blue eyes twinkled. "Tea?"

The crone perked up. "Yes, thank you, Burgette. Do we have some of those little cakes?"

"We do, Mistress," the woman, Burgette apparently, responded.

The crone clapped her hands. "Do try the little cakes, Madam Lares. Especially the pink ones."

I wanted to tell her no and leave, but I hadn't seen the mare return, and I wasn't going anywhere without her. "Thank you," I said to Burgette, taking a pink cake and popping it into my mouth. The crone was right. Tasting of rich cream and strawberries, the tiny pink cakes were delicious.

Burgette pulled a chair over and motioned for me to sit. "The Beautiful One returns within the hour. You might as well rest and refresh yourself in the interim."

I gathered she was talking about the mare. "I will. Thanks again." I shortened my staff and shoved it into the waistband of my dancing pizza pants. It was probably a good idea to remove the temptation to blast the crone with it.

Bowing to us both, the woman left, closing the door quietly behind her.

"So, did everyone come with you from the castle beneath the sea?" I asked, curious about the change.

The crone nodded. "Everyone who matters is here."

I refrained from asking about those who didn't matter for fear she'd tell me she'd fed them to the

Leviathan. And speaking of the Leviathan... "Did you ever figure out how to keep your giant sea monsters from ganging up on you?"

The crone made a face and popped a chocolate cake into her mouth. "Not so much."

We ate in weird silence for a beat, and I tried again. "Is that why you moved?"

Chewing a yellow cake, the crone sighed. "I see you're not going to let me enjoy my treat. She stood. "Come. I'll give you what you need to defeat the Trickster."

I jumped to my feet. "You know how to defeat him?"

The ancient witch hurried toward the door, ignoring me. I grabbed three more tiny cakes and hurried after her. After all, a woman has to feed her fluffy.

We emerged into a hot sunny day on the opposite side of the treehouse. Down below us, the two dogs scampered around a teen boy wearing trousers that tied at his waist and stopped just below his knees. His feet and chest were bare, and his tousled dark hair hung to his chin. He was adorable. Wanda would definitely be a fan. He looked to be about seventeen years old.

The boy laughed as the small dogs sailed after the ball-shaped seedpod he'd thrown for them, clapping his hands when the black and tan dachshund leaped on the ball and her piebald sister leaped on her. The two dogs rolled in the dusty grass, making growly noises that were too cute to be scary.

The crone waved at the young man as she hurried past.

"What are their names?" I asked the crone. "They're so cute."

"Laverne and Shirley," she responded. The crone stepped onto the ramp I should have seen before and started down.

"What great names!" I exclaimed. "Which one is Laverne?"

The crone hit the ground and started toward a round hut built under the shade of the trees surrounding the compound. "Whichever one responds when you call out, Laverne."

I stared at her, speechless, and followed her inside. Entering the hut was a delightful surprise. The room was ten degrees cooler than the exterior. The floor was covered in rugs, and there appeared to be nothing but dirt beneath them. The room was octagonal, with floor-to-ceiling shelves, and looked like an exact replica of the wonderful library we'd made use of in the crone's undersea castle.

Anticipation flooded me at the sight. "Wanda would wet herself if she saw this room."

The crone narrowed her vibrant gaze as if assessing whether I was speaking euphemistically or telling her that Wanda had a bladder control issue. For my ward's sake, I decided to clarify. "Being a historian like you, she adores magical reference books."

The crone nodded. "I, of course, have the most extensive magical library in existence."

"Of course," I murmured, drawing another narrow-eyed look.

"Because you are the most powerful historian in existence," I appeased. At that moment, I wished I had my sister's ability to talk smack with the ancient witch. Bev and the crone had hit it off when we'd visited the undersea castle. She could say the most outrageous things, and then she and the crone would link arms and have tea.

The crone nodded regally. "Truth." Her aura flared purple and then sifted away into silver sparkles that left a glittery pile on the rug. She walked to the nearest bookshelf and reached for a single, thin tome, tugging it free from the rest. She skimmed a look through the pages, frowning and then shoving it back onto the shelf. Her aura flared again. That was when I realized she was accessing her powerful magic to locate the book she was searching for.

I dropped into a chair and waited, hoping she'd be done before the mare arrived to fetch me.

I'd dozed off on the table, my head on my arms, by the time she found what she was looking for. I became aware that she'd found it when she slammed it down onto the table an inch from my head.

I jolted awake with a shriek, surging out of my chair with magic dancing in my palms. A beat later, the air whispered behind me, and I threw out a hand to catch my staff.

The crone laughed with delight. "Jumpy much?"

I gave my heart a few beats to calm down before asking, "Was that necessary?"

"Yes. It was. The Beautiful One is here. You need to go."

Thank the goddess!

She shoved the book toward me with an outstretched finger. "Take this to your historian. She'll know what to do with it."

The book looked just like the one she'd originally rejected. I picked it up and opened it...to nothing but empty pages. "Um..."

She slammed it closed. "It's not for you to interpret. Give it to the girl."

"Right." I turned on my heel and headed toward the door.

"How rude!"

I jolted to a stop, leery of retribution from whatever slight the crone was imagining. I turned slowly, already calling my magic forward. "I'm sorry?"

That might have sounded like a polite attempt to discern the source of the crone's displeasure. What it really was, was an effort to cut the discovery process short. I'd start with an apology, then move on to an explanation if that seemed the right solution. Followed by a correction if I managed to get that far.

Hopefully, I could get out of there alive.

"You didn't thank me for the book."

"I'm so sorry. I'm still a bit dazed from waking so abruptly."

"So, it's my fault you're rude?"

I stood there, flapping my lips for a minute, unsure what to say that wouldn't result in my head being lopped off, Queen of Hearts style. Finally, I sent power into my staff, prepping for war, and said, "Yes. It's your fault."

The crone shrugged. "All right then. Have a nice trip."

Goddess in a girdle.

The woman was well and truly nuts.

"Aggy?"

I wove the voice into my dreams and clung to sleep.

Something poked me on the arm. "Aggy? Are you going to sleep all day?"

Groaning, I pulled the pillow over my head. "Go away."

Hot breath bathed my ear, followed by a wet

tongue. I swiped a hand at Monty. "Can you feed him for me, please?"

Wanda gave me an all-suffering sigh. "I did. Three hours ago."

I groaned. That meant it was eleven-ish, and I had no more excuses to stay in bed. Unless... "I think I'm sick."

"Nice try. Come on, get up. The world is ending, and you're not going to sleep your way through it."

I didn't like the tone of her voice. Cranking my eyes open, I narrowed them on the teen. "Shouldn't you be at school?"

She cocked a hip and gave me attitude. "School's closed because there are no doors or windows on the building. Nobody can get inside."

I closed my eyes again. "Swear, swear, swear."

"Ditto," Wanda said. "The fairies have blanketed the entire town with a 'nothing to see here' spell, but they're running out of ideas for keeping the non-magical ignorant."

I sighed. It was an ongoing problem. A little less than half of the residents in Rome, Indiana were non-magical and blind to the fact that magic even existed. Keeping them blissfully unaware had been a challenge since I'd become Lares, a.k.a. ancient guardian deity for the town. Before I'd taken on the role of guardian, nothing magical ever happened in Rome.

Or, maybe it had, and I'd been blissfully unaware since I hadn't even known that *I* had magic.

I rubbed my eyes. "Okay. You can kill the disgust. I'm not a slug. I was up half the night dealing with a summons from the crone."

Wanda's eyes went wide. She jittered with excitement. "You saw her again? Did you have to fight the sea monsters?"

Since saving her life had been the reason we'd nearly lost some of my council to those very sea monsters, I'd been reluctant to tell her about the adventure. Unfortunately, my advocate, whose idea of tough love was to rip a wound open wider before healing it again, had spilled the beans to the kid. Wanda had been understandably fascinated by the idea of massive sea monsters. But she'd been even more interested in learning about the crone.

I hated talking to her about the crone, probably because I knew that someday I might lose my ward to the ancient witch. Wanda needed to be trained for her role as a magical historian. I couldn't train her since I knew nothing about her magic. Nobody else on my council could train her. The crone, being a magical historian herself, was the obvious choice to do it.

I really wasn't looking forward to that day.

"No sea monsters. The crone moved into a compound in the woods."

Wanda frowned at that. I sort of shared her

disappointment. I hadn't liked fighting the monsters, but the castle under the sea had been pretty cool. "What did she want?" the teen asked.

Her question reminded me of the book. Feeling around under my covers, I found it near the bottom of the bed. I barely remembered stumbling into the room and falling into bed in the wee hours of the morning. "She gave me a riddle about the Trickster that was not helpful." I pulled the book free of the sheets. "And this. For you."

Wanda took the slender volume from me and opened it up, frowning down at the blank pages. "She gave you a blank notebook?"

I nodded. "When I tried to look at it, she slapped my fingers just like old Mrs. Troutfish had in second grade." I grinned at Wanda when she snorted. "Minus the ruler, fortunately." Shoving the covers back, I shuffled toward the door. "Coffee."

"What am I supposed to do with this?" Wanda asked as I made a left at the hallway and shuffled like a zombie toward the kitchen.

"Don't know. She said you'd know what to do with it. Have fun."

8

THE TRICKSTER'S JEST WILL GIVE
NO JOY

"Any luck deciphering the notebook?" I asked Wanda later that morning. I'd had a shower and eaten a couple of day-old muffins from Tilly's Bakery. Even having been in my refrigerator since before the Trickster got to her merchandise, the muffin still tasted as moist as if it had been freshly baked that morning.

It was magic. But, I realized as I opened the fridge and stared at the lone remaining muffin that Tilly's special brand of magic wasn't going to light up my day for much longer if we didn't stop the Trickster. "We need to get this guy," I told Wanda. "He's seriously cutting into my poor eating habits."

The teen grunted softly in response. That was when I really looked at her for the first time since coming into the kitchen. "That isn't the crone's journal." Wanda had a large, leather-bound book spread open in front of her and was staring intently at it while twirling a stick-straight ribbon of hair around her finger.

She grunted again. What we had was a failure to communicate. It was like dealing with the crone. Only less full-on crazy. I walked over and looked down at the yellowed pages of what appeared to be a really old book. Someone had scribbled in the margins, and parts of the text were underlined and starred. "Is that one of your history books?"

Wanda's response mechanism seemed to be on a timed delay. A full thirty seconds later, she said, "Huh?"

I opened my mouth to repeat my question but was interrupted by my ringing phone.

Yo mama, ho mama, don't let this call go, mama.

I sighed. I was going to put a nanny-cam in the kitchen to catch Mavis in the act of messing with my ringtones.

Yo mama, ho mama, don't let this call go, mama.

I hit *answer*, "One of these days," I threatened. I expected Mavis to laugh and congratulate herself. She didn't.

"Aggy, we need you out here right now."

Wanda looked up, concern in her dark gaze.

"What's wrong, mom?" I headed toward the front door, pulling my purse off a bat-shaped hook Wanda had installed for our purses and keys.

"We need your help, honey. Get here as fast as you can."

"Get where?" I asked. "Where am I going?" I opened the door, and Wanda scooted through ahead of me. I gave her a stern expression, but she shook her head.

"The park. The wizroom situation has taken an ugly turn."

N iele, Mavis, and Gren were standing near the road when we arrived, staring out at a sight that was unlike anything I'd ever seen before.

Wanda and I climbed out of the car with our mouths open, astonished. "What happened?" I asked after a moment to take it all in.

Niele frowned. "The wizrooms are intoxicated."

"Intoxicated?" I murmured in disbelief. "You mean they're drunk?"

Mavis shook her head. "Magically speaking, it means supercharged, revved up. Somebody fertilized them with magic."

We stood on a patch of grass about twenty feet wide that ran along the road. It appeared to be the only part of the park that wasn't covered in the wizrooms. The things ran up to the edge of the pond in the distance, climbed the sledding hill, and crowded around the base of the trees. I even saw a few sticking out of the bark of those same trees. "They're growing like weeds."

Gren nodded. "They are weeds. Magical weeds."

"They're oddly...pretty," Wanda said.

She was right. The mushrooms ranged in size from a few inches tall to nearly a foot in height. They stood on pulpy stalks with oversized caps that varied in color from the lightest pink to the palest lavender, with several shades of darker pink and purple in between. Like the array of colors, they had a range of patterns on their caps. Some had leopard spot shapes covering them. Others were covered in stripes shaped like lightning bolts. Others were covered in what could only be described as polka-dots. The adornments were all a fleshy color, not pretty and not flashy, but the variety was interesting and made me wonder what other differences they had. "Does this mean they're more potent?"

Gren glanced at Wanda. "We're not sure. From what I've read of past infections, the magic wanes as they grow and spread, until they eventually burn themselves out and die. But I've never heard of a crop expanding this quickly. These aren't normal wizrooms."

"Of course not," I said, my tone bitter. A warm wind sifted through the park, carrying with it the unpleasant scent of mildew. I covered my nose. "What's that smell?"

Niele nodded toward the wizrooms. "It's them. Their spores smell like an old, wet basement."

"Spores!" I threw my arm over my nose and mouth.

"Too late," Mavis said with a sigh. "By now, all of Rome has been infected."

"Everyone will be purple or polka-dotted?" I asked, horrified.

"Not everyone," Wanda said. "Though I'm sure some will."

"She's right," Niele said. "The magic is probably too weak for that now. But we have a bigger problem. As long as these things are giving off spores, we're in danger of having a rampant outbreak of respiratory issues."

"Is there a way to stop them from shedding the spores?" I rubbed my head, feeling as if I might explode from problem overload. *What else could possibly go wrong*? Even as I had the thought, I mentally thrashed myself. There was no need to tempt fate.

"The fae could lay a barrier spell over them," Gren said, wincing. "But the queen won't even discuss it with us."

"Why not?" I asked. "Doesn't she know her people will be in as much trouble as the rest of us if we don't get this under control?"

"That's the thing," my protector said, his handsome face creasing with worry. "They won't be. She's planning to restrict them all to Fairy."

"What?" Wanda exclaimed. "She can't do that." She looked at me, her expression filled with outrage. "What about Trish?"

That was a really good question. I put my arm around Wanda's shoulders, hugging her. "I'll talk to the queen. We'll figure this out." Except that I'd never talked to Queen Das before. From what Trish had told me, the queen was a raging recluse who thought all other species were stupid and unworthy. It wasn't exactly optimal breeding ground for satisfactory negotiations. But I'd do it. I had no choice.

"So, what do we do in the meantime?" Mavis asked, frowning.

"There's nothing the witches can do?" I asked.

"With the fae bugging out..." Her lips twitched. "Sorry about the word choice."

I snorted.

"We have our hands full. Niele basically kidnapped me to get me to the park because I told him I was too busy to help him."

I looked at the gnome, and he shrugged. "I won't apologize."

I patted his shoulder. It was gritty with dirt from his underground travels.

"But the good news is, we've sorted out the barking cats and meowing dogs mess."

"That's great," I said in my most supportive cheerleader voice.

Mavis wasn't cheered. She gave me hangdog face. "It would have been if the squirrels hadn't immediately started mooing."

"Are the cows chittering?" Wanda asked with a grin.

"Goddess knows. I'm not going near any cows right now. I've got enough to do." My mom's tone was uncharacteristically pessimistic. Things were getting to her.

"Can we bring more witches in from around the state?" I asked.

Mavis crossed her arms over her chest, frowning. "We can try. But after what happened with Dell..." She glanced my way, letting me fill in the rest of the thought myself.

Dell had been a witch from Chicago who'd come into town, supposedly, to help us find Wanda when she'd been hexed. Aside from Dell's sour personality, her presence in the situation turned out to be less than helpful and downright detrimental.

"Okay, I'll leave that to your judgment. In the interim, any ideas on what we can do to slow these things down?"

Niele nodded. "I have a thought. It's a little weird, and I don't like the long-term effects on the park grounds, but I think we need to do something."

"I agree. What is it?"

He took a deep breath, his homely features softening with my agreement. "I think we should salt the ground."

My brows lifted. "Salt it? Why?"

"Ah." Gren nodded. "That might work."

"Salt kills anything growing in the ground," Wanda told me. "Historically, it's always been viewed as an act of aggression."

"Yes," Gren agreed. "Magically, it's a good deterrent against evil. I'm hoping it will work both ways here. The idea is to make these things fight for their lives, so they have no energy left to send out spores."

"Let's do it," I agreed. "Where are we going to get enough salt, and how will we spread it?"

"That's where you and your staff come in," Gren said.

"I've ordered the salt," Niele told me. "The truck will dump it on the road here. I need you to create a windstorm to spread it over the ground. Can you do that?"

I was really better at destroying things than moving them around, but I'd forced my magic in gentler roles in the past. "I'll do the best I can."

"I can help," Mavis said. "But I don't have enough energy to do it alone."

While we waited for the salt to be delivered, I leaned against my car, glancing down at Mavis, who'd decided to sit inside until we had to go to work. She had her head back and her eyes closed, and I noted some new lines of fatigue on her face. I touched her shoulder. "You okay?"

Mavis nodded without opening her eyes. "I've just done too much magic over the last couple of days. We all have," she quickly clarified. "I should stop whining."

"You're not whining," I said.

Mavis shrugged. "The Trickster's magic is made of complex twists of energy. Unraveling it has been harder than anything I've ever done before." She opened her eyes and looked up at me. "It's really slow going, Aggy. By the time we unravel one mess, two more spring up. We can't keep trying to tackle this one problem at a time. We need a global solution."

I nodded. "The crone told me something that sounded way too much like the contents of a fortune cookie. I need to spend some time trying to decipher it. Maybe that will help."

"That sounds like her."

"Add that to the blank notebook she gave me for Wanda, and we have a smorgasbord of not helpful."

The rumble of a large engine pulled my attention down the road. "Truck's coming. It's showtime."

"Yee-ha," Mavis said, yawning widely.

9

THROUGH WEARINESS AND
DESPERATE TIMES

I sent Mavis home with orders to rest until morning. She fought me on it, but I needed her at her best so she could help me figure out how to fix our Trickster mess. Bev arrived at the house in the late afternoon, after I'd spent a couple of hours trying to decipher the crone's cryptic warning.

She rolled down the hallway into the kitchen, Monty bouncing alongside. "Hey," she said, settling a weary gaze on me. "I heard you and mom took on the magic mushrooms this morning."

I nodded. "We gave it the old college try. We just need to wait and see if it works."

Bev nodded toward the message I'd scrawled onto a lined pad of paper. "What's that?"

Expelling a weary sigh, I said, "This is the crone's idea of helping. I've been trying to figure out what she's telling me."

Bev moved closer, reading over my shoulder. "The Trickster seems a random thing. But chance is rarely the author of happenstance. All revolves around the sylph. The corrupt one holds the world at her fingertips. Do not allow her perfidy, or all will cease to be as you know it."

I watched my sister's expression as she read. She read it through silently a couple of times, her lips moving. A moment later, recognition lit in her gray eyes. "Do you know what she's trying to say?" I asked.

Bev lowered herself into the chair next to me, reaching a long, slender finger toward the word, *Sylph.* "I don't know what this whole mess means. It's too prophecy-esque, but I recognize the word, *Sylph.* That's fae. It's probably safe to assume this is referring to Queen Das."

I thought about that for a bit, realizing the queen of the fae had been a recurring theme since the Trickster arrived. Could she be behind his presence? I lifted my gaze to Bev's. "I need to talk to Trish."

"I agree. Talk to Trish. But her loyalties are divided, Aggy. She's been walking a very fine line between performing her duties as a member of your council and dealing with the brittle ego of her queen."

I realized as I heard the words that I should have seen it coming. Queen Das was like many of the fae. She was a powerful creature with a delicate psyche.

From some of Trish's random comments, I'd gathered Das was a difficult leader. But I'd never given
the problem the attention it deserved. I'd never
stood before the queen face to face. Das, I suddenly
realized, would consider that a great slight.

Das would have expected me to make an effort to
meet with her. She would be threatened by my
guardianship. She would also be jealous of my relationship with Trish. I'd never asked for her blessing
to include one of her people on my team. Trish
represented both of us. And I hadn't given a single
thought to what that must be doing to her. "Swear,
curse, swear."

Bev patted my hand. "Before you start kicking
yourself in the butt, consider everything we've had to
deal with since you became Lares. You're new to the
magical world. You wouldn't have understood the
fine points of dealing with its leaders." She hesitated
a beat and then added, "That's why you have Ferral."

She was right. Why hadn't my advocate schooled
me on Queen Das? "I need to talk to him."

The front door opened, but I didn't hear it close.
Bev and I shared a look and I stood. Monty was way
ahead of us, he was tearing down the hall, tail
drooping and a strange whine distorting his bark.
The feeling of impending doom sliced through me
just as the bell in the tower decided to ring.

Gong!

Monty circled the man lying on the floor in front

of the door. His tail was wagging low and fast. It was his worried wag. He sniffed Luke's face, nudging him with his nose.

Bev and I skidded to a stop beside Luke's unmoving form, and I hit my knees, placing my hands over his head and chest.

I sent a gentle stream of magic into him, seeking information and getting a snout full of it. "He's barely breathing. His heart is beating too slowly, and there's something dark...." The magic infecting his body flared suddenly and exploded, smacking me hard in the face. I flew backward, slamming into the wall and sliding down to my backside. My thoughts went muzzy for a beat, and pain sluiced down my spine. My poor, battered sacroiliac throbbed.

"Your what?" Bev asked, bending over me.

Oops. I must have said that last part out loud. I rubbed my achy tailbone. "Never mind. There's some kind of dark magic inside him. It..." I blinked rapidly, trying to wrap my mind around what had happened. "It threw me out."

Bev helped me to my feet. "He's unconscious. I can't rouse him. We need to call mom."

I knew she was right, but I hated to disturb Mavis. She'd only been resting a couple of hours. I sighed. "Okay."

While Bev called Mavis, I sent out a call to my council. *I need you.*

A large, black bird fluttered through the open door and landed on Luke's hip. "Pee!" Ray screeched.

Irritation burned through me. "Get off him, heathen!" I made shooing motions with my hands. "Can't you see, he's hurt?"

Ray lifted his wings and fluttered them, then danced sideways and back, still atop Luke. "Rude!"

"You're rude," I said, feeling like a five-year-old arguing about who started it. "Get off him."

Ray flew away and landed in the hallway, waddling toward the kitchen. I shook my head, looking at Monty. "Go make sure he doesn't do something he shouldn't in there."

With a happy bark, my hero took off after the raven.

"Mom's on her way." Bev eyed the man on the floor. "He's too heavy for us to move without hurting him."

"The others should be here soon."

Ferral arrived first, his usual arrogance on full display. He looked a little rumpled and a bit harried. "What's happened to the wolf?"

I glared at him. "His name is Luke."

Ferral shrugged and crouched down beside Luke, sniffing. "Dark magic. Has he had a run-in with Bathos?"

"I don't know anything. He just showed up and passed out on my floor." We all stared at the unmoving man on my floor. Worry dug its sharp claws into my lungs, making it suddenly hard to breathe.

Mavis showed up at a run, panting with flushed cheeks. "I got here as soon as I could." Her gaze landed on Luke. "Oh, no." Lowering herself next to him, she started to run a hand over his chest. I grabbed her hand, stopping her. "Be careful. When I did that, something threw me out."

A pair of delicate blonde brows lifted in surprise. Gray eyes narrowed. "Threw you out?"

I nodded. "Ferral thinks Bathos might have had something to do with it."

"He always thinks my dad's involved," Wanda said, slouching down the hall toward us.

I glanced back and found her glaring at the advocate. "Were you in the belfry?" I asked the teen.

She nodded, dismissing Ferral with a final glower. "Batty and I were trying to figure out the empty notebook."

A deep sense of failure swept through me at the renewed knowledge that the bat in my belfry wouldn't talk to me but held long and frequent conversations with my ward. "Did Bathilda have any insights?"

"Nope," Wanda said. Her gaze fell on Luke. "Is he sick?"

"We're not sure," I started to say.

"No," Mavis said, standing. "He's been attacked."

The deep thrum of large wings pounding the air

made my heart quicken. I recognized that sound. "Gren's here. We can move Luke to the couch and try to figure out what's wrong."

A tall, dark form filled the doorway, the sunshine behind him creating a halo that suited my favorite angel's personality perfectly. Gren's dark brown eyes found mine and settled, warming to smooth, melted chocolate. His gaze asked a question directed only at me. *Was I okay?* I let my answering gaze fill with all the emotions I needed to hold deep inside. Fear, confusion, frustration, and worry. His jaw tightened, sharing my pain.

"Luke has been attacked," I told my own personal angel. "Can you help Ferral carry him to the couch?"

Ferral grunted. "I don't need his help."

"I don't want you flinging him over your shoulder like a caveman. We don't know if jostling will hurt him."

Ferral shook his head and scooped Luke up like a bride. "Will this do, *Madam* Lares?"

I kept from baring my teeth at him. Barely. Ferral swept past me with Luke held gently in his arms. I gave Gren a look and he smiled, his gaze warming and sparkling with humor.

Rolling her eyes, Mavis followed the advocate into the living room.

With the world turning inside out around us, at

least we could still count on Ferral's asshatery to keep us centered.

I looked at Wanda. "Can you get blankets and pillows from the closet?"

The teen disappeared into my room.

"I'll get water and first aid things in case we need them," Bev announced.

I watched my sister head for the kitchen. She looked worn out. Warmth bathed my side, and I turned to find Gren standing close enough to almost touch. He reached out and swept a strand of hair out of my eyes. "You will find an answer, Aggy. You always do."

Tears burned my eyes at his unwavering faith in me. I wasn't sure what I'd done to deserve it.

"I'm sorry to be late," said a voice behind us.

We turned to find Niele, covered in dirt and naked as the day his mother expelled him from her womb.

"Another house turned bottom-up and we had to rescue the people inside."

I rubbed my face. "Is everyone okay?"

Niele nodded. He put hands on hips and closed his eyes, looking as weary as I felt. When he opened them again, his gaze had sharpened. I knew what he was thinking. It was what all of us were thinking. We needed to solve the Trickster problem before innocents were killed.

And everybody seemed to be looking at me for the answers.

"Why did you call us in?"

If the question came out harsher than usual, I chose not to notice. "Luke's hurt. Something attacked him."

Niele inclined his frizzy head. "How bad?"

"We aren't sure. Mavis is checking him out now."

Monty barked as he ran past Niele, but didn't stop to greet him. He was hot on the trail of the raven, who'd apparently decided that flying through my house would be fun.

Watching the two animals disappear into the sanctuary, the gnome rubbed a grubby hand over his face, leaving dirt smears behind. "Is everyone here?"

"Everyone but Trish. I'm sure she'll be here soon."

He nodded. "I'm just going to go clean up."

"Of course." I placed my hand on his beefy arm as he turned away. "How long has it been since you slept?"

He shook his head and covered my hand with his. "I'm fine." Shifting out of my grip, Niele moved away from me down the hall.

I watched him go, something painful flaring in my chest. My people were all exhausted, and their spirits were flagging under the weight of frustration. A sudden wave of fear and grief made it hard to breathe.

"Aggy?"

I turned to Gren, who stood in the doorway to the living room. "Luke's awake."

Hurrying across the room, I found the shifter on his back on the couch, trembling under a blanket. Mavis was kneeling beside the couch, her hand on his chest and a gentle glow of magic pulsing from her palm. Bev and Wanda stood nearby, their expressions filled with worry and fear. Monty lay near Luke's feet, snuggling with his buddy, and Ray stood on the back of the couch, his round black eyes skimming to me as I approached.

Ferral leaned against the wall, his muscular arms crossed over his chest and a glower on his face. His intense silver gaze followed Gren and I across the room.

"Hey," I said to Luke as I approached. "You scared us."

"Pee!" Ray said, bobbing his head and dancing sideways down the couch.

Mavis pulled her hand away from the shifter and moved back, sitting on the coffee table.

I glanced at her and she frowned. The healing evidently wasn't going well.

Luke's color was bad. He was gray beneath the usual stubble. His lips were ashen. By contrast, his golden-brown gaze looked feverish when it rested on me. He tried to sit up and collapsed backward with a pain-filled groan. Holding his middle, Luke reached for me with his free hand, his grip painful. "Aggy…"

I clasped his feverish, trembling fingers. "What happened? Did the Trickster do something to you?"

Luke's gaze glowed with intensity. He shook his head, the dark brown tangle of his hair glossy in the light from the oversized windows. "They took her, Aggy." He stopped, swallowing hard as fresh pain etched its way across his features.

"Who took who, Luke?"

His fingers tightened to the point that my finger bones ground painfully together.

I must have winced because Gren reached down and grasped Luke's wrist. "Lighten up, wolf."

Luke did, but only barely. He tried to sit up again, but Mavis gently pushed him down.

"You need to stay put," she scolded.

Luke's gaze never left mine. Fever throbbed in his eyes, and tension rippled through his muscles. "It's Trish," he said on a gasp. "They took Trish."

10

A RABID ROYAL WILL CROSS THE LINE

"Who took her?" Bev demanded.

Luke never looked away from me. "The fae," he responded. "Queen Das sent soldiers to get her. I tried to stop them..." His chalky gray pallor deepened. He fell back, gasping for breath.

"Do you know why they took her?" Ferral asked.

Luke shook his head. "Something's going on with the fae. There's been a lot of activity, and Das hasn't been seen for weeks."

I was pretty sure I knew what was going on. Bev and I shared a look. "I might have some insight into this," I told my council about the prophetic-style information the crone had given me.

Ferral looked even crankier than usual by the time I was done. "Das is not above political machinations," he said. The advocate's dense brows lowered over his intense silver eyes. "But what is she playing at now?"

His voice was low as if he were talking to himself, but Mavis spoke up, offering a possible motive. "From what I've heard, Das is arrogant and mercurial. Her ego demands that everyone treat her with supreme reverence." She glanced at me. "Aggy hasn't presented herself to the queen since becoming Lares. Is it possible she's mad about that?"

Since Mavis was voicing my exact thoughts, I frowned.

Ferral grunted, skimming me a look I couldn't interpret. By the goddess's favorite goblet, if he blamed me...

He sighed. "My apologies, Madam Lares. I've fallen down on my duties. I should have overseen a meeting between the two of you."

Shock made me blink. For a moment, I couldn't respond.

"It appears you'll have that opportunity now," Gren said, moving up behind me for support. "Because we'll need to meet the queen to negotiate Trish's release."

Ray settled his beady gaze on Luke and shuddered, all his feathers rippling as he lifted his wings and danced away. "Bad," he squawked far too loudly.

Nobody responded to the raven's succinct appraisal. He wasn't wrong.

Mavis stood. "Now, you all need to give me room

to work. I can't cure Luke of this because I don't have any power over fae dark magic. But I can make him more comfortable, and he can try to shift. That might finish the work I can't do."

I nodded. "I'll do something about a meal. Then I'll need a report from everybody on where we stand with our many crises." I glanced around at my exhausted council. "We can't keep going as we have been. We're going to have to work up a schedule with hours off, so everyone can get some sleep." I looked at Niele. "Starting with you. I'm ordering you to get some rest."

To my surprise, he didn't argue. He had to be exhausted.

"I'm fine," Bev said, frowning. "I don't need sleep."

"I'm fine too," Mavis agreed. "I got a couple of hours of rest. I could use some food, though."

"Ditto," I said. "I'd love something from Tilly's. But there's no telling when she'll be back in business."

Falling in with me as I headed to the kitchen, Bev looked grim. "That's actually in my report. She's had to shut Tilly's down for the foreseeable future. Her stock is poisoned, and her employees have all quit."

"Why don't we let her work out of this kitchen until we come up with a solution?" Wanda asked. She sat down at the table, opening the blank notebook and settling it in front of her.

I stared at her, my mind unable to wrap around what she was suggesting. "You want Tilly to come here?"

Wanda poked skinny shoulders toward her ears. "Why not? She needs a kitchen. We need food. Win-win."

"The kid has a point," Ferral said.

We all stared at him as if he'd sprouted a nipple ring.

If Ferral liked the idea, it couldn't be good... right? "My kitchen is so small," I told them. "She'd probably hate it here."

"She'd probably be grateful for the help," Mavis said as she came into the kitchen. "Tilly lives in an apartment with a tiny kitchen. If she worked here, we could set up the shop as a cooling and wrapping station."

"We could even allow people to come here to buy the food," Wanda said. "The shop has a separate entrance."

Something inside me rejected the idea of giving my soon-to-be candle shop to another entrepreneur, no matter how temporary. But they were right. I hadn't had a chance to open my shop yet. There was no sense letting it sit vacant. "I guess we could get a used oven to put in there, then she'd have the whole space to herself."

Mavis rubbed her hands together. "I'm loving this idea, honey. You could even sell Tilly's baked goods once you open your store. Her goodies will double your traffic in the shop."

The idea was growing on me too. "Will you talk to her? If she wants to do it, have her come out and assess the space and tell us what she needs. We'll get her set up as quickly as possible. It would be good if we could offer Rome some joy in the form of delicious baked goods during this current mess."

Mavis nodded. "Consider it done."

"I'll take care of getting any supplies she needs," Gren said.

I plucked my phone off the kitchen counter. "And I'll order takeout."

Bev gave me a jaunty wink. "You always have your priorities in order."

I winked back. "Of course."

After ordering more Chinese takeout than any ten people should be able to eat, I pulled Mavis aside. "How's Luke?"

"I've done all I can do. I've encouraged him to shift, but he only seems to want to sleep. We might want to have Ferral talk to him."

I thought about that. As a shifter himself, of the moon hound variety, and an overall bossy personality, the advocate might be able to harass Luke into shifting. Which gave me a thought. "Doesn't Luke have a pack around here?"

"According to Trish, he left his pack behind. Apparently, the alpha was a bit too...alpha," Mavis said, smiling. "They're up north somewhere, Vermont, I think."

"Well, that's no help then."

She shook her head. "Honestly? I'm not sure shifting will help. Maybe Luke's doing the best thing by sleeping."

I glanced at Ferral, who was sitting at the table with Wanda, watching her stare at the notebook. As I approached, he said, "Maybe she meant for you to write something in it."

Wanda gave him a teen-sized eye roll. "That would be dumb."

"Yes. It would be. But the crone is an illogical creature. She is, however, quite cunning."

Wanda's response was to scoop up the notebook and head for her "room," which currently consisted of the old pastor's office that I'd intended to turn into a walk-in closet and bathroom.

We were still working on making the decision about where the teen's very own room would be. Wherever it was, it would require Trish to build it. With everything that had been going on, we hadn't drawn up the plans yet.

I sat down across from the advocate. He looked at me, his expression surprisingly free of derision or dislike. "Madam Lares."

"Advocate."

His lips curved upward in the corners. Just a

little. "I owe you an apology. I should have realized you needed to address Queen Das."

I bit down on my instinct to dismiss his apology. First, because I'd never gotten one from him before and the apology needed to be cherished, and second because he was right. He should have realized. "Let's remedy that. Give me a crash course on Das. We need to figure out why she's taken Trish and what she has planned. The crone's warning seems to suggest that the queen is behind the Trickster's arrival in our lives."

Ferral nodded. "I would agree with her assessment. I think we can assume that Das is throwing a temper tantrum. She's five hundred years old, with the temperament of a teen. At sixteen, your ward is far more mature than Queen Das."

I grimaced.

"But that doesn't mean she has a child's proclivities," Ferral went on. "Das has led one of the bloodiest reigns in recent fae history. She has no compunction about killing her own people or the non-fae. Which is why your arrival on the scene has probably vexed her."

"I don't understand."

"You are the guardian of all people in Rome, human and magical. Technically, your dominion covers Das and her people, a fact that no doubt burns like acid in her soul. Especially since Trish is a member of your council."

"And has been spending a lot of time here, working on the renovations."

He shook his head. "Das is jealous, but not in the way you're thinking. She isn't jealous that Trish might favor you, even have loyalty to you. She is simply angry that you deign to usurp her province."

"Okay, two things. It doesn't sound like she's big on protecting her people."

He inclined his head in agreement.

"And I didn't usurp anything. I'm here to help."

"Ah, but Das would not see it like that. She believes you see yourself as superior to her. I'm afraid my faux pas in not introducing you has probably fed into that illusion. She clearly believes you think you're too good to come to her."

"She could come to me."

"Das would never do that. She is what she accuses you of being. She is too arrogant to lower herself. She would see that as admitting you were superior."

I rubbed my head. "I'm getting a headache."

"And that, Madam Lares, is what it's like inside Das' head. her entire psyche is headache-inducing, for herself as well as everyone else."

"Then her goal in sending the Trickster...?"

"Was likely to overwhelm you with problems, thereby ensuring you'll fail. Then she can gloat over that failure and proclaim that, due to your obvious incompetence, Fairy is no longer under your aegis."

"If she's abusing her people, she needs to be under my guidance."

"Therein lies the crux of the problem. You cannot simply wish the fae under Queen Das well and turn your back. And she will not allow you to protect her people as you need to."

"So, what's the grand plan," I asked. "She destroys Rome and presumably demoralizes me so that I run away sobbing. Then she's the queen of what? Nothing. Those who survive the Trickster's ugly deeds will move away, and Rome will be a ghost town. How does that enrich her small, mean life?"

"She cares not about the world of humans. Her people live in an in-between place that is anchored in Fairy. They have created a gate from Rome into Fairy because Rome is a place of magical power. But Das has never liked having that connection with the earthly plane. She is likely already making plans to break the gate and return her kingdom entirely to the fairy realm."

"But, wouldn't that solve our problem?" I asked in a spurt of hope.

"Not at all," Ferral responded. "Das won't withdraw her Trickster. She fully intends to destroy your dominion, Madam Lares. Whether or not she continues to allow the connection to Rome has nothing to do with that goal. She'll be watching and enjoying the fruits of her machinations. Don't think she won't."

Curse, swear, curse. "I need to speak to her. Can you arrange it?"

"*We* need to speak to her," Ferral corrected me as he stood. "I'll start the process to get a face-to-face meeting with Das. In the meantime, you have much to learn about the niceties of the fairy court. We'll start that training as soon as I get back."

It was on the tip of my tongue to tell him I could give a rip about the niceties. That nasty woman kidnapped my friend. I fully intended to get Trish back from her. And if solving the Trickster problem came back to dealing effectively with Das, I'd somehow manage that too.

After all, I really had no choice. It was my job to protect the town of Rome, Indiana. And I was fully invested in doing it.

THE JESTER'S EVIL AT THE HELM

B ecause I needed to feel as if I was doing something...anything...to help, I headed into town and paid a visit to Chief Marshal. I parked my Range Rover on the street in front of the police station and looked around. At first glance, every-thing in the picturesque town looked normal-ish.

Closer inspection showed me a cardinal hanging upside down from a tree branch like a bat and a small tree in a pot near the alley with starfish sprouting from its slender branches like flowers. Even as I saw the oddities, the air around them quiv-ered. When it stilled, the bird was right side up and the tulip tree sported pink flowers again.

I'd have to tell Mavis and Bev the witches' glamour spells were failing. I hated to do it, but we had a few hundred non-magic humans in Rome and, though that number was steadily dwindling as the magic world continued to invade the calm normalcy of their human world, I was intent on keeping as many of them happily ignorant as I could.

The harsh reality was that the witches were good at many things. Glamours weren't their strong suit. The fae had always done that kind of thing for Rome. Apparently, we could no longer count on them for help.

My steps were slow and heavy heading into the station. I knew that nothing good would come from the visit. The number of people in the public area had shrunk from the last time I'd been there, but there were still people lined up and down the alley leading to the station's door.

Rather than budge in front of them, I called Davis Marshal from the street.

"Aggy," he said when he answered. "Where are you?"

"I'm outside. I didn't want to jump to the front of the line. How's it going? Are things getting any better?"

He grunted. "Define better."

"Less horrible than before?"

"Maybe a titch. Can you meet me at the back door? I want to talk to you about something?"

"Sure."

"I'll see you in a minute."

I walked around the building and arrived at the

door leading to the private parking lot for the Rome Police as Davis opened the door and stepped out. He pointed to a boxy white SUV. "Climb in. Let's go for a drive."

I did as he suggested. We drove in silence for several minutes as Davis took us the back way out of town. I didn't initiate a conversation because, honestly, the quiet was soothing. For a blissful few moments, no crisis required my help. Nobody expected me to fix anything. It was nice.

I lay my head back on the seat and sighed.

Davis glanced my way. "My feelings exactly."

I snorted. "The last couple of days have been worse than my seating, and believe me, that's saying something."

He nodded. Chief Marshal had been ignorant of magic when I'd first ascended to my dominion as Lares. But our adventures since then had probably given him an idea of the crazy that had become my life.

I studied his attractive profile as he drove. With his thick mop of dark hair, graying on the sides, and tall, leanly muscled body, Davis was a good-looking guy and still solid despite his sixty-some years. He had the sharp gaze of a cop and a no-nonsense way about him that was comforting in a crisis. At the moment, he also had a fresh set of lines around his eyes and a tightness in his square jaw that told me he'd felt every painful moment of the last forty-eight hours.

"What did you want to talk to me about?" I asked him.

He turned into the park and drove toward the lake.

I bit my tongue on a warning, hoping that the work Niele, Mavis, and I had done earlier had slowed down the wizrooms enough to disable their poison.

"I hope you don't mind this little ride. I had to get out of that station for a while, or I was going to lose my mind."

"That bad, huh?" On a normal day in town, Davis wouldn't spend much time in his office. As the sole on-duty cop during the week, he spent most of his time either walking or driving the streets, dealing with problems as they arrived. It had to be horrible for him to be cooped up with the cauldron of problems life in Rome had recently become.

"I'm not complaining. But..."

"But you're dealing with a roiling mess that seems to have no end?"

He skimmed me a look, a grim smile on his craggy face. "It's like you can read my mind."

I barked out a surprised laugh. "I'm living your reality myself."

"Any idea yet on how to deal with this Trickster?"

"Not yet. We're looking at all options."

"If we could lure it to the jail, we could lock it up in those special cells the witches hexed for me."

We'd had to add three more of those special cells recently. I suddenly wondered if Davis blamed me for all the magical problems. It seemed like all Hades had broken loose since I accepted the Lares job. Probably because it had. Literally, in some cases.

I nodded. "If we could find him, that might work. Unfortunately, none of my people have been able to set eyes on him, despite seeing his handiwork all over the place."

"Do you think he's invisible?"

"Not invisible, no. But as good as. From what I've read, Tricksters can blend into their surroundings, and they can move so quickly they're little more than a blur on the air."

Davis drove in silence for a moment. Then he sighed. "It breaks my heart looking my people in the eye and lying to them about their problems as if I have no conscience."

"If you didn't have a conscience, you wouldn't feel bad about it," I reminded him.

"Maybe we should just tell them all about magic. They probably deserve to know."

I chewed my bottom lip, looking for the right words. "Do you remember when I told you about magic?"

Davis skimmed me a look, the first tendrils of

doubt sliding through his gaze. "I do. It threw me for a loop."

"Yes. And, it took you a while to get over it, as I recall."

His jaw tightened, a muscle ticing in his cheek. "My world was turned upside down. I won't deny it. But, I needed to know, and maybe these people in Rome need to know too. Wouldn't it be safer for them?"

I'd had the same thought many times. "You might be right, Davis. I'd like to talk about it with you and my council. But I don't think this is the right time. Not with everything else going on. It will just add another layer of complexity and chaos to an already unmanageable problem."

He expelled a breath, inclining his head. "Okay. But when this is over, I want to have that conversation."

"You have my word."

He took his eyes off the road to look my way. "What about putting them all in stasis until this is over?"

I caught movement out of the corner of my eye and turned. A small figure stumbled into the road in front of us. I screamed Davis' name, bracing myself on the dash.

The cop slammed on his brakes and swerved to avoid the young woman, who'd turned to us with wide eyes and outstretched hands as if she would stop the big car herself.

Too late, I realized I should have used my magic. It had happened too quickly, and my brain locked up. By the time I reached for a power word, the girl's frail form had bounced off the car, sailing into the air and landing out of sight at the side of the road.

"No, no, no, no..." Davis chanted as the car skidded to a stop. He was out of the car and running toward the girl before I even managed to unbuckle my seatbelt.

I ran after him, pulling my phone out of my pocket as I ran.

He stood on the shoulder, staring down into a grassy ravine that ran along the road. His shoulders drooped, and his head was lowered.

"Is she alive? I'm calling 9-1-1."

He shook his head. "Don't bother, Aggy." His tone of voice was dead, beyond miserable. I braced myself for what I'd see as I skidded to a stop beside him, a spray of small stones pinging away from my sneakers as I looked down into the ravine.

I blinked, confused. "I don't understand." The grass was dented in the shape and size of the girl. There even looked to be a little blood on the glossy blades of grass.

But there wasn't a body. My head came up and I scanned the area, looking for the girl. "Did you see her walk away?"

Davis didn't answer me. He stared into space as if the incident had finally broken his stalwart brain.

I touched his arm. "Davis?"

He continued to stare at the grass where there should have been a body.

A truck roared past, blaring its horn at the abandoned car in the middle of the road.

I squeezed Davis' unmoving arm. "Come on, Chief. I'll drive. Let's go to my house. I think Mavis is cooking."

She wasn't. But at that point, I'd say almost anything to pull Davis out of his catatonic state. And the combination of Mavis and her cooking seemed like just the ticket.

I'd expected my house to be quiet, mostly empty. Those who weren't on rest would be out tackling the Trickster's handiwork. It would probably just be Wanda and Monty at the house. But, as we stepped inside, voices came to me from the back of the house. Relaxed and happy voices.

Monty bounded toward me, eyes bright and tail wagging. He touched his nose to my foot and then spun around to return to the food…er…I mean people in the kitchen.

I headed toward the sound of voices, Davis's footsteps following in my wake. The scent of spicy tomato sauce met my nostrils as I stepped through the door and looked around.

Bev was chopping salad ingredients at the sink while chatting amiably with our mom. Layla stood next to her, a beer in one hand.

Ferral's deep voice came from the mudroom, where I assumed he was on his phone, trying to get us a meeting with Das.

Niele was all cleaned up and wearing his moss shorts, his stick and berries appropriately covered for polite company and dinner.

None of them noticed Davis and me at first.

Wanda was spreading butter on slices of Italian bread, chatting with her companion at the kitchen table. Sitting across from her, Luke had a blanket around his broad shoulders. His golden-brown eyes were bright, and he favored me with a smile when he saw me. The smile became hesitant when he spotted the chief but then strengthened. "Hey, Chief Marshal."

Davis nodded at Luke, his gaze sliding over the people in the room and landing unerringly on Mavis. She'd been stirring the spaghetti sauce I'd smelled, but she turned with a surprised expression when she heard Davis's name. "Oh. Hey, Davis. I hope you're hungry."

Guilt swept over me. I'd promised to handle

dinner. "What happened to the Chinese food I ordered?"

Niele flushed. "I hope you don't mind. My gnome crew was hungry. They've been working day and night. I took the food to them."

A guilty flush heated my cheeks. "I don't mind at all. I just feel bad I didn't think of feeding them. Please, give them whatever they need. Tell them all to go home for a few hours and rest."

Niele nodded. "Thanks. I'll make sure that happens."

I walked over and hugged Mavis. "Sorry, you got stuck cooking again."

She kissed my cheek. "No worries, honey. You know cooking helps me think. It's all good."

"Stop thinking. You need some downtime."

She moved closer, lowering her voice. "I see you brought me something else to think about."

I grinned. "Davis needs a good dinner and some rest too."

Mavis nodded. "Chief," she called across the room. "Would you like a beer?"

Davis walked past everyone else as if they weren't there, approaching Mavis with a heated look. "I'd love a beer. What is that delicious scent?"

"My homemade spaghetti sauce, with meatballs. I hope you're hungry. I made enough for an army."

His gaze heated further as he said, "I'm starving."

Mavis's cheeks turned pink. "Aggy, will you get Davis a beer?"

"My pleasure." I got myself one too. I generally preferred wine, but the icy beer felt good on my parched throat. "Has anybody heard from Gren?"

"He's looking into a rash of spirits popping up around town," Layla said, giving Davis a finger wave. At his blank look, she laughed. "Princess Layla? I've changed a little."

Davis skimmed me a look.

"It's her. Remember her and me going into the vortex?"

"He nodded."

"Layla got hit by a magic attack on the way out. It...changed her."

"I've since rediscovered my devilish side," the princess told him wickedly. "But I've learned it's easier to eat spaghetti without all those teeth."

We laughed.

Bev nodded enthusiastically. "She's not kidding. I still have nightmares about the one time she tried it with her terrifying maw. The sauce went everywhere."

"I found some in my hair later than night," Niele agreed.

Wanda lifted a hand. "Behind my ear."

Monty barked enthusiastically, a delighted light in his bright eyes.

"Monty loved it," I said. "He was cleaning

spaghetti sauce off the floor and cabinets for a week." We all enjoyed a good laugh at Layla's expense.

"Har, de, har, har," the princess said. But her lips twitched with an answering smile.

Davis laughed with us, leaning against the wall near where Mavis worked. He seemed to visibly relax, as if the burden he'd been carrying was lightened by spending time with others who shared some of the secrets he'd been carrying around.

I suddenly realized what I'd done to him by leaving him out there on his own. He couldn't talk to anyone at the station about magic. As far as I knew, the cops under him were human, as Davis was, and I had no idea if they knew about magic. I'd thought I was doing him a favor, trying to keep his life like it had been before the knowledge was forced upon him. But there was no putting that genie back in the bottle. His life had been irretrievably changed, and he deserved a support structure to help him navigate the new challenges I'd forced on him.

A shadow flitted past the kitchen window. The soft throb of wings on the air. An awareness, like a zing of electricity, shot through my system, followed by an elevation in my heart rate. My mouth opened, and I spoke without thinking. "Gren's here."

The back door opened. My gaze locked onto the tall, strongly made man with wavy, dark hair and piercing brown eyes. His gaze found mine, warming to melted dark chocolate. For just a heartbeat, the world stopped. My perception of our surroundings fell away, and everything spun down to an awareness of him.

Something was changing between us. Something powerful and hungry. And I wasn't sure how to control its effects on me. Or even if I wanted to try.

You're okay? He asked inside my head.

I smiled at the question, a soft smile filled with all the emotion I was holding deep within me so no one else would see. The secret was mine to keep. It was Gren's to hold. And nobody else needed to know. *I'm good.*

Luke's voice interrupted our moment like a splash of cold water on my face.

"Gren, what's the deal with the ghosts?"

Gren turned toward the shifter, his hands sliding into the pockets of his jeans. "A dozen sightings. All over town. People who saw them believed they were alive until they disappeared before their eyes."

Davis and I shared a look. Something that looked like relief slipped through his eyes. "Make that thirteen," he offered in his husky voice. "I thought I'd hit a young girl on the park road. But when I went to check on her, she was gone."

"Do we think the Trickster is behind the ghost sightings?" Mavis asked the room at large.

Gren frowned. "I'm not sure. Inadvertently, probably. Our graveyard isn't the only one in town that was flipped around."

Davis's eyes widened. "Flipped around?"

I nodded. "The stones are all gone. The grass is unmarred. Gren couldn't even feel the bodies beneath the surface anymore."

"The one aspect that makes me think maybe he's involved," Gren offered. "Is how lifelike they are. Ghosts are usually easily identified, especially in daylight. They're insubstantial, wispy. These ghosts look like they're alive in the brightest sunlight."

Davis nodded. "And solid. I was sure I'd hit a living woman."

"Have the specters hurt anybody?" Layla asked.

"One man thought he saw his dead wife. He walked blindly into the street and was clipped by a car," Gren said. "But there have been no attacks." He glanced at me. "Just some very confused non-magical humans."

I closed my eyes. "We can't block them from seeing spirits, can we?"

"We can't," he agreed. "Spirits aren't magical. They're..."

"Spiritual," I finished for him. "Anyone with a soul and an open mind is capable of seeing them."

He inclined his head. "If the Trickster wanted to make sure the people we've been trying to protect were affected, this would be a really good way to do that."

I dropped into a chair at the table with Luke and Wanda, suddenly exhausted again. We needed a breakthrough on the Trickster mess, and we needed it soon. Every minute seemed to send us more deeply into chaos and confusion.

"I've been thinking," Layla said.

We all turned to look at her.

"This Trickster...he hasn't actually harmed anyone, has he?"

I frowned. "Yes. Emotionally. I assume you meant physically, though. Why do you ask?"

She stared at the floor, seemingly in deep thought. After a moment, she said, "I once met a witch whose special power was chaos magic. She was very...talkative...about her craft." Layla glanced up, looking sheepish.

I narrowed my eyes at her. "Talkative, huh? I'm guessing you were motivating her to be cooperative?"

Layla shrugged and grinned. "Devil, remember."

Luke and Bev chuckled.

"Do we want to know how you motivated her?" Wanda asked. She rose from the table with a baking sheet covered in garlic bread, sliding it into the oven that Mavis opened for her.

"I didn't perform violence on her if that's what you're afraid of. She was torturing someone I cared about. I just needed to impress upon her what a bad idea that was."

Ferral came into the kitchen. He gave me a meaningful look that told me he wanted to speak to me privately after dinner.

I inclined my head, my attention caught on movement in the back yard.

"Anyway," Bev spurred. "What did you learn about chaos magic?"

Layla set her empty beer bottle on the counter. "That it's very successful in taking down an adversary, often without any real violence."

I didn't like the sound of that. "Did she give you any tips on how to defeat it?"

"Actually, she did. Though, I don't think she really meant to. On the demonic plane, I was well known for my interrogation abilities. I can make anybody talk given enough time and interest."

"Again with the things that will make a sixteen, almost seventeen-year-old have nightmares?"

Layla grinned at Wanda. "I'll keep my nightmares to myself. In this case, the solution to your problem is...simple."

We all waited for her to go on. She didn't. After a moment, Ferral, whose patience was the length of a snake without a tail, said, "What exactly is this simple solution?"

Layla seemed surprised by the question. "That's it. Simplify the range of problems you're having and taper your response to address the narrower target. The thing about chaos is that you lose sight of key details because you're pulled in too many directions at once. You become frantic and lose even more focus. When it feels like you're being attacked on twenty different fronts, you can't focus on any one thing long enough to fix it."

Silence pulsed through the room as we all considered Layla's advice. A knock on the door ended our thoughtful silence. "Come in!" I called out to the two enormous males I'd seen crossing the backyard.

The nearly eight-foot-tall creatures had straight black horns that stuck out to the sides of their heads and narrow, triangular faces. Their charcoal-gray skin had a scaled aspect to it, the scales more texture than actual scaling. Their eyes, exotically slanted, were black with fiery centers. Their massive hands bore thick, black claws and their legs were bent, like a goat's hind end, with split hooves like a farm animal.

They were Matthew and Glenn, Layla's most loyal guards. My council had grown used to their devilish appearance when we'd recently worked together to save Wanda from a witchy plot. Davis, however, hadn't seen enough lost ones to become immune to their terrifying appearance. He stiffened and straightened away from the wall when the two guards came inside my house, shifting closer to Mavis as if to protect her.

I smiled at the two devilish creatures. "Hey, guys. You're just in time for spaghetti."

There was an audible gasp, and I turned to find Wanda and Bev hiding grins behind their hands. But it was Layla who named the elephant in the room. "Spaghetti ala splatter for two, please."

Monty was going to think he'd died and gone to heaven.

12

A HUMAN COP IS OVERWHELMED

I watched Davis and Mavis...the rhyming thing was just too cute for words...chatting easily with their heads together, and smiled. Maybe it was just nice to see two people I cared about having a pleasant, stress-free moment. Or maybe my poor brain was trying to escape the stupendous *Ugh* that was my current activity.

A training session with the snotty advocate.

"Madam Lares, if you don't pay attention, you're not going to be prepared when we visit Queen Das."

I sighed, dragging my attention away from happier things and diving head first into the swamp of obligation. "I am paying attention."

He sat back in his chair, crossing massive arms over his broad chest. "Repeat my last five words."

"Repeat my last five words."

His silver gaze narrowed threateningly on me.

I sighed. "Das will kill us all."

He seemed surprised that the happy prediction had found a spot in my brain. "And that possibility doesn't worry you?"

"Of course, it worries me," I said, losing patience. "But nearly every moment of my time since becoming Lares has been weighed down under the possibility of everyone I know and love being in danger. I won't say it's getting boring..." Because dying was definitely not on my near-term bucket list. "...but with all our current problems, dealing with a spoiled brat of a fae queen just doesn't seem like a priority."

Ferral said, "And Trish?"

I closed my eyes, guilt flooding me like adrenaline. Just for a beat. A very short time. I'd forgotten about Trish. I expelled a breath. "We need to get her back. You're rrrrr..."

His lips twitched. "I'm what?"

I glared at him. "You're rrrrr..." I swallowed hard, then cleared my throat. "You're ri...right. I'm paying attention." It nearly killed me to tell him he was right. What did that say about me? That I wasn't stupid?

Ferral nodded. "Good. Now, here's what I think is going on with Das. I believe she wants a place on your council."

My eyes went wide. "You're kidding, right?"

"Not at all. I don't mean a physical place there. She'd never lower herself to sit on a council of which she was not the lead. But she believes she should have a say in everything that happens in Rome. She does not respect nor recognize your dominion over her."

"I don't want to have dominion over her. My job has nothing to do with her."

"And that is the key," he said, relaxing. "We must convince her you are not trying to rule over her people in any way, shape, or form."

"I don't rule over anybody," I argued. "I protect. Or, try to protect." I frowned, thinking of all the stuff currently going on for which I was providing little to no protection.

"You and I understand that. But to Das, your interference...and make no mistake, that's how she sees it...is as good as proclaiming that she cannot keep her people safe."

"So, that's ridiculous. How am I going to convince her that I'm not trying to interfere?"

"The answer to that is both simple and complex. To put it succinctly, you must declare her people outside of your authority."

I frowned.

"You must convince her that you don't want to help the fae."

"What if a fairy needs my help? I can't just..."

"You can and you must."

I shook my head, not wanting to commit to that. Then I had a thought that was almost worse. "Trish can still be on my council, right?"

He stared at me, his expression set in stone. His intense silver gaze was brittle and hard.

My hopes sank. "I can't lose her. She's invaluable and..." I swallowed hard. "She's my friend."

"Until we defeat the Trickster, you must do this, Madam Lares."

"For goddess sake, Ferral! Why can't you just call me Aggy?"

"We are *not* buddies," he said in his snottiest tone. "I am your advocate. You are my Lares."

I threw up my hands. "Fine! Whatever." Good goddess. I was channeling the sixteen-year-old. "Have you heard back from the fae about our visit?"

"Yes. We go at midnight."

I sighed. "Why must all of these things happen in the middle of the night?"

His response was a single, raised brow.

I spun away from him, calling out to Mavis and Davis...heh. "Does anybody need anything?"

Davis stood. "I should get going. I need to check in at the jail and make sure everything's okay there."

Mavis stood too. "Can you give me a ride home, honey?" she asked me. "I came with your sister, and she already left."

"Of course."

"I'd be pleased to give you a ride home," the chief said.

Did he have extra color in his craggy cheeks? Or was it my imagination? Nope, he was flushed. And his pretty friend was blushing too.

I thought I might melt from the cuteness.

"That would be wonderful. Thank you, Davis."

"It's my pleasure."

"Night," I told them. "Mom, I'll call you in the morning and tell you how our visit to Fairy went."

Mavis stopped to give me a hug. "Be careful, honey."

"I will."

She linked her arm with the chief's, and they started for the door. Mavis stopped suddenly, turning back to me. "I forgot to tell you," she said. "Tilly will be here in the morning to start baking. She's decided to use your oven until the one Bev bought gets here in a couple of days. I hope that's okay?"

My mouth watered at the thought. "Are you kidding? Tilly's treats warm from the oven...it's going to be pure heaven."

Mavis laughed, her eyes twinkling. "I know, right?"

"I love Tilly's," the chief said hopefully.

Mavis patted his hand as he opened the front door for her. "I'll bring you some goodies later."

His smile made my whole body warm with plea-sure. Any residual worry I was carrying around for the chief fell away. He was in good hands. And I hadn't seen Mavis that happy in a long time.

Suddenly aware of a presence beside me, I turned to Ferral.

His lips curved in a pleased smile. "You did a good thing...Aggy. They are good people. They deserve whatever happiness this world allows for them."

I found myself giving him an answering smile. "Yes. They are. And they do...advocate."

He barked out a laugh. "I'll be going. I have preparations to make before we leave. Get some rest. You'll want to be fresh and sharp for this meeting."

The night was darker than usual, with only a crescent moon to light our way. The trees of the Mystical Wood darkened it even further, their enormous, overarching presence like silent sentinels not entirely approving of our approach. Even the pixies, with their athletic airborne dancing and happy rainbow colors, were sparse. The wood was eerily quiet. The wind rustled the branches of the massive trees high above our heads, but only the soft rustle of the leaves broke the unnatural quiet.

Despite the unnerving lack of sound, the pleasant scent of night-blooming flowers accompanied us through the forest, their delightful perfume pulling us gently along the path.

Ferral seemed to know where he was going, in spite of the fact that there was no map or signage declaring the location of Queen Das' queendom. After asking him three times where we were headed and receiving only grunts and murmured non-answers, I'd given up and simply followed where he led.

I was just about to try again, certain that Ferral had miscalculated our route somewhere along the way, when the path ahead of us started to glow with a rainbow of colors. Stepping onto the first of a long line of moss-covered stones, I examined them for the source of the glow. There was nothing.

All around us, dancing lithely through the trees in bursts of vibrant color, pixies flitted with manic energy. Their athletic displays were punctuated by the graceful flickering of massive butterfly-like flutterflies. Where the pixies left bright, exuberant colors in their chaotic wake, the flutterflies glowed with soft pastels and moved in sweeping, gentle arcs and waves.

The trees, I realized, were not the same kind I was used to seeing in the woods. Their pale, smooth-barked trunks were pocked with hundreds of small dark spots I recognized as pixie burrows. Some of the giant trees were impossibly pitted with the hideaways. Like Swiss cheese. To the point where it seemed they shouldn't be able to stand upright. But they were whole and hearty, seemingly unaffected by the myriad of lairs. Instead of leaves, the trees' graceful branches sprouted a dense display of the sweet-smelling flowers I'd scented as we approached.

Frothy drapes of silver moss lightened the darkness with a lacy radiance that was as gentle on the eyes as it was illuminating.

I hadn't realized I'd stopped to watch the show until Ferral's voice spurred me from my trance. "Fairy is a beautiful place, unlike any other."

I blinked in surprise. "We're in Fairy?"

He nodded.

"But I didn't even feel a barrier or spell."

"We are expected."

On the heels of his statement, the rhythmic thump of booted feet filled the silence. We stood and waited as they approached, determined not to give Das any excuse to offer violence. A moment later, the darkness peeled away from a dozen men, all dressed in heavy boots and a shiny silver fabric that looked vaguely like chain mail.

Marching toward us in formation, the group wore stern expressions on their perfect faces, the delicate features and wispy blond hair making them seem unlikely warriors. Though Trish shared the same delicate features, and she was one of the finest warriors I'd ever seen.

Das' soldiers carried few weapons. The fact would have made me feel better, except that I knew they themselves were weapons. The fae's magic was as unexpected as it was deadly.

They approached in perfect formation, stopping a mere ten feet away. As one, they bowed their heads. The soldier in the middle of the front row stepped forward. "Queen Das welcomes you to Fairy. Your presence here will be allowed under the Fae Charter for Non-Fairy Ambassadors, Article Twelve Hundred and Fifty-One. Do you agree to abide by the Charter on the threat of execution for any failure to do so?"

I swallowed hard, opening my mouth to ask what constituted "not abiding."

Ferral stepped in front of me and inclined his head. "We do."

"State your title and purpose."

I opened my mouth to speak, but Ferral furtively touched my arm and gave me a tiny shake of his head. Then he returned his attention to the soldier. "I am Sir Ferral of the Guardian Assembly. I serve as Advocate to Madam Lares, Guardian of Rome and its people." He stepped back and indicated me with a flourish of his hand. "Madam Lares requests an audience with Queen Das."

"You are expected," said the soldier.

With that, the three rows of soldiers, four in each row, spun on their heels and marched into the darkness.

I gave Ferral wide eyes. He frowned, his lips formed in a tense line. Then we moved out after them, no longer enjoying the beauty of Fairy.

I expected some kind of castle. Or, really, any kind of building. What we saw when we got to the end of our march was an enormous, raised pavilion. The center of the building was dark, offering only the barest suggestion of the throne at its center.

I couldn't tell if the queen was occupying her throne at the moment. The shadows were too deep.

Hundreds of fairies were arrayed around the pavilion, their sharp, hostile gazes stabbing at us like blades.

I barely looked at the assembled fae. My gaze had caught on a single figure. The slender woman with wispy blonde hair stood before the pavilion, a guard on either side of her. Each guard held a slender sword, the blades crossed beneath their prisoner's dainty chin. The weapons were no doubt there for our benefit since I knew they didn't need blades to kill.

Trish stared at us as we approached, her pretty

face tight with anger. I looked into her vivid green eyes and felt the sting of that anger like a lash across my skin. I realized with a jolt that she was mad at me.

"You shouldn't have come," she ground out when we stopped a few feet away. "This isn't your fight."

To my surprise, Ferral spoke before I could. "It is very much our fight. You are a member of the Lares council. You have obligations to Madam Lares. You have neglected your duties."

I stared at him in shock. "I don't think…"

"You are correct, advocate. I have been remiss in my duties to the Lares. I've allowed personal problems to waylay me." Trish gave me a slight bow. "I beg your forgiveness, Madam Lares."

I just stared at her, confused.

"How dare you come into Fairy and reprimand one of my people," a strident voice spoke from the depths of the massive pavilion. I lifted my gaze as a line of pixies entered the pavilion, meeting in the center and shooting skyward. Like a Vegas dance line, the colorful pixies bent away from each other at the top of the arc and circled away from the throne, performing a complex dance that left bright tails of color in their wake. The small fae ended their chorus line routine by forming a perfect arc of silvery illumination over the head of the squat, diminutive creature sitting on the throne. Their light was like a living aura that was far prettier than the creature it adorned.

Responding to some unspoken command, Trish and the two guards stepped to the side, opening a clear path to the creature whom I had to assume was Das. The fairy queen.

Das inclined her small head. "You may come before me."

Though I recognized the gamesmanship in Das' command, there was no denying the power that throbbed against my skin at the directive. I felt its concussive force in the center of my chest, and I was surprised to find my feet moving forward of their own volition.

Whatever my interactions with the fairy queen... whatever my opinion...I could not forget that she was a magical force to be reckoned with.

At that moment, I understood exactly how much trouble we were in. If Das was responsible for infecting Rome with the Trickster, it was going to be all but impossible for us to rid ourselves of him while keeping my dominion safe.

The queen peered at us through cold, black eyes that shone with a strange inner light through the shadows. Far from the tall, beautiful queens of fairy-tales and movies, Das was a terrifying creature that resembled, more than anything, a very large bug.

Her small head bore a wispy aura of pale blonde hair, the strands so soft and fine they rose above her skull as if infused with static electricity. Her nose was small and rather flat, twitching constantly as if she were assessing her environment through the sense of smell. But her mouth was her most disturbing feature. When she smiled, it was intimidating rather than reassuring. Her pale, thin lips stretched around a terrifying array of triangular silver teeth.

Das' body was thick and wide, covered in a gauzy gown that fluttered in a breeze I couldn't feel. The fabric of her dress was so thin it barely hid the dark, splotchy skin beneath.

Tiny feet clad in soft, flat shoes stuck out from under the gown's wispy hem, and a pair of pale, membranous wings lifted from her back.

"Have you come to beg for the return of my warrior fairy?" she asked in a smug, haughty voice.

I hadn't expected such a blunt question and was ill-prepared for it. Fortunately, Ferral was much better equipped for bargaining with the queen than I was.

He bowed to her. "Queen Das, thank you for being magnanimous enough to speak with us. We are grateful for the opportunity to meet."

Das blinked her blustery gaze at him and then inclined her head. "It is good you afford me the respect I deserve." The winter-like gaze slid my way. "But I notice the Lares has not properly addressed me."

"That is my fault, I'm afraid," Ferral said, sounding contrite. I wished I could bottle the Ferral I was watching at that moment for all our future interactions. The advocate offered me his hand. Per his instructions, I put my hand in his. "Queen Das, most excellent ruler of fairy-kind, may I present Madam Lares, guardian of the dominion of *human* Rome."

I wondered if Das caught the advocate's slight inflection on the word human. It seemed her scary gaze sharpened at his introduction.

I inclined my head, enough to be deferential but not enough to appear a supplicant. "It is my great pleasure to meet the most excellent queen of the fae," I told her. "I am both honored and humbled that you have allowed me to visit your beautiful land."

Das regarded me for a long moment. Around us, dozens of fairies held silent vigil over our meeting. There was an air of anticipation in the waiting fae as if they expected fireworks to erupt at any moment.

I hoped they were wrong.

"Why have you come now, after all this time?" Das asked me. She cocked her head with the question, the action making her look even less human. If that was possible.

"I apologize that it took me so long. My only excuse is ignorance. I was unschooled in magic when I took on the role of Lares. I am learning as I go. It has been...interesting."

It was a calculated risk giving Das the impression of weakness, but Ferral and I had decided it would be worth it. We could use her perception of my weakness against her in the future.

"Am I to believe you have not come to beg for the return of Trish, Ancient Warrior? That seems unlikely, does it not?"

I bit back a sharp retort. I was not going to beg the nasty queen for anything. But I would request Trish's release. If Das refused, we'd have to figure out how to get her back without creating a major war. I inclined my head. "You are right. My visit to you is twofold. I did wish to remedy my oversight in meeting with you. And I do wish to request Trish's return. She is a valuable member of my council."

"The warrior stays with her own people. You must do without your token fairy." The rage in her statement momentarily put me on my heels. I'd expected her to stay within character, play the benevolent but tough ruler. Bargain. But her words told me there was more at play than jealousy or hurt feelings. We'd underestimated Das' rage.

I took a beat to consider my response. Finally, I said, "Trish is not just a member of my council. She is my friend. I care about her. I miss her."

"Baa!" Das exclaimed, flipping a clawed hand into the air. "No fairy is a friend to humans. We are a far superior race. Befriending cattle is beneath us. The warrior stays with me. You must go."

We were at an impasse. Das had painted me into a corner. Everything I could think of to say would be taken badly or discounted. She'd not only resisted any argument I might have made. But she'd portrayed me as a person having no value with the utterance of just a few words.

The soft murmuring of the surrounding fae told me more than anything that I'd lost the argument before it had even started.

Finally, I said the only thing I had left to say. "I'd like to speak to my friend before I leave. I wish to say goodbye."

"The warrior does not wish to speak to you."

"Please," I said, biting my tongue against the angry words I wanted to say.

"I will speak to the Lares," Trish said behind me, her tone soft but confident.

I turned to find Trish standing sans guards. Had the guards and blades only been for show?

Das stared at Trish for a moment, their gazes locked on each other. I got the distinct sense that they were communicating somehow. Finally, Das' horrible mouth curved in a toothy smile.

I shuddered from the sight. "Very well, you may walk a ways with the human and the dog. You will return to me before they reach the barrier."

Trish gave a low bow.

I inclined my head to Queen Das. "There is one other issue I'd like to speak to you about."

Das flipped a hand. "Go. We are done."

I shook my head, setting my jaw. "Queen Das, I recognize your rule over the people of fairy. I respect and support your monarchy. You have nothing to fear from me on that score."

Das' face darkened and her wings fluttered in agitation, lifting her off the throne. "I do not fear you!"

I closed my eyes, realizing what a terrible mistake I'd made. Opening my eyes again, I lifted my hands, palms out. "My mistake, poor choice of words. Of course, you don't fear me. What I meant to say was my job doesn't give me any dominion over the free fairy race. I would never imply that it did. My duty is to the people of Rome. Any and all who live there can count on me to protect them to my best ability. I have no jurisdiction in Fairy. I wish no power over or input into your queendom. But should you ever need an ally, please consider me as such."

"I do not ally with cattle."

Charming to the end.

My smile was tight. "Noted."

Das glared down at me. "Go now."

"Yes. But, before I go, please answer me one thing. Do you have knowledge of the Trickster currently turning my dominion on its head?"

Something gleamed in her black eyes. "I know nothing of your Trickster."

I held her gaze just long enough to let her know I didn't believe her. Then I inclined my head. "Thank you for meeting with me, Queen Das. May your life be long and filled with the beauty of natural things."

I turned away and strode back toward the wood without looking back. Ferral fell in just behind me, guarding my flank. I was pretty sure the soldiers who'd escorted us into Fairy were following at a discreet distance.

I smelled Trish's flowery perfume when she joined me. "Are you crazy?" she whispered.

I laughed, my nerves making the sound wobble. "Some have told me I am." I turned to her, giving her a close look for the first time since seeing her again. "They haven't hurt you, have they?"

Her expression tightened. A shadow passed through her eyes. "I am fine, Aggy. You shouldn't have come."

Quick anger overcame me. "Of course, I should have come! You're my friend, and you were taken prisoner by a crazy lady! I wanted to know you were okay."

Ferral made a soft sound of censure. "Keep your voice down."

I pulled air into my lungs and expelled it slowly. When I was calm again, I asked, "Why did they take you?"

She glanced behind us and lowered her voice. "Das is up to something. I agree with you that she sent the Trickster. With Das, you never know. It could just be something someone said that she didn't like." Trish shook her head. "We walk on tenterhooks around her, Aggy. It was very dangerous for you to come."

"I had to come," I told her. I stopped and turned, pulling her into a hug. "We were all so worried. Luke is beside himself."

Trish pulled out of the hug. "Is he okay? They hit him hard. If he hadn't shifted, they might have killed him."

I nodded. "He's fine. Like the rest of us, he's worried and wants you home."

She sighed. "Home. It sounds wonderful." Her expression hardened. "I can't come back, Aggy. You need to adjust to that reality."

I shook my head. "You have to come back. How am I going to figure out where Wanda's bedroom should go without you."

Trish laughed, her eyes glittering with unshed tears. "Luke can help with that."

"No. You started my renovations. You will finish them."

"Stubborn woman."

I sniffed, my own eyes overflowing. "Yes, I am stubborn. And I'm not giving in on this. One way or another, you're coming home."

She scraped her palms over her wet cheeks. "I won't argue with you. I only want to tell you this. Das is up to something. The Trickster is part of it. You need me here to be your eyes and ears."

"How will you get information to us?" Ferral asked.

Trish whistled softly. A tiny pixie shot out of the trees and buzzed closer, landing on Trish's outstretched palm. The pretty little dark-haired pixie fluttered her wings, sending bright white dust into the air around her. "This is Mari. She will come to you if I have a message."

"Hello, Mari."

The pixie rose into the air, her snow-white dust forming a cloud around her. "Ma'am."

"I have to go," Trish said.

More tears slipped down my cheeks. I hugged her again. "Take care of yourself."

"I will." She turned away, and I had an irrepressible need to keep her there a moment longer. "Tilly is moving her bakery into the church."

Trish stopped mid-step and spun. "Seriously?"

I nodded, a grin curving my lips. "I'm gonna get so fat."

Trish looked wistful. "Maybe you could send me something through Mari."

I nodded. "Chocolate, chocolate chip muffin?"

Trish groaned. "Yes!"

"It's a deal."

She nodded, her eyes gleaming wetly in the light

from Mari's dust. "Take care of everyone, Aggy. I'm counting on you."

Words wouldn't come to me, so I simply nodded. Then I watched my friend walk away, heading right back into danger. And there was nothing I could do to stop her.

13

A TERRIBLE WRONG, A FAIRY'S PLIGHT

I woke to the decadent scent of chocolate and yeast. Monty had long deserted me. His spot on the mattress next to me was cold. I didn't blame him. If the scents permeating my room were any indication, Tilly had arrived.

Five minutes later, I shuffled into the kitchen and found my little dog parked as close to the brownie's small feet as he could get. He barely skimmed me a look when I came into the room, his frilly tail giving one quick swipe across the floor in greeting.

"I see my dog has already left me for you."

Tilly turned in surprise, a look of worry flitting across her fine features. "I think he just likes the smells."

I held up a hand. "I was just teasing. He's a chowhound like his owner."

Tilly grinned, looking relieved. "I didn't wake you, did I? I was trying to be very quiet."

I shook my head. "My brain is hard-wired to come online when there's chocolate nearby."

Tilly's soft laughter made me smile. "Have you had coffee?" I asked her.

"I have, thank you. I brought some pods from the bakery. I hope you don't mind. It's my special blend."

"Dark roast?"

"Of course."

I sighed. "Perfect."

The door into my shop closed softly and I glanced down the hall to find Mavis hauling a really big bag of flour in my direction. "Hey." I hurried to take it from her. "You're here early."

She beamed, swiping a ribbon of graying blonde hair off her flushed cheek. "I'm Tilly's kitchen slave."

"Helper," Tilly called from the kitchen. "Not slave."

Mavis and I shared a grin.

"Do you get free samples? Maybe enough for a friend too?" I placed the flour on the kitchen table.

"You're saving my business," Tilly said, placing an enormous chocolate, chocolate-chip muffin in front of me. "You get as many samples as you'd like."

"Oh no!" Mavis exclaimed theatrically. "She'll eat you right out of business."

I gently smacked her arm. "Stool pigeon."

She cackled happily.

I made my coffee and sat down with my muffin, watching my mom and Tilly perform their combined magic. The smells filling the kitchen sank into my bones, infusing me with a peace I hadn't felt since the Trickster hit town.

That thought sucked the happy right out of me. For a few blissful minutes, I'd actually managed to forget the nasty scoundrel.

I thought back to my study of the fae information Ferral had assigned me in preparation for our visit to Queen Das. I'd learned something in *The Big Book of Fairy* he'd given me. Yes, that was actually the title. And it wasn't false advertising. The aged volume was three inches thick, the pages covered in tiny, tiny print. I'd skimmed over most of the fae described within the book's yellowed pages, spending a few minutes reading about brownies. Strangely, brownies had been described as being small in stature, with oversized ears and noses. Nothing at all like Tilly. I wondered if she wore a glamour. Or maybe she was only part brownie.

I couldn't ask, of course. That would be rude. But I was nosy enough to wonder.

The more important part of that "brownies are fae" thing was that...well...brownies were fae. Tilly might know something about Fairy or the queen that could help.

As Tilly slid another large sheet filled with cookies into the oven and straightened, her face flushed pink from the heat, I asked, "Have you ever been to Fairy?"

She blinked in surprise. Clearly she hadn't expected the question. "Of course, Madam Lares. All fae live there until we go out on our own."

"Please call me Aggy."

She glanced at Mavis for verification that it would be okay.

Mavis nodded. "She prefers Aggy."

Sighing, I tore off another hunk of muffin and popped it into my mouth. After swallowing, I tried again. "How well do you know Queen Das?"

Tilly suddenly became agitated. She wouldn't look me in the eye, and she seemed not to know what to do with her hands.

Mavis and I shared a look. Mavis wrapped an arm around Tilly's shoulders. "It's okay if you don't want to say anything. Really."

I nodded. "It's just that I met the queen last night. I was wondering if you could tell me anything about her that might help with this Trickster mess."

"I didn't know about the Trickster, Madam... Aggy. I swear I didn't."

"I believe you."

Tilly nodded, her slender fingers twining nervously together. "Queen Das is volatile. Unpredictable. She is threatened by you."

"Yeah." I sighed. "That's what we thought. I tried to reassure her last night. I don't want to take over

Fairy. But I do have an obligation and a right to protect the people of Rome. She needs to understand that."

Tilly shook her head. "Das understands only what Das wants to understand. She believes all non-fairies are just so much clutter in the universe. Even within the fae, many of us are deemed beneath her notice."

"What about the warrior fae?" I asked. "What do you suppose she wants with Trish?"

"Leverage," Tilly said without hesitation. "She is just a way to mess with you. Das doesn't value her warriors because they are not of fae royalty. And she has never had to defend her queendom against an attack."

I felt my eyes go wide. Mavis and I shared a look. *That might work in our favor,* I told her through our mind link. Mavis nodded.

Aloud, Mavis asked, "How do her warriors feel about that?"

Tilly shrugged. "Most are complacent for the same reason. They train as if it is simply conditioning, and they play at battle. They have no use for anything outside their purview. I doubt they even study tactical warfare." She flushed violently, glancing around as if afraid she might have been overheard. "I shouldn't have told you all that. It is treasonous."

"We will keep the secret," I told her. "You're safe

here, Tilly. You have my word."

The brownie sighed. "I have not felt safe for many years, Aggy. As I said, the queen is unpredictable. At any moment, she may decide I shouldn't be here and force me back to Fairy." Tears glistened in her eyes. "I do not wish to go."

In an effort to lighten the mood, I made a horrified face. "That can't happen. I'd die without your muffins and cookies."

Tilly laughed, scraping tears from her face.

I stood and walked over to her, pulling her into a hug. "You are my people now, Tilly. I will do everything I can to keep you safe. You have my word."

She nodded, then stiffened and exclaimed. "Ah!"

'What's wrong?" I reached for my magic only to find Tilly grabbing oven mittens and diving for the oven door.

"My cookies! They nearly burned."

Relieved, I stepped back. "I'm distracting you. I'll get out of your way."

"No. Please stay," she said. Settling the sheets on the stovetop, she pulled off the mittens. "Do you have a plan for getting rid of the Trickster?"

"I've been told it can't be done."

Tilly bobbed her head back and forth. "Technically, that is true. But if you could find a way to reverse the spell that gave him access to Rome, you might be able to send him back."

Hope flared in my chest, then died. "That would

be a fairy spell, right?" I shook my head. "Trish was the only one who might have been able to work with a spell like that."

Tilly's gaze turned mischievous. "Perhaps."

"Do you think you could do it?" Mavis asked.

Tilly shrugged. "You might not know this, but brownies have a bit of a reputation for mischievousness. It's possible I might be able to find and interpret the spell you need."

"You'd be willing to have a look?" I asked, hope turning to excitement.

"I would."

***

"Every pane of glass along Main Street is broken," Layla reported two hours later. "We've been cleaning up glass since five this morning. It's a mess."

I'd called another meeting of the council, intending to make the meetings short and frequent until we got things under control.

I looked at Bev. "Is that something the witches can fix?"

She grimaced. "Normally, yes. But with everything else we need to do, I suggest we go with a non-magic fix."

I sighed. "Who wants to be in charge of getting a glass company here?"

Luke raised his hand. "I have a buddy in the business. I'll ask him to bring a couple of his competitors with him."

"Good. And boarding up the windows until they can be fixed?"

"The lumber company outside of town has already offered to donate the wood and a couple of his guys," Luke told me. "I'll help pound nails too."

"I'll help with that as well," Davis said. "That's something I can do." He frowned, clearly feeling less than useful in the magic world.

"Good. Bev?"

"We're working on a spell for the wizrooms damage. Willy thinks she might have a way to remove the body staining." Her lips curved upward. "I'll let you know when we have a cure for your purpleness."

I looked down at my purple arms and hands. I'd rejected Bev's offer to renew my glamour. Her energies were needed elsewhere at the moment. I sighed. "Thanks. Anything else?"

"So many things," Bev said wearily. "We fixed the fake pregnancy epidemic but couldn't wipe the women's minds about it, so we have a lot of emotional, confused human women in Rome right now." She shook her head. "Dogs now sound like dogs. Cats sound like cats..."

"And squirrels?" I asked, my lips twitching.

"They stopped mooing," Bev said on a sigh. "Now they're talking."

I felt my eyes go wide. "Like actual words?"

Bev nodded. "It's creepy as all heck. We left them for now. In the grand scheme of things, talking squirrels seemed fairly harmless."

"I agree."

"The backward buildings have been the biggest challenge," she went on. "The Trickster put an elastic hex on them. When we fix one building, the magic tugs on something else and yanks it around. We've about exhausted all our energies on that particular problem."

I rubbed my forehead as a headache started to throb there. "Niele?"

The gnome jerked as if I'd woken him up. I realized with a slash of guilt that I likely had. He'd refused to rest as I'd demanded and looked even worse than he had before. "Huh?"

"Give me your report and then lie down on the couch and take a nap. If you won't go home and rest, you'll do it here."

He rubbed a big hand over his eyes. "Yes, ma'am."

I almost smiled. He sounded like a ten-year-old accepting a rebuke from his mother. "Do you have anything to report?"

He sat up straighter and stifled a yawn. "Trees."

I lifted my brows. "Trees?"

He nodded. "An entire street of trees sank into the ground and disappeared. We've been lifting and anchoring them back into place."

"How many trees were there?" I asked, appalled.

"Forty. They weren't all huge. But some were. I had to call a couple of my cousins in for help."

Thank the goddess for Niele's cousins. "Please ask them to stop by here for coffee and cookies when they need a break. You too." I looked around the group. "Tilly has temporarily moved her bakery operation here because her shop was poisoned by the Trickster. She's graciously offered us anything we want from her stock."

Everyone's eyes lit up. Even Ferral's. It was a small joy but even more special because of it.

I looked at Gren. "What do you have for us?" I asked him.

"The ghost situation has worsened. Several more popped up on the highway a mile down from Rome. Their sudden appearance in the road caused three fairly minor crashes and one large one. I've been trying to find the source of the ghosts but haven't managed it yet."

"You've spoken to Father Ignacious at Saint Paul church?"

"I have. His graveyard suffered a similar upheaval to yours. In fact, every cemetery for ten miles around the town has been flipped. I'm sure that's where the ghosts are coming from. But, until we can figure out how to flip them back around, I don't see the specter problem going away."

"Awesome," I murmured. I glanced at Niele. He and his cousins would need to evaluate the ground beneath the graveyard to see if it was something they could fix. As I looked his way, a soft snore sifted out from between his gaping lips. He was out like a light.

"I'll speak to Niele about that when he wakes up."

Gren nodded. "I'd like to be part of that conversation."

"Of course." There was a tap, tap, tapping on the big, arched windows at the front of the room. I turned to find Ray standing on the outside sill. "I'll let him in," Bev said, unfolding her slender form and stretching before heading that way.

A moment later, the raven flew into the house, made a circle high above our heads, above the lights and fans, and then landed on the floor in the center of the room. He strutted toward me, head bobbing and wings flapping with apparent irritation.

"What's up?" I asked the big, black bird.

"Caw!"

We all winced at the super-sized cry in the contained space. "Use your inside voice, Ray," I scolded. I watched him for a moment, a niggling feeling of wrongness filtering through my system. I waited expectantly for the raven to call me rude or do the pee dance. He did neither. Reaching the space at the end of the couch, the raven flapped its wings and landed in the center of my big, square coffee table.

"Caw!"

Peering more closely at the bird, I felt unease crawling up my spine. Then the raven's beak opened and clacked together a few times, his eyes glowing with an eerie green light.

"Back!" I yelled, jumping up and grabbing Niele by the arm to awaken him. "That's not Ray."

14

FRIEND OR FOE? TRUST DOTH TAKE FLIGHT

We all jumped from our chairs and scuttled backward. An instant later, Gren was by my side, easing in front of me with his big body. In a flash of gray light, Luke burst into his wolf, growling and snapping at the imposter raven. A flare of heated silver light told me Ferral had become his hound. Bev and Mavis stood across from me, pale green magic dancing on their palms.

In the distance, Monty sounded the alarm, his barking sharp and fast. I could tell from the muted sound that Wanda had him closed in her room with her. I was glad. I didn't want either of them anywhere near the lethal mischief-maker.

The raven hopped across the table, feathers rippling as its beak opened wide again. "Very good, Madam Lares," the raven said. Its throat rippled over an unnatural-sounding laugh. "I'll admit, it seemed unlikely that you'd actually invite me into your home. I thought I'd have to settle for drawing you out." The large bird flapped its wings, lifting a few feet off the table before settling down again. Its beady green gaze lit with inner fire as if it were preparing to attack but then turned flat again. "I'd say it's a pleasure to meet you, but..." The thing seemed to shrug, a singularly strange sight when performed by a creature with no shoulders.

"We're speaking to the Trickster, I presume?" I said.

The bird cackled wildly, hopping across the table and then back again. "Very good. You're not nearly as stupid as you look." With a ripple of air and light, the raven stretched, its feathered form elongating as it widened. A long, curved nose replaced the beak, a wild bloom of bright red hair replaced feathers on the top of the head. Arms stretched to its sides, legs sprouting from its base, and a shapeless middle formed the body.

When it had finished transforming, a strange little man stood before me, still standing on top of my table. "There. That's better. Isn't it?"

"Is it?" I asked, calling magic to dance at my fingertips.

The table beneath his feet creaked and the Trickster looked down. "Oh, no. That won't do. It won't do at all." His long nose twitched, and the table exploded into light so bright it blinded me for a few seconds. When my vision returned, I was shocked to see a fat little pony standing where my table had been, the Trickster perched atop its wide back.

Luke and Ferral lunged after it, snarling and snapping their oversized teeth.

The pony leaped the couch and galloped to safety at the other end of the large room. Its tail swishing as Luke approached, the pony kicked out, its tiny hoof connecting with Luke's broad, furry chest and sending him flying.

In a flash of golden light, the pony turned into a Unicorn. Despite how they were depicted in fairytales, the unicorn was not all rainbows and flowers. It rose up with a scream and pawed the air. Then landed and galloped in my direction, horn lowered to gore me. With a panicked shriek, I shoved a nearby upholstered chair toward the charging animal, infusing the shove with magic.

The chair flew into the air, smacking into the creature's horn and sticking there. The unicorn shook its head, and the chair shattered around it, falling to the floor in a spray of kindling.

The Trickster cackled from the mythical creature's back, urging it on with kicks to its sides.

I reached for more magic and hurled it, a blast of golden energy as big around as my arm.

Bev threw a wave of pale green magic at the same

time, the force of it slamming into the unicorn and taking it to the ground. Somehow, the evil prankster stayed on the horse and it was back on four hooves within the blink of an eye.

The Trickster flicked his fingers and hit my energy with a blast of oily black power. The two energies smacked hard into each other, causing an explosion that rattled the glass in all the room's windows.

In the blink of an eye, my magic was transformed. A dozen large knives sailed back at me.

Gren's wings snapped out and compressed the air in front of me. The barrier created by the compacted air stopped the knives in mid-air, only a couple of feet away from where I stood. They fell harmlessly to the floor with a clatter.

Luke lunged at the unicorn, snagging a pristine white leg between his teeth.

The Trickster flicked his fingers at the wolf. Luke yelped. He dropped to the floor with a snarl and began chewing on his own flesh. I watched in horror as something rolled beneath his fur. Luke bit frantically at whatever it was, drawing blood.

"Somebody do something," Niele yelled. "He's going to hurt himself."

"Oblivion!" Mavis screamed, a wave of green magic sliding over the werewolf and putting him to sleep.

Niele rushed over and picked Luke up, carrying him to a spot away from the fray.

The Trickster flicked his fingers at the unicorn. A swirl of magic engulfed him, the creature beneath him thickened, its skin changing from white to gray. The creature forming beneath him was massive, its form blockish. Horns grew from its massive face and its small tail flicked with irritation.

I gasped as a full-sized rhinoceros stomped and snorted beneath the Trickster. The monster fixed its dark, beady eyes on me, and its ears twitched forward. The rhino snorted again, gathered itself for a charge, and disappeared behind the form of my protector as he put himself between us.

Gren snapped his wings, lifting off the ground, and slammed into the rhino at an angle. He barely missing being gored by the animal's horns. Growling with the effort, he shoved the massive creature, trying to push it to the other end of the room.

Niele slammed into it from the other side, reaching for the Trickster.

Laughing gaily, the prankster turned translucent, like an overlay riding the air. Niele's strong fingers slipped right through him.

The Trickster flicked his fingers and Niele flew backward, slamming into the wall. Two framed pictures of a pixie-laden forest fell to the ground, the frames shattering.

The animal lowered its head and dug in, my

beautiful oak floors groaning and cracking beneath its efforts to gain purchase.

But it was no match for my determined angel. Gren's wings pulsed against the air, each powerful stroke carrying enough muscle to drag the rhino backward an inch at a time.

On its back, the Trickster continued to cackle with delight. Killing people...harming innocents...it all seemed to be a game to him.

Foul creature.

Ferral shot past me and leaped, his strong, lithe form flying over Gren's head and landing on the rhino's back.

Its empty back.

The Trickster was gone, leaving only the sound of his shrill, hated voice behind. *Until we meet again, Madam Lares.*

The monstrous animal went rigid as soon as the Trickster's magic left it. Ferral leaped off its back as it began to shrink back down to the floor, transforming back to my table in the blink of an eye. My broken, completely destroyed table.

Footsteps danced along the hallway. For a beat, I thought the Trickster had returned. But it wasn't the deadly prankster. It was a wide-eyed, breathless teen.

I expected her to ask what was going on...to eye the damage to my beautiful room with horror. But she skidded into the room and held up the empty notebook the crone had given to her. "I've got it! I've figured out how to use this thing."

More footsteps sounded, and Tilly stuck her head in behind Wanda. "Is everything okay? I heard roaring and crashing."

Bev snorted, shaking her head. "That's just Tuesday around here."

Wanda took a huge bite of a still-warm chocolate chip cookie and moaned. "Thish ish amashing."

"Don't talk with your mouth full," Mavis and I said in unison. We shared a grin.

Wanda rolled her eyes. She swallowed and looked at Tilly across the room. "This is the best cookie I've ever tasted," she told the brownie.

Tilly beamed with pleasure. "I hope you're up for trying the peanut butter chocolate chip next."

Wanda grinned widely, her teeth covered in melted chocolate.

"We might actually fatten her up with Tilly here," Bev said. She took a sip of her coffee and moaned herself. "Tilly, this coffee is wonderful. What kind is it?"

"It's my own special brew. You can only get it at my bakery." Her eyes sparkled with mischief. "Or in the Lares' kitchen."

Bev looked at me. "That's it. I'm moving in."

I paled. "Um, ah..."

"Me too, honey," Mavis announced. "This sandwich is ridiculously good."

I sagged in my chair. "I guess I can subdivide my shop into bedrooms. Who needs to follow her dreams, anyway?"

Wanda snorted. "If you're trying to guilt those two, don't bother. They'll take baked goods over you any day."

Bev and Wanda bumped knuckles. "Word," Bev said with a grin.

I sagged lower. "And, I'm unloved to boot."

"Aw," Mavis cooed, patting my cheek. "We love you, honey. We just love Tilly's food more."

Wanda giggled.

It was time for a change of conversation. I fixed my ward with a look. "Okay, little piggy. Can you stop eating long enough to tell me what you found in that ridiculous notebook?"

Tilly picked up the tray she'd been arranging and headed toward the door. "I'll take Luke a snack."

"What's that wonderful smell?" Mavis asked.

"Just a little something I learned at my mum's knee for curing a werewolf's ailments. Wolfsbane soup."

We all stared at her, our eyes wide.

"Um," I finally said. "Isn't wolfsbane bad for wolves?"

"Normally, yes. It's also a powerful antidote for other poisons. This soup contains several other herbs that counteract wolfsbane's toxicity while fighting the poison the Trickster injected into Luke."

I frowned. "Do you know what that is under his skin?"

She shook her head. "Not specifically, no. But it seems to be using Luke's lycanthropy against him. I believe this soup will help calm that down."

I nodded. "I'll be in shortly to check on him. Thanks, Tilly."

The brownie nodded. "Of course, Aggy. Anything I can do to help."

I watched her go, the tiniest seed of doubt taking root in my gut.

"What is it?" Bev asked.

I shook off my thoughts. "What?"

"You look worried about something."

I sighed. "I'd be crazy at this point if I wasn't worried, don't you think?"

Bev's expression told me she wasn't convinced, but I had nothing else to give her. I was just generally uncomfortable about everything. Scared, and yes, worried. There was nothing for it but to keep moving forward. And on that note...

"Tell us what you've discovered," I told Wanda.

She opened her mouth to speak, and my cell phone rang. I frowned down at the number, not recognizing it. "Hold that thought," I told Wanda, hitting the *answer* button.

Wanda shrugged and went back to her cookie.

"Hello, this is Aggy."

"Oh, thank heaven!" a woman said on the other end of the line. "I need to talk to you. I think the world is ending."

15

A CHILD IS BORN? THE PRANKSTER'S WILL

Aside from her wild prediction, Doctor Meredith Lawson did have a point. "Are you sure?" I asked the, once again, wild-eyed physician.

"There's the proof," she all but screamed at me. "You can see it for yourself."

I narrowed my eyes at the blurry gray x-ray on the reader, still not sure exactly what I was looking at.

"For heaven's sake, Aggy!" the good doctor screeched. "That's a baby."

To me, it looked like a Mr. Peanut, minus the hat and cane. "But that's not possible."

Her eyes wide, she juddered her head as if to say, "Duh!"

"Who's the guy?" Bev asked, leaning closer to Mr. Peanut to get a better view. Maybe she was looking for his monocle.

"I can't tell you that. Doctor-patient confidentiality and all."

"Does he know he's..." Mavis shook her head. "...pregnant?"

"He's human," the good doctor said as if that explained things. It kind of did.

"How'd you get the ultrasound?" I asked. "I assume he didn't come to you for it."

"A colleague over at the hospital sent it to me. The man came in complaining of nausea, constant pressure on his bladder, and something trying to climb out of his belly through his skin." The doctor looked a little green around the gills. "He told the physician at the emergency room that he thought a giant worm was in his stomach leeching off him."

Mavis nodded. "He wasn't far from the truth with that."

Dr. Lawson nodded.

"Any pickles and ice cream cravings?"

"Mom!" Bev said. "Not helpful."

Mavis shrugged. "I can only speak of that which I know." She looked at Doc Lawson. "Chinese food made me want to hork for the whole nine months. To this day, Beverly won't eat Chinese food."

"I do too eat Chinese food," Bev argued.

"Egg rolls don't count," Mavis disagreed. "Anything fried is delicious. But that doesn't make it real food."

I lifted my brows at them, and they both fell

silent. "Is this guy the only one?"

"So far. But this does not bode well."

Understatement of the century.

"Okay, will you get with your emergency room doctor friend and keep tabs on this? Let me know if any more pregnant men turn up?"

After getting Doctor Lawson's promise to keep us apprised, we left the office. We stood outside under a leaden sky, shivering as a cold, wet wind whipped around us, a portent of the rain to come.

"What are we going to do about that mess?" Mavis asked.

"You don't think it's real, do you?" I asked.

"It sounds like it's kicking him," Mavis reminded me.

We stood in miserable silence for a minute. Then Bev said. "I say we wait and see. Hopefully, it's an illusion and, once we defeat the Trickster, it will just go away."

Since we really had no choice, we all agreed.

"Back to the bat cave," I said.

"I should check in at work," Bev said. "I haven't been there for two days."

"Okay, honey," Mavis said, giving her a big hug. "Take care of yourself."

I hugged her too, and Mavis and I watched her walk off down the street to her car. Bev was a pharmaceutical representative who mostly worked through her phone and car. Her hours were flexible, and her company didn't monitor her activities very closely. But not showing up to work for two days was really pushing it.

"What's up next?" Mavis asked as we started toward my ancient Range Rover.

"I need to hear what Wanda found."

A large man appeared in front of me, his super-sized form covered in a dusty black hoodie and dark blue sweatpants. He wore a ball cap over dark, curly hair, and a dark stubble peppered his chalk-white face. His eyes were dead, black and empty like a shark's, and he moved with a rapid shuffle that was not unlike a zombie's.

"Aggy?"

"It's okay," I told her. I tried to step to the side and let him pass, but he plowed right into me before I could move. Ice bathed my skin and pierced my mind. Agony cut a path through my body. My mouth opened in a soundless scream and I convulsed against the pain and cold.

The overcast day transformed around me in the beat of a heart, the landscape desolate and cold. The lines and planes of the space where I stood were as foreign to me as they were foreboding.

Ice sank beneath my skin, scraping along my nerve endings as if someone was slicing through me with a machete carved of ice. Thoughts that were not my own slashed through my mind; ugly, terrifying, and bloody.

A woman's cruel death. A child's heart-rending hopelessness. A long life filled with loneliness. Someone else's devastation ripped through me, an inch at a time, until ice coated my back and pain sheared through my knees.

Then it was gone. The cold and horror had passed entirely through me.

The scream died in my throat. When I came back to myself, I realized I was on my knees, panting in the aftermath of the attack.

"Aggy! Honey, did it hurt you?"

Mavis bent over me as pain pulsed in waves from my knees. I shivered so violently my teeth were clacking together.

She held out a hand and I grasped it, gasping from the pain in my knees as I stood. "What just happened?"

"Ghost," Mavis said, her gray eyes focused in the direction the specter had moved. "He walked straight through you. So weird."

I shivered violently. "Weird is one word for it." I looked at my knees. Thank the goddess I'd been wearing jeans. There was gravel stuck to the fabric, but I didn't see any blood. Still...I bent one leg and then the other, wincing at the residual pain.

"You landed hard on your poor knees," Mavis said. "Let's get home, and I'll heal them for you."

I nodded. As I limped toward my car, my gaze swung around the area, looking for more ghosts. I didn't see any. That was good. Because I never wanted to experience that nightmare again.

We arrived home fifteen minutes later to a long line of people at my shop door and a full parking lot. I parked on the shoulder of my road rather than trying to find a spot in the lot. Mavis and I climbed out. "I'll move the car later," I said, taking in the line of people. It stretched toward the small parking lot and into the grass beside it.

The sweet scent of sugar and cinnamon wafted toward us on a light breeze. I inhaled with a sigh. "I'm going to gain a hundred pounds if Tilly's here for very long."

Mavis looped her arm through mine. "I'm willing to take one for the team and eat your portions as well as mine."

I laughed and tugged her into my side. "Have I told you today that I love you?"

"Right back atchya, honey." Mavis kissed my cheek.

"Hey, Aggy!" a pretty blonde woman called to us from the line. The adorable toddler clinging to her leg waved at us with a soggy fist, then stuck her chunky thumb back into her mouth.

I waved back, recognizing the neighbor across the street who was keeping Mrs. Twimblee's cat while the older woman was in the hospital. "How's Rufus?" I called.

"He's good." She pointed to the shop as the line

advanced and gave me a thumbs up. "Great idea on the bakery. Tilly's magic with baked goods."

I blinked at her words before realizing she hadn't meant it literally. "She definitely is," I said, grinning. "Enjoy."

Mavis and I made it into the house without any other slowdowns, and I hobbled to the kitchen.

"Sit," Mavis commanded. "I'll see what I can do to make those knees feel better."

I didn't argue. They'd started to stiffen up on me. I closed my eyes as the heat of healing magic infused me. Tilly must have been done with her baking for the day. The kitchen had been cleaned to spotlessness, and there was a basket in the center of the table with a checked fabric cloth in it. I tugged a flap of the cloth away from the contents and nearly swooned. "Peanut butter chocolate chip cookies."

The cookies were as big as my palm and teased my nose with their decadent scent. "I'm definitely going to have to diet after she leaves."

Mavis patted my knee, sitting back on her chair. "Smart girl. I noticed you didn't say you were going to diet while she's here."

"I know my limitations."

"Knock, knock!" said a familiar voice. The mudroom door opened after a quick double-tap. Layla stuck her head inside. "Can we talk?"

I bit back a groan. The lost princess rarely visited unless she had bad news. "Sure. Come on in."

Layla eyed the basket, her eyes gleaming.

"Help yourself," I told her. "Coffee?"

Layla nodded. She accepted a hug from Mavis and sat, plucking a cookie from the basket. Her eyes rolled back in her head and she moaned. "I should have offered Tilly a spot at *my* compound," she said while chewing.

"You snooze, you lose," Mavis said.

I made three cups of Tilly's special coffee. For a few minutes, we contented ourselves with drinking and eating, our discussion centering only on gastronomic subjects. Which, for us, was pretty normal. I briefly wondered where Wanda was, thinking about going to look for her. But I knew I was just trying to put off Layla's update. "Okay," I said. "Give me the bad news."

Layla's blue eyes shifted away, focusing on her cookie. She frowned. "As you know, I've been monitoring the demonic realm and earthbound demons."

I nodded. We'd decided it made sense for Layla to stay on top of the demonic world since she had connections and knowledge we didn't have in that area.

"Things are not going well."

"Please don't tell us the vortex is opening up again," Mavis said. Her expression showed such horror I thought she might run screaming from the room if Layla gave her the wrong answer.

"Not that. Like I told you before, it will take them

a while to get it open again. I've been more focused on Trickster activity that sets the dark element off and sends them gunning for innocents."

That was always a danger. Magical humans could mostly take care of themselves. It was easier... though not infallible, as I learned from my encounter with the ghost...for us to see magical trouble coming. But humans were sitting ducks.

"Has something happened?"

She eyed me. "How much do you know about Bathos' business?"

I shook my head. "Not much." Which, I suddenly realized, was not good. Bathos and his ilk were potentially very dangerous. I should have known everything there was to know about them. I mentally kicked myself. I'd allowed his relationship with Wanda to color my treatment of him.

I had a feeling I was about to regret that. "What has he done?"

"He hasn't done anything, personally. But his associates have been causing quite a stir in the Mystical Wood. Several magical creatures have been affected by their activities."

"Associates?" Mavis asked.

Layla nodded. "Bathos is a Barrister for the dark world. What that means is that he takes demons in and keeps them contained until their trials. Then, he deals with the outcome of the trial." The look she gave us made my palms sweat.

"And by deals with you mean...?"

"You don't want to know."

I dropped my head into my hands.

"He gets paid quite handsomely for his services as a barrister, jailor and, where necessary, executioner."

"He kills people?" Mavis asked, appalled.

"Not people," Layla corrected. "Monsters. He deals with some of the darkest, most dangerous demonic criminals on this plane."

I suddenly found it hard to swallow. Pushing my cookie away, I marveled that Layla had done the impossible. She'd actually made me reject sweets. "This is bad."

Layla nodded enthusiastically. "It is. But not for the reason you're probably thinking. It's bad because Bathos had a really bad hombre in his prison beneath the ground when this all started."

All the blood fled my face. "And now?"

"Now." She frowned. "Now, he has an empty prison."

Curse, swear, curse, curse!

"No wonder Bathos wanted us to engage an amalgamation spell," Mavis breathed.

Layla nodded. "He doubled his security measures in the prison caverns and hired more air and ground guards for around the house, but the Trickster found his setup." The lost princess frowned. "I don't know how he found out where

Bathos kept his prisoners. Other than you all, who followed your own people to the jail, nobody has been able to find the prison."

"What about a previous prisoner?" I asked.

Layla shook her head. "They don't come out of there with the capacity to return. Either they're executed, or their minds are wiped so they can start a new life." Her frown deepened. "Bathos leaves nothing to chance. Once a prisoner has been in his jail, he shuts it down and moves it to another area. The system should have been foolproof."

"But it wasn't," I said, stating the obvious.

"No. It wasn't. Somehow the Trickster found it."

"Could Bathos have a mole?" Mavis asked.

"Not likely. First of all, nobody who works for him knows the exact location of the prison at any given time. It's a moving target. But..." She caught my eye and held it. "The Trickster might have caught Bathos in a weak moment and gleaned it from his mind."

My eyes went wide. "He can pull information from our minds?"

Layla nodded. "If you're ever face-to-face with him, you need to make sure you block him from your thoughts. Otherwise, there's no end of damage he can do."

Swear! Curse! Curse! Swear!

"Too late for that," Mavis said, her worried gray gaze sliding to me.

16

LOSS OF CONTROL A BITTER PILL

I spent the next hour trying to think of anything the Trickster might have gleaned from my brain. Terror, horror, confusion, feelings of ineptitude... probably all things he could make use of. My greatest fear was that he would have pulled thoughts of Wanda from my mind. Mavis or Bev. Monty. What if he tried to target them?

I jumped up suddenly, realizing I hadn't heard from my two roomies for a while. Hurrying down the hall, I opened the door to the cluttered former pastor's office and expelled a relieved breath. Wanda was draped over her new twin-sized bed writing something in her journal. Her narrow feet hung off the end, bouncing to music from the earbuds stuffed into her ears.

Monty's head popped up, and his tail hit the mattress a couple of times. Then, probably noticing I didn't have any food and didn't appear to be going on any adventures, he lay his head back down and went back to sleep with a sigh.

Quietly closing the door, I made a sudden decision I hoped I wouldn't regret. Moving with purpose, I headed down the hall and wrenched open the door into my new shop. As I pulled it open, a wave of delightful scents enveloped me. I shuffled into the store like a zombie, saliva pooling in my mouth.

Glancing around in awe, I tried not to gawk as I took in the shelves and display cases filling my future candle shop. Each shelf and every display was filled to the brim with baked goods and savory foods. Cookies, cupcakes, muffins, and pies filled the enclosed display cases. The colors and shapes were a delight for the eye, even as the scents were a smorgasbord of gastronomic temptation.

Shelves filled with yeasty bread, biscuits, croissants, and flatbreads lined one side of the shop. A large refrigeration unit was filled with soups, meat pies, and assorted savory delights. A second shelving unit held boxes of Tilly's special coffee, her home-made sauces, syrups, and flavorings, dry noodles, and too many other items to list.

"It's pretty spectacular, isn't it?" Mavis asked as she came out from behind the counter.

"How did you guys set this up so fast?" I asked, my tone filled with awe.

Mavis shrugged. "A little elbow grease and a lot

of magic. Wanda and I are taking turns manning the register until you need us."

Which ripped me out of my food delirium and back to reality. "That's why I came in here. I think we need to go talk to Bathos again."

Mavis nodded as if she'd been expecting it. Turning to a young woman who had her arms filled with goodies, she said. "How would you like to work off the cost of those items?"

The woman beamed back at her. "I'd love it."

Mavis touched her shoulder. "Come with me." Addressing me over her shoulder, she said, "I'll be out in a couple of minutes. I just need to tell Tilly she has a new helper."

I nodded and then found myself reluctant to leave. Finally, with a wistful sigh, I left the room full of deliciousness behind and went to prepare for our outing.

I need your help, I thought at Gren.

His response was quick. *I'll be right there.*

I considered who else to bring, deciding Luke needed to rest and heal. *Advocate, I need your help.*

Of course, your majesty. I'll just drop what I'm doing and fly to your side.

I rolled my eyes at his snotty tone. *Thanks.* Grinning at the pique thrumming through our mind link, I headed to my room to change.

Ten minutes later, both Gren and Ferral were in my kitchen, and I was dressed in my battle leathers.

Both men met the sight of me in my leathers with a lift of a brow. "We're going to see the demon Bathos." I quickly explained what Layla had told me. The end of the story left Gren looking concerned and Ferral glaring his disapproval.

"Madam Lares, we can't just go haring off into what sounds like an extremely dangerous situation on a whim. We should call the council together and discuss it."

"My council is busy trying to contain the chaos in Rome. Between the three of us, we should be able to handle anything."

"Let's at least include the wolf."

I shook my head at the advocate's suggestion. "He's taken major injuries twice in less than a day. He needs to rest and heal."

"What about Niele?" Gren asked.

"He's dead on his feet, and he refuses to rest," I informed my protector. "He'll be more of a liability in his current state than a help."

"You're going to see my father?"

I flinched, turning to find Wanda standing in the door, her journal clutched in her hand. Monty sat down by her feet, his bright, brown eyes somehow reflecting the irritation in Wanda's gaze.

"Yes. Layla says he's been hit by the Trickster. We're going to make sure he's okay." A partial truth. Technically, not a lie. I felt okay about my phrasing until it came back to bite me.

"My dad's in trouble? I'm coming too."

Goddess in a gondola!

"That's not a good idea," I said.

Wanda stuck her chin in the air, her dark brown gaze flashing. "I. Am. Coming."

I looked at the two men for help.

Ferral opened his mouth. "This could be dangerous..." he began.

"If my dad and Aggy are in danger, they might need me. I'm coming."

"Aggy has us," Gren said gently.

"What about my dad? Will one of you save him if it comes down to him or Aggy?"

I bit down hard on the desire to remind her about all of Bathos' cruelties against her. I knew she wouldn't hear them. It was healthy and good for her to be with me...with the council. She had a relatively safe, healthy life with school and friends and normal teen things. But the one downside was that her distance from the demon Bathos had smudged the sharp edges of her knowledge about what he was.

She'd glamorized him. Whitewashed his lethal tendencies. I didn't have it in me to disabuse her of her feelings toward her father. That seemed like the cruelest truth of all. "You're not coming, and that's the end of it."

She glared at me for a long moment and then spun on her heel, stomping back down the hallway.

"Tilly could use your help in the shop," I yelled to her rigid back.

Her only response was to slam her temporary bedroom door.

I looked at Gren. "I think that went well."

He grimaced.

Monty trotted over and jumped up on me, his fat little paws resting on my sore knee. He gave me soft eyes. Unwilling to disappoint both of my house-mates in one shot, I got him a dog cookie, kissed him on his nose, and we headed out of the house.

The mudroom door slammed closed as we crossed the grass, and I turned to find Mavis running after us. "Sorry, I got hung up. I'm coming too."

I chewed my lip, wanting to tell her to stay home with Wanda. I wanted her to be safe too.

"She'll be no good as a council member if you insist on constantly protecting her," Ferral said softly enough that Mavis didn't hear.

I knew he was right, but I didn't like it. I nodded just enough to let him know I agreed.

"You were just going to leave me?" Mavis said as she joined us. I could tell by her tight smile that she was a little insulted.

"To tell you the truth," I said, dropping my arm around her shoulders, "I was fleeing the wrath of the teen."

Mavis's expression softened. "She wanted to protect her dad. That's sweet."

"And extremely misguided," Ferral growled out. "You're doing the child a disservice by not telling her the truth about him. She's weaving flowery fairy-tales and making him Prince Charming in her mind."

I doubted that was strictly true. Wanda was entirely too sensible for that kind of silliness. But the gist of his point was true. She was definitely soft-ening Bathos' image. "I can't tell her that her dad is a murdering savage. She'd be devasted."

Ferral inclined his head. "Initially, yes. But it would be a kindness in the long term."

I knew he was right. But I also knew I couldn't do it. Our relationship was still too new...too fragile. That might well shatter it completely.

"Does anyone else think the girl gave up way too easily?" Gren asked.

My gaze shot to his. I didn't see the teasing light I'd expected in his gaze. "You think she's scheming something?"

"You do know her, right?"

I sighed. I knew her well. "Would you mind trav-eling aloft where you can see if she follows us?"

"Of course." He took three long, running strides and leaped, his enormous wings snapping out on either side and pounding the air to give him lift.

I stared after him for a beat, admiring the length of his charcoal wings and the ease with which they carried him into the sky.

"I'm going to shift," Ferral informed me. "I can scent danger better as my hound."

"Okay."

His form disappeared in a flash of silvery light, and the moon hound was suddenly there. As his hound, Ferral's head reached nearly to my shoulders and he was half again as long as me.

Mavis and I watched the powerful creature lope away, and I sighed. "I guess we'll be walking alone."

Mavis tucked her arm through mine. "It will be nice. We can have a long talk about your love life."

Ugh!

There was a teasing gleam in her eyes I knew all too well.

Mavis and I chatted easily as we entered the woods. Beneath our conversation, I slowly became aware of the sound of large hooves pounding toward us. We stopped, tensing as we tried to identify the location.

A beat later, the White Mare broke from the tree line and galloped toward us.

I smiled at my friend, happy to see her.

"Saved by the mare," Mavis said, laughing.

I turned my grin on her. "Yes. And thank the goddess she's here. Because I just realized I don't know how to get to Bathos' house." The mare had guided us there the last time we'd visited the demon's lair.

Snorting and sweaty from her gallop, the White

Mare eased to a stop and lowered her head to nuzzle us.

"You're my best friend in the world," I whispered into her silky ear as I scratched under her heavy mane. "You saved me from talking about embarrassing things."

"I'm going to tell your sister she's not your best friend," Mavis teased.

I ground my teeth and hid my face. There wasn't a thing I could say to get myself out of that quagmire. So I didn't try. "We should get going," I said instead.

———

The soft sound of the mare's oversized hooves met the forest floor with muffled thumps, occasionally sending small creatures scurrying into the undergrowth. I'd noticed an unusual lack of magical and natural creatures within the forest as soon as we stepped beneath the trees.

Something was off about the Mystical Wood. I wondered if it had anything to do with the Trickster.

Mavis clung to my waist, her head resting on my back as the mare moved at a sedate walk through the woods. We'd been discussing the problem of Wanda's fixation with her father as we made our way toward Bathos' place.

Mavis had grown quiet over the last quarter mile

or so, her weight on my back growing heavier. Soon, I heard a soft, whistling snore, and I smiled.

Reaching forward, I ran my hand over the mare's sleek neck. "Apparently, you're as good as a rocking chair or a lullaby," I said quietly.

The mare snorted with amusement.

"Are we there yet?" I asked with grim amusement. I'd been teasing her with the question since shortly after we'd left my property.

The mare offered me a soft nicker, tossing her head...her version of "don't make me stop this car!"

The truth was, the last couple of times we'd traveled to Bathos' home, we'd been moving a lot faster. I had no idea why we were currently moving at such a sedate pace, but the mare seemed tenser than usual...more on edge. Her head turned from side to side as we stepped across an invisible barrier into another part of the wood.

A much darker part of it.

I'd learned since the first time I'd travelled the Mystical Wood's verdant paths that it wasn't just one enormous forest. Its magical acres were subdivided among several magical factions. Magical borderlines delineated one faction's area from another's.

I felt the bite of magic along my skin like the sting of a thousand mosquitos as we entered one such area. The magic was heavier than what I was used to...darker. The trees that stood sentinel there were perfectly still. Their branches, which towered high above our heads, didn't sway gently in the wind as they had in other sections of the woods. There was no rustling of leaves above us, no lively canopy of life skittering to and fro.

I shivered as the temperature cooled around us, the air made chillier by the dampness permeating the space.

I had the uncomfortable sensation that someone or something was watching us.

The mare's head shot up and she screamed at a large figure perched in a branch about thirty feet off the ground. The sharp-beaked predatory bird looked like something from prehistoric times, its lethal-looking beak mirrored by the horn-like protrusion on its small head. The bird's big body was covered in frilly gray feathers that reminded me of an ostrich's plumage, and its legs were unusually long, also like an ostrich.

But the threatening red gaze told me it was no ostrich. I'd bet money the creature had originally come from the demonic plane. Maybe it had escaped from the vortex before we'd managed to seal it. Maybe it had been here a long time, living in the impenetrable obscurity of the wood.

Mavis woke with a start, lifting her head. She unwound one arm from around me and rubbed a spot on my back. "Sorry, honey. I drooled a little on your battle leathers."

I snorted out a laugh. "I'm glad you got a nap. I have a feeling you're going to need it."

"Huh? Why?"

I jerked my head toward the thing watching us pass, and she gasped. "Is that a pterodactyl?"

"It sure looks like it."

I stared into the terrifying red eyes and tightened my muscles against another shudder.

Under our perusal, the bird opened its beak and gave a strident cry. Lifting its wings, the creature danced sideways along the branch, like a bigger, uglier Ray.

But that was where any resemblance to my raven ended. Like the prehistoric bird it resembled, the creature's wings were more like a bat's than a bird's, featherless and leathery. Deadly finger-like bones protruded from the wrists at the top of the wings, no doubt meant to attack and hold prey while the lethal-looking beak ripped it into bite-sized pieces.

I shuddered violently. "I hate dinosaurs."

"Really?" Mavis asked. "I think they're kind of cool."

"You would," I said, chuckling.

My adopted mother was about as fearless as they came. In her early sixties, Mavis seemed even less afraid of things that go bitey in the dark than she'd been ten or twenty years ago. When she brought me into her heart and home as a lost and lonely teen, I'd thought moonlight paled in her presence. As I'd grown older, my awe of her strength and resilience had only increased. She'd tackle anything without concern for her own safety or health. Which was why trying to keep her safe was giving me ulcers.

The bird screamed again and flapped its bat-like wings, lifting off the tree.

The mare tensed beneath me, her head lifting in an answering scream, then she gathered her legs beneath her, and I yelled, "Hold on, Mom!" just as the mare took off at a terrifying gallop.

Mavis gave a little yelp, and her slender arms tightened around me, compressing my ribs.

I grunted from the pressure on my middle but had no time to worry about it. A rush of wind from above presaged the appearance of the flying monster.

Mavis screamed, ducking sideways and nearly pulling us both off the horse as three-inch-long talons grasped for her.

She flung up a hand and magic slashed over the talons, setting them on fire.

The bird reared back, flapping its wings hard on a scream of pain. But the fire soon went out, and the creature was attacking again within seconds.

The White Mare turned her head as we approached an area of tighter trees. Fear made the whites of her eyes glow in the low light. She bared her teeth in another scream that was quickly answered by the bird.

I called my staff to me, flinging out an arm as it smacked into my palm. Without thinking, I yanked my power forward and fed it through the weapon, compressing it into a narrow stream of pure energy that glanced off the monster's left wing and shot past it to sheer off an oversized branch of a nearby tree.

The bird dropped toward us again, talons slashing the air. Agony sliced through one arm as the lethal talons encircled it, digging deep into my flesh. The monster pounded its wings, trying to pull me into the air.

Mavis threw out a hand, and a pale green web of magic wrapped around the bird's pointed head. She made a fist and yanked it back. The magic compressed around the monster's head, pulling tight enough to slice through leathery skin.

The bird reared back again, clawing at its own face, and the mare dug in more, shooting forward to make the best use of the time Mavis had gained us.

Trees flew past at a dizzying speed.

I bent low over the mare's neck, clutching a thick hunk of mane in my hands as I dug in my heels on sheer instinct. It wasn't necessary to cue the mare to run. She was already running at full speed, dodging trees and leaping over fallen logs. It was a hair-raising run and only slightly better than the alternative, which was us on the ground with that monstrous bird bearing down on us. If she ran any faster, we'd be flying.

Flying!

I leaned close to her ear. "Can you take off? Fly?"

The mare grunted, her chest heaving beneath my legs. She spun to the right without warning, and I gave a little scream, wrapping my arms around her neck to keep from sliding off and taking Mavis with me.

A vision filled my mind, quick and sharp. It was a visualization of an aerial battle between the mare and the bird. I watched as Mavis and I fell off the horse's back, slamming into the ground in twin, crumpled heaps. In the vision, we were the victims of the mare's nearly vertical flight pattern in her effort to escape the bird.

"Right. No flying. Got it," I told her.

"Aggy!" Mavis screamed, bringing my attention back to the bird, which had overtaken us again, and was stretching its deadly talons toward Mavis.

"Can you give us some breathing room?" I asked Mavis. "I have an idea."

"Yep!" Mavis yelled back. I eyed the sky above us, picking my spot. "On the count of three," I yelled.

Wind buffeted us from above. The sour stench of the monster slid over us, blanketing us in evil. I fought to keep my mind on what I needed to do and sent a mental picture to the horse. Her head bobbed up and down as she made a slight adjustment to our course.

"One."

The bird screamed again, its foul breath painting our skin.

"Two."

A talon ripped toward my head, snagging some of my hair and ripping it from my scalp.

"Three!" I screamed in a panic-stricken voice.

Mavis blasted the air in front of the bird with sizzling green magic. It exploded into a hundred tiny pinwheels of fiery energy, which burrowed into the bird everywhere they touched its body. The creature screamed with agony, writhing under the biting magic.

I waited until the mare had put three strides between the bird and us, then sent an arrow of power into the largest branch I could find that was directly over the bird's head. The magic sheered across the branch, and it dropped like a thousand-pound rock, slamming into the bird and carrying it to the ground.

We didn't slow or look back. Whether it was dead or not, we wanted to put as much distance between the nasty thing and ourselves as possible.

Five minutes later, we broke through the edge of the woods and onto Bathos' acres of gently rolling lawn. The mare slowed to a trot, her sides heaving and foam lathering her entire body.

I tugged on her mane. "Let us off. You need to cool down, and we can walk."

She stumbled to a halt, and I worried that she'd

done too much. We'd just managed to get clear before the beautiful horse's legs buckled and she went down.

"No!" I dropped to my knees beside her. "You have to get up. You need to cool down."

"Aggy," Mavis said, her tone heavy.

"Help me get her to her feet," I barked at Mavis. "She'll colic and die if she doesn't cool down properly."

"Aggy, honey."

I tugged ineffectually on the horse's thick mane. "Please, please, please get up."

Blood-flecked foam coated the horse's muzzle and chest. That couldn't be good. "Mavis!" I screamed. "Help me."

My gaze shot angrily to Mavis's, and my stomach filled with lead. Tears shimmered in my mom's pretty gray gaze.

I followed her line of sight and gasped. The horse's beautiful white flank was torn and bloody, the tracks bone-deep.

The horrible bird had ripped her to shreds.

17

THE DEMON'S LAIR A DEADLY GOAL

"No, no, no, no!" I started toward the enormous home in the distance, intending to force Bathos to help my fallen friend. But something stopped me. I was unwilling to leave the mare even to find help. I ran back, dropping to the ground beside her.

Laying my hands on her haunch, I felt a frantic quiver beneath her skin. Her sides were still heaving, and her green eyes rolled to me with a plea in them. "We have to heal her," I told Mavis. Neither of us had that kind of healing power, but we had to try. Maybe working together, we could get her on her feet. We'd figure something out from there.

Mavis placed her hands on the skin near the wounds, and I closed my eyes, pulling my magic forward in a thin strand that I knew wouldn't harm... even if I wasn't sure it would help. My control over my magic was weak at best, but I'd been working on levels and strengths of energy expulsion and felt fairly confident I could find the right mix. I eased the channel open a bit more, allowing a wash of gentle gold energy to cover the wounded area. Mavis's magic slid against mine, heating and energizing it.

I pictured my magic healing the wounds...knitting the torn tissue, and easing the pain. In my mind's eye, the wounds flared with angry color, the red of blood, the green of putridity. The horse's sides began to heave faster, her breathing growing labored as she snorted with panic.

Her panic made mine flare. Tightness banded my chest. Sympathetic pain blossomed in me, and I gasped under its razor-sharp claws.

"Aggy?" Mavis said, her magic stuttering.

"I'm okay, don't stop." When she still hesitated, I opened my eyes, pleading with her through tears. "Please?"

She frowned but nodded.

I bit down on the pain and eased more magic past my fingertips. And then more. And more.

The mare's body began to twitch. She grunted in pain as we pushed more and more magic into her body.

A foul stench rose from the wounds. I gagged under its horrible influence. Mavis groaned.

Black ooze slid from the wound and ran down the mare's trembling side, sizzling as it hit the grass.

The horse's body erupted in a seizure, her strong legs flailing to the point where Mavis and I had to jump away from her or be taken down by the power of her legs and hooves.

We stood, pale-faced and shaky, as the horse fought her own body to overcome an array of seizures. One after another, for way too many minutes, she jerked and spasmed, every muscle in her body as tight as steel.

Just when I was ready to do something drastic, the attacks started to ease. The large muscles of her haunches softened. Her legs flailed one last time and went still.

I pulled air into my burning chest, realizing I'd forgotten to breathe.

Mavis was wringing her hands together, her gaze locked onto the horse. "Do you think we helped at all?"

I was afraid we might have done more harm than good, but I nodded toward the gashes, which were still open and angry, but appeared narrower than before. "The wounds are closing," I said. The tissue around them was still swollen and red, but I got the sense that the black venom we'd watched ooze out of the injuries had been the worst of the problem. "They look better."

"That thing had poison on its claws," Mavis said, her voice angry.

I nodded. "Hopefully, we killed it with that branch."

The mare's eyes opened, and she tried to lift her head. Fighting to get her legs underneath her, she managed to get partially upright. But her back end was apparently too weak for her to stand. I chewed my lip, fighting panic. I was out of ideas.

The woods exploded in a blaze of white light. The trees bent under the power of the explosion, and the scent of ozone blasted over us.

I sighed, feeling more than tired. "What now?" I groused.

Mavis swiped hair off her sweat-coated face and turned to meet our next challenge, her slender form straight, magic spitting from her palms.

I joined her, pulling my own energy forward again. We were a united front against whatever was coming our way.

A small figure with wild white hair emerged from the woods. Mavis and I shared a shocked look as the slightly bent figure stalked toward us across the lawn. She wore torn jeans over her skinny legs and a tee-shirt that said, "Dachshunds are like potato chips. You can never have just one."

I smiled at the sight of that tee, knowing the cavalry had arrived.

The crone didn't bother to look at us as she knelt beside the beautiful mare, running gnarled fingers over the quivering white coat. "What did this to her?"

"It was a big bird thing," Mavis said, watching the ancient witch carefully. "It looked like a pterodactyl."

"We managed to take it down," I said, feeling a bit defensive that we'd allowed the crone's friend to be hurt. "But when we came out of the woods, she collapsed. That's when we saw the wounds."

The mare nickered softly and nuzzled the crone. "That's right, pretty one. I've come to take you home."

Her words struck sudden terror in my heart. "She's not..." I swallowed hard. "She isn't dying...?" I couldn't finish the question, but it didn't matter because the crone had already dismissed me. She stood and stepped back, her hands cupped in front of her. A wave of multi-hued magic emerged from her hands and washed over the mare. The crone slowly lifted her hands, and the mare lifted with them, her legs finding the ground as her body was raised off the grass.

The horse wobbled on her legs, her muscles quivering violently from pain or weariness.

"Come along, my good friend. We'll get you home to rest and heal. Laverne and Shirley are missing you."

Slowly, the mare started to turn, the crone seemingly aiding her movement with a hand on her sleek neck.

I stepped forward, touching the horse's back. "Will she be okay?"

"She'll be fine. She just needs to regain her strength." The crone frowned over the slowly closing wounds. "Crude work, but it will suffice." Her sharp gaze swung from Mavis to me. "You removed all the poison?"

"I think so," I said.

The crone nodded. "Good." She gave me a bright smile. "You did well, Lares...Witch." Then she turned on her heels, and the two of them returned to the woods. I watched as another explosion of light bent the trees away from what I assumed was the crone stepping through the barrier between her dimension and ours.

"Okay then," Mavis said brightly. She frowned. "Where are Gren and Ferral? Shouldn't they be here by now?"

And just like that, Mavis took my defrazzling nerves and jazzed them right back up again. I forced insta-panic away and called to Gren in my mind. *Where are you?* No response. I tried Ferral. *Are you at Bathos' place yet?* Static scraped across my mind, and the panic ratcheted up a few notches. "There's something wrong. They're not responding."

Mavis rubbed her hands over her face, clearly

trying to tamp down on worry. "Okay. Let's not panic..."

"Too late for that," I told her.

"Let me rephrase that. Try not to lose your ship. Things are cray-cray right now. We know this. They probably just got waylaid and will join us soon. In the meantime..."

"We need to go talk to Bathos. Right." I nodded. "Thanks for dragging me back from the edge. My *ship* was just about ready to sail."

Mavis laughed. "Just doing my part to help you with your anti-swearing pledge."

"Your efforts are entertaining."

We started across Bathos' massive backyard, heading for the pool area and the back door we'd used the last time we were there.

"Do you find it odd there were no guards at the edge of the woods like last time?" Mavis asked me a few minutes later.

I nodded. I'd been skimming a look over the sky above, thinking it was strange the giant guard hawks that had attacked my raven friend, Ray, the last time we'd been there weren't at the very least watching us as we approached.

My apprehension tripled as we got closer to the house. Bathos' elegant mansion stood tall against a backdrop of the setting sun. Its doors and windows felt menacing as I began to imagine malevolent gazes peering at us from each one.

The air was still and quiet. Too quiet. And as we stepped onto the concrete area around the pool, I picked up a scent that made the small hairs along my arms and the back of my neck rise in warning.

Glancing at Mavis, I saw the lines between her brows that told me she'd smelled it too. I placed a finger against my lips and pointed to the glass door leading to a large common room on the lower level of the big house.

I pictured the space as I pulled the door open, seeing the big room filled with leather couches and a large fireplace on the outside wall at one end. Down a wide hallway was the kitchen, and beyond that, the door leading to Bathos' subterranean prison caverns.

Walking into the subdued lighting in the family room, I squinted in an attempt to see the room. My vision was poor after the bright sun outside, and I nearly tripped over the first body, actually kicking it with the toe of my sneaker before jolting to a stop.

I gasped, backtracking at the sight of an unknown dead man. He was dressed in the "uniform" of one of Bathos' servants. His features were twisted in stark terror, and his skin was already mottled with death. I saw nothing that would explain the poor man's demise, only the expression of horror on his face, and the outstretched hand that looked as if he was trying to keep something at bay. The fingers were curved like claws in death.

I grabbed Mavis's hand, and we stepped carefully around the man. Another servant was down in the hallway, and two more in the kitchen. I forced myself to check the entire house, hoping to find Bathos.

Twenty minutes later, we had to admit defeat, having found no sign of the demon on any of the three levels.

Mavis stared at the young woman who was draped over the large kitchen island. "We need to check the caverns." Even as she said the words, she shuddered, telling me just how much she didn't want to do that.

I nodded. "Do you have your phone?"

She pulled her cell out of the pocket of her capris khakis. If someone saw Mavis in a non-murdery place, they'd just think she was an attractive older woman heading out to play bridge with her friends or running to the grocery. She certainly didn't look like a kick-butt monster masher witch. Of course...I glanced down at my own clothing...I was wearing yoga pants and sneakers, hardly Lara Croft, Tomb Raider™ myself.

"I'll hit the caverns. You stay up here and keep calling council members until somebody answers the phone."

She shook her head. "You're not going down there by yourself."

I didn't bother arguing with her. Heading across the room, I wrenched open the door leading down into the caverns. "I'm just going to do a quick look around. I doubt there's anything down here."

Mavis got a funny look on her face. "It's going to be a lot quicker than you think, honey."

I followed her line of sight and groaned. It was a pantry, not the steep and slippery wooden staircase I'd been expecting. "What the...?" I closed the door and looked around. Had I opened the wrong door?

"Bathos moved the location of the cells," Mavis said.

Curse, swear, swear!

I rubbed my brow. "That's just great."

"The question is," Mavis went on, "did he move it before or after all this happened?" She swept an arm around the room, indicating the two dead women.

"His escaped prisoner could have done this," I pointed out.

Mavis nodded. "Seems likely."

Would Bathos have put himself into the caverns and then moved them to hide from the monster who'd escaped? The demon had faults. Many, many faults. But I didn't think cowardice was one of them. And he wouldn't have reached the trusted position of barrister for the worst of the worst in the demonic world by being a deserter.

Aggy...?

I jumped at the sound of Gren's voice in my head. *Gren! Where are you?* I waited for a response and didn't get one.

"What's wrong, honey?" Mavis asked.

"Gren's trying to reach me. Wherever they are, there's some kind of interference."

"What could interfere with your mental communication? We're not talking cell phones here."

I had no idea. But whatever it was, I couldn't shake the feeling it wasn't good. "Let's finish up here and go find out. I'm worried about them." On a whim, I dialed Wanda's cell phone. She didn't answer, but that could just be because she was mad at me. I ended the call, sighing. "I don't know how you did it," I told Mavis as we started out of the kitchen.

"Did what, honey?"

"Raised two teenagers." I was pretty sure that however much Wanda pushed my buttons, I'd been even worse at her age. I knew Bev had been. My sister had been a wild child, and I'd had a huge chip on my shoulder.

Mavis gave me a one-armed hug. "You *were* moody and sometimes resistant to my excellent life lessons."

I snorted.

"But you were never unkind, and I always knew you loved me. No matter how mad I made you."

I realized she wasn't just talking about me. I sighed again. "I know she loves me. I love her too. But I have no clue what I'm doing."

Mavis opened the first door we came to in the

hallway, peeked inside, and then closed it again. "Kids never like to be told no, Aggy. No amount of parenting skill will ever change that. Wanda will get over it and...someday, far, far from now...she might even thank you for it."

I opened a door and glanced inside, finding a dining room. "Oh, I like that table."

Mavis stuck her head in and nodded. "That's really pretty."

We checked all the doors on the first and second levels and trudged up to the third floor. At that point, I was pretty sure we weren't going to find a door to the dungeon. Only an idiot would attach a prison for monsters to his bedroom. Magical or not.

The entire third floor appeared to be Bathos' private quarters. The main portion in the center held a larger-than-king-sized bed with four tall posts, each of which had a gauzy drape attached to it. The floor was brilliant white marble, covered by a vivid red rug that was so thick my feet sank when I stepped onto it. There were two sets of French doors with heavy red velvet curtains on one wall and a massive, old-world-style dresser against another.

An active fireplace crackled and popped pleasantly from the wall leading into a large bathroom. Through the open door, I could see a white claw-footed tub draped with plush red towels and a long counter with two raised copper sinks.

The wall behind the four-poster bed was covered

in terrifying, violent images done in stark shades of blood-red and black. The paintings seeming to depict a level of Hell where demonic creatures guarded the unfortunate victims of the fiery pits.

Bathos' apparent addiction to fireplaces became suddenly more clear. It was an odd fascination for an earthbound demon, since it could be assumed he'd never set foot in the Hades dimension. But apparently, he'd enjoyed enough man-made stories about Hell to have pieced together his own version.

"I'll check this closet," Mavis said, reaching for a lever-type door handle.

I nodded and started to look away, only to catch movement out of the corner of my eye. My gaze shot back to the door, and I watched in horror as the smooth wood boiled outward, rippling from top to bottom like molten metal.

And speaking of molten metal... As Mavis's hand hovered over the handle, it suddenly flared red-hot, mere centimeters from her fingers.

"No!" I screamed, lunging in her direction.

Gong!

18

TERROR DIGS THE DEEPEST HOLE

G *ong!* My internal warning bell was either too late, or something else was going sideways in another part of my dominion. I didn't have time to figure it out at that moment. Mavis touched the handle and screamed, her body twitching as smoke rose around her hand. She didn't seem able to pull her hand away.

I started to run, but the distance across the large room felt like miles. In sheer desperation, I screamed, "Release!" and sent a bolt of magic into the door. The magic hit hard enough to judder the door in its frame.

Mavis jerked away, stumbling backward and looking down at her hand. Her palm was fire-red, and blisters were already starting to form across the surface. As I watched in horror, the redness and blistering spread to her wrist, with every sign of moving up her arm.

Mavis stopped screaming long enough to draw a breath and then screamed again, the sound like razor blades slicing my nerves.

I reacted without thinking, terrified about what was happening to her. I touched her forehead and said, "Sleep!"

Mavis went silent and still, her eyes closing, and she dropped like a rock. I barely caught her, dragging her toward the hallway and propping her up against the wall. Inside the bedroom, the closet door blew open, shattering against the wall. Something shuffled across the floor, the sound heavy and wet.

Dread turned my feet to lead. I eyed Mavis quickly, determining that she was breathing and her heart was working, and then turned and ran back into the bedroom, slamming the door behind me.

I searched frantically for whatever had come through the door and saw...nothing.

Beyond the closet door was a yawning, musty-smelling darkness. I recognized that smell.

It was the caverns.

Had we just released Bathos' prisoner from the subterranean prison?

If the monster had been down there, loosed from its cell, where was Bathos? Why hadn't he imprisoned it again?

There could be only one answer. Bathos was down.

I shoved my first thought...of Wanda...away. We'd created a problem, and I needed to fix it.

Somehow.

Movement skittered across the wall to my left. I spun to face it, my hands spitting with defensive magic.

There was nothing there.

A fretful moaning sound lifted through the room. For a moment, I thought it was Mavis, moaning in pain. But the sound had been nearby, too close to be her.

Something cold and sour-smelling brushed against my skin. I itched to slam the closet door shut but resisted. I needed to leave it open. Somehow it had kept the creature from leaving. If I could get it back inside the door....

Movement slashed through my peripheral vision on my right.

I turned my head quickly enough to see a shadow flash past the bedroom door.

Panic clamped icy fists over my heart. I couldn't let the monster get out of the bedroom. My only hope of saving Mavis was keeping whatever it was contained.

With me.

My throat suddenly wouldn't work. When I tried to swallow, it got stuck.

Think, Aggy. Think.

First on the agenda was figuring out what I was dealing with. On the tail end of that thought, the room went completely dark.

The moaning rose up around me. It slid over my skin like oil, leaving me feeling tainted and cold.

Movement from above my head had me flinging a fistful of energy at the ceiling. The magic hit the pristine white plaster and left a large black burn mark behind. A shadow danced away as if gleeful that I had failed.

Feel your death... a phantom voice hissed into my ear.

With a yelp of fear and surprise, I jerked sideways, stumbling backward until I hit the wall.

The shadow slid from the ceiling and melted down the wall as if it lived beneath the paint. I threw more magic at the ever-moving glooms with the same result. A large black blot splatted across Bathos' wall, but my magic never came close to touching the shadow.

I noticed that the thing avoided the doorway leading to the caverns, oozing upward and skating across the ceiling rather than coming within feet of the opening.

The door had been spelled with something that kept what I could only assume at that point was a shadow demon contained. If Mavis hadn't opened it, the thing might never have escaped.

The realization of what it was turned me to ice. I'd fought a shadow demon once before when the vortex had been bleeding demons onto the earthly plane. And I'd barely survived the experience. I'd only managed to beat it with the help of my council. Alone, I wouldn't have a chance.

The shadow slid down the wall and plunged beneath the marble. I watched in horror as the shadowy figure skimmed through the floor, moving right at me. I ran, making it only a few steps before the floor buckled up from underneath me. Screaming, I stumbled and barely caught myself before a cold, black hand reached out of the crack and wrapped around my ankle.

I screamed again, the sound filled with desperation and terror. The shadow's touch burned me like fire, and I found myself being yanked downward, through the crack, and into the scorching heat of what looked like a Hades dimension. At the last moment, I managed to grab the marble, my downward plummet jerking painfully to a stop. Immediately, my sweaty fingers started to slip. Through sheer desperation, I managed to hold on.

The heat was unbearable, scorching my skin despite being far below me. Sweat popped out all over my body, and my clammy hands threatened to lose their grip on the floor.

Growling with the effort, I clung to the edge of

the crack, wishing I could let go with one hand so I could scald the demon with magic.

But I didn't dare. I was barely holding on as it was.

Somewhere in the distance, a door slammed open, crashing against the wall, and energy flared over my head, hot and sizzling.

I felt its touch on my skin as I fought to drag myself upward. The demon's grip lessoned for a beat and then tightened again as soon as I started to rise.

More power seared the air above me, followed by a single word, barked in a voice I knew all too well. "*Cedo!*"

The monster's grip on me loosened again. "No! Mavis, get out of here."

"*Apage!*"

The monster moaned, the putrid stench of burning brimstone rising up around us. The creature gave me another yank and, to my horror, one of my hands slipped off. I screamed as the other hand gave way and I was suddenly falling, plunging downward into the stifling heat and sizzling flames far below.

My screams ripped at the tender flesh of my throat. Fear stole my mind, turning me rabid with fear.

"Aggy!" Mavis sounded so desperate, so worried. I wanted to tell her it would be okay. It would be a lie, but I couldn't bear the thought of how my fiery death would make her feel.

The heat below me scorched my legs, blistering the flesh and charring my skin black.

A sharp pain slashed across my face as the heat melted the skin there.

I was still screaming, but my throat was too raw to emit much sound.

"Aggy! Wake up!" Pain lashed my cheek again.

Wait a minute. Why did that feel like a slap?"

"Wake up, Aggy. You're okay. Stop screaming... please?" Mavis's voice was filled with tears, and the sound finally got through to me.

Slamming my lips closed, I realized my eyes were shut and opened them, just as Mavis slapped me again. "Hey!" I said, indignant. "That hurts."

Mavis deflated, "Thank the goddess. I couldn't take much more of that shrieking. What in the world were you going on about?"

I stared at her in shock. "I was falling into a fiery pit. The shadow demon yanked me through the floor."

Mavis's blonde eyebrows lifted. "Through the floor?" She shook her head. "Have you been reading *Alice in Wonderland* again?"

I forced my sore, weary body upright and pointed to the crack in the marble floor. "I'm not lying, look, there's the cr...." The floor where I was sure the demon had broken through was whole and unblemished.

"You were having a bad dream," Mavis told me.

I stared at her for a moment as her words sifted slowly through my brain. Then I grabbed her hands, turning them over. "You're not burned."

She tugged her hands out of my grip. "I wouldn't say that. I'm pretty steamed right now. You dragged me out into the hallway and locked the door. I've been out there listening to you scream and couldn't do anything about it."

"Wait, I was in here by myself? There was no monster?"

Her gaze darkened with something that looked like fear. "I wish. No, when I broke the door open and came in, there was something leaning over you."

"Something?"

She nodded, fidgeting and avoiding my gaze.

"What did it look like?" I asked.

Mavis continued to refuse to look at me until I grabbed her arms and gave her a little shake. "Mom, talk to me. I can't stop this thing if I don't know what it is."

She turned a haunted gaze to me, her pupils huge as if she were on the razor edge of going into shock. Her lips opened and closed a couple of times. Finally, she closed her eyes, dropped her head back, and took a long slow breath. When she opened her eyes again, she looked calmer. "Aggy, honey, it was horrible," she said in a voice that was almost too soft to hear. "It looked like a phantom with cold, dead eyes. Kind of man-shaped, but without any features or physical attributes. And when I finally got it away from you...." She swallowed hard. "There was still a shadow moving in your eyes."

I frowned. "A shadow?" I thought of the shadow I'd seen skittering across the walls, elongated and humanoid one minute, then amorphous and disjointed the next. "It was in my eyes?"

Mavis nodded. "What did you see in here, honey?"

I shook my head, trying to dispel my confusion. "You reached to open the closet door." I glanced toward the handle of the door in question. It no longer glowed with heat. In fact, it looked perfectly harmless. It was just a closet. "You burned your hand when you touched it. I panicked and yanked you out of the room, locking you out so it couldn't get to you."

As I said the words, I realized my reasoning was off. Locking the door would only keep Mavis out.

My frown deepened, and I shook my head to dispel my doubts. "Something shadowy moved through the walls and the floor. I thought it was a shadow demon."

"And the screaming?" Mavis asked.

I explained to her about the monster opening the floor up and trying to pull me down into the fiery pit. By the time I finished, I realized how crazy I sounded. "None of it was real, was it?"

"No. I was standing at the door, reaching for the handle and you screamed, 'No!' The next thing I knew, you had hold of my hands, and you were pulling me out into the hall. I let you drag me out because I thought you'd seen something dangerous. But when you came back inside and locked me out...." Mavis's haunted look remained. "Then you started to scream." She shuddered. "You sounded as if someone was tearing you into pieces. I never want to hear that sound again."

"Aggy?"

Mavis and I turned in surprise at the sound of Gren's voice.

"Thank the goddess?" I said, pushing to my feet and running to wrap my arms around him. "We thought something had happened to you."

"Something did happen to me. And to the advocate."

I looked behind him. "Ferral? Is he all right?"

"Mostly, yes. He's taken the girl home."

"Wanda?" My hands tightened in his shirt. "She followed us?" *Swear!* "Is she hurt?"

"She's shaken, but otherwise fine, Aggy."

"What happened to you?" Mavis asked. Her thoughts flew across her face, easy to read. Confusion, curiosity, realization, and fear. "Was it that horrible pterodactyl thing?"

Gren slid his hand into mine and looked deep into my eyes. He must have seen something in them he didn't like because two worry lines appeared between his molten chocolate eyes. "No." He narrowed his gaze on Mavis, assessing her. "We were set upon by a nest of huge snakes. There were dozens of them, fast and lethal. I'm afraid the girl suffered quite a bit of trauma over it."

I closed my eyes. "She's terrified of snakes," I said.

Gren nodded. "Anyone would have been terrified of these snakes. I've never seen their like. The smallest one was fifteen feet long and had red eyes. They were white, with fang-shaped markings on their snouts. Ferral and I managed to dispose of all but two of the nasty things. Unfortunately, those two got away."

We stood in silence for a minute, lost in contemplation of our adventures. Finally, Gren asked, "Did you find Bathos?"

"No," I said reluctantly. "The prison caverns have been moved, and there's no sign of him in the house or grounds." I described my experience with the shadowy thing.

"Fear-eater," Gren said, his expression dire. "That's the last thing we needed to have set loose right now."

I chewed my lip, feeling guilty. "Did we release it somehow?" I asked.

"From what you told me, it was already loose. And it's been busy. Those people downstairs...."

"The dead bodies?"

He nodded, his handsome face bathed in sadness. "I couldn't see any sign of injury on any of them. All showed extreme signs of fear."

"Are you saying they were literally scared to death?"

Gren shrugged. "It looks that way."

I reached out and pulled Mavis into a hug. "You saved my life. If you hadn't shooed that thing away, it would have killed me."

She hugged me back, her grip almost painful. "But where did it go?" Mavis asked. "Did I send it out there to hurt other people?"

Gren squeezed her arm. "You didn't set it loose, Mavis. Bathos somehow did. I only hope, for the girl's sake, he didn't end up like those people downstairs."

"We need to do something with the bodies," Mavis said.

"I suggest we don't bury them until the Trickster is caught and the whole cemetery/ghost thing is set to rights," my protector said.

"Good idea," I said. "I'd like to find their people first anyway."

"What should we do with them in the meantime?" Mavis asked.

"I'll bet Bathos has an oversized freezer or two in this house," I said.

Gren nodded. "Let's go find out."

But, before we could do that, the soft swish of footsteps on carpet had us all whipping around, magic dancing at the ready.

I watched in horror as the levered knob on the closet door started to depress.

Thinking of the fear-eater's attack, I had to fight an overwhelming impulse to turn and run.

It didn't make me feel any better when Gren moved closer, putting his big body in front of Mavis and me.

Tension filled the room, hemorrhaging from each of us like blood, as the door began to open.

I waited for the putrid stench of evil to fill the room. When it didn't, I frowned, doubt displacing some of the fear in my mind.

A tall, slender form dressed in a slightly rumpled black suit and a wilted white shirt stepped out of the closet. Bathos twitched in surprise when he saw us. He frowned. "What are you all doing in my bedroom?"

19

THE WARDEN'S POW'R A FOOL DOTH THWART

I allowed the magic to die on my fingertips. "Where have you been?" I demanded, earning myself a glower from the demon Bathos.

"I've been dealing with my business, Madam Lares. I live here, remember? I have duties. Now answer my question. What are you all doing in my house?"

"You moved the prison caverns," Mavis said.

Bathos arched perfect black brows at her. "I did. Not that it's any business of yours."

Mavis cocked a hip, her peaches and cream complexion flushing with anger. "When your monsters nearly kill Aggy, it is definitely my business."

Bathos glanced at me, a question lurking in the arched brows.

"Are you missing a fear-eater by any chance?" I asked.

He didn't react at first, but then he slowly closed his eyes and went very still, barely breathing. His eyes snapped open a beat later, and I flinched from the rage there. "Please tell me you didn't let it out of this room!"

Gren moved in front of me again. "Back down, demon. If you'd been doing your job, the thing wouldn't have been able to escape the caverns in the first place."

Flames flared to life in Bathos' black eyes, a single fiery point in the center of each one. His jaw tightened, and his fingers curled, the perfectly mani-cured nails lengthening into claws.

Mavis and I yanked magic forward, ready to defend ourselves.

But before Bathos started a war he didn't need, he reined himself in and took a step back. The fire disappeared from his eyes, and he shoved his clawed hands into the pockets of his suit, ruining the perfect lines. "I apologize. This damnable Trickster has me on edge. Please forgive me."

I didn't entirely trust his abrupt about-face, but I let my magic go and nodded. "Understandable. It's got us all on edge. Please tell me you can get that thing back."

He inclined his head. "I can."

As calm and self-assured as his voice sounded, I

spotted the flicker of unease in his gaze because I had been looking for it.

"You didn't, by any chance, lose a nest of over-sized albino snakes too, did you?" Gren asked.

Bathos paled.

"And a pterodactyl?" Mavis added.

Bathos lost another shade. "It's been a trying time."

"All of your people in the house are dead," I told him, my tone gentle. I doubted the demon had formed any attachments to his staff, but my reverential tone was for their deaths, not his probably non-existent feelings.

The quick flash of pain that crossed his handsome face surprised me. He seemed to deflate, moving awkwardly to a chair and dropping into it. "What killed them?" he asked in a defeated voice.

"The fear-eater," Gren said.

Bathos lowered his head into his hands, clearly affected by the loss of his people. "I'll notify their families."

I nodded. "I'm sorry for your loss."

Bathos didn't acknowledge my words. He sat with his head in his hands for a full minute before straightening and looking me in the eye. "As you can see, I have much to do here, Madam Lares. What can I help you with?"

"First," Gren said, "...tell us what happened here? How did all of these creatures escape?"

Bathos' face turned hard, his gaze brittle with rage. Fire flared in the center of each eye again. "The Trickster. I warned you we needed to get rid of that thing."

"Yes, you did," I admitted. "But your plan was untenable."

He nodded angrily. "Yes, well, you see the result."

"You didn't answer my question," Gren said. "How did they escape?"

Bathos seemed unwilling to share that information with us. "You tend to your business, and I'll tend to mine, *angel*."

Gren's smile was a warning. "As Ms. Adyms just said, if it endangers the Lares or her dominion, it *is* our business."

The two men glared at each other for a moment. Bathos' expressions clearly told me he was considering digging in his heels. But then he sighed. "I tried to capture the Trickster myself. It actually worked better than I'd hoped." He winced. "Until I realized he'd allowed me to capture him."

I realized what he was saying. "The Trickster wanted you to imprison it, so it could bust out your other...guests."

Bathos looked miserable. "It was definitely a humbling experience."

I knew all about those. Something that felt like pity slid through me. "We're actually here to talk to you about the Trickster. I was wondering if you'd considered any other options for getting rid of it?" He lifted a brow and I shrugged. "I'm feeling a little desperate at the moment." When his eyes lit with hope, I clarified. "Not desperate enough to open a portal to the demonic plane."

Anger replaced hope on his handsome face. "Then you and I have nothing to talk about."

"I think we do," I told him. "Why does it have to be the demonic plane?"

"Because, do you really want to unleash this thing on another realm? In the demonic plane, the Trickster will be just another monster in a world of monsters. He won't even be the worst monster there. If we're lucky, one of the other fiends will eat him."

I smiled a little at that thought. "I get that. But I can't open Rome up to the demonic realm again. That's a non-starter."

"What about recreating the demonic plane here?" Mavis asked.

We all looked at her with varying degrees of horror.

She held up a hand. "Hear me out on this. I think I have an idea that might work."

"I'm listening," I responded.

Mavis nodded. "All of these monsters we keep bumping into everywhere, we've been viewing them only as problems...dangerous obstacles. But what if we could make them useful?"

"Still listening," I said, frowning. "But preparing

to make a run for it." Anything that required revisiting that dinosaur-bird thing, a nest of giant albino snakes, or the fear-eater was not my idea of a good time.

Mavis rolled her eyes as Gren chuckled.

"What if we could assemble a bunch of deadly fiends in one place and then lure the Trickster into it? We might not be able to take the Trickster down, but I don't think he'd fare as well against a bunch of mindless monsters. For one thing, their minds are too simple for trickery except at the most basic level. And at that level, the Trickster's going to be hard-pressed to keep his A-game in place against them."

Gren nodded. "It's definitely an intriguing idea. But the logistics are formidable."

"That's the problem I see," Bathos chimed in. "Believe me when I tell you the Trickster is impossible to contain. I'm the best monster jailer on the earthly plane, and I couldn't manage it for more than five minutes."

"The way I see it," Mavis said, "We have two main issues. First, we need to create the perfect place to cage him. One that will, hopefully, lead to his demise so Das can't sic him onto some other unlucky population. I might have a solution for that."

"Reluctantly still listening," I said with a smile.

Mavis narrowed her gaze on me. "The next ringtone I program into your phone is going to be a doozy."

I flung my hands up in surrender. "Just teasing. I'm intrigued."

"The coven has been working on creating inter-planar spaces. We're very close to locking the spell down and have started doing small experiments." She winced. "This would be a whopper of an experiment. It would be a risk trying it out before we've perfected it. But given the destruction this nasty creature has managed to cause in a short amount of time, I think it's an acceptable risk."

"How long do you think it would take you to finish the spell?" I asked.

She sighed. "That's a good question. Losing Trish has put a crimp in the process, for sure. We'd relied heavily on her fae magic in the spell. It was the glue that held it all together."

"That actually might be a good thing," Gren told her. "If your spell used fae magic as the main component, Das could potentially break it."

Mavis nodded. "I had thought of that. But that leaves us without the glue. I'll need to give it some thought, but it has potential."

"What about using demonic magic," Bathos asked.

We all turned to him, our expressions filled with distrust. "We're not opening a portal to the demon realm," I reminded him.

He held out his hands. "I'm not suggesting that. I have warden magic. I run a magical prison. Perhaps my magic might strengthen this bubble the witches are going to create."

I looked at Mavis. She was staring at the demon, a speculative gleam in her eye. "The process to extract your magic would be painful."

Bathos didn't hesitate. "I'm not afraid of pain, witch." He appeared insulted by Mavis's warning.

After a moment, Mavis nodded. "That might work. Are you willing to let me draw some magic from you and test it with our witch magic. If it's incompatible, the idea's a non-starter."

Bathos inclined his head in agreement.

"Good," Mavis said. "We'll do that before we leave then."

"So..." I said. "How do we get the monsters into this inter...." I frowned.

"Inter-planar space," Mavis said. "Think of it as a bubble of existence that isn't part of any known plane," she clarified. "There is an unknown multitude of these spaces, like little islands that float between the planes. We've been trying to create a spell to capture one of the islands and lock it down. The how of capturing the monsters is fairly simple. Once we have the bubble locked into place, we simply tag anything we want to go into it. The tag locks onto our bubble and yanks them inside."

"How would you get the tag on them?" Gren asked.

She shrugged. "We can hex a dart or an arrow and shoot it at them. Simple."

"Sounds simple," I said. "In theory. But how do we find the Trickster so we can tag him?"

"That's the second part of the issue. It's not going to be easy. We'll need the help of a good magical historian for that." Mavis grinned. "Know any?"

———

Ferral looked up from reading when we came into the house. He closed the well-worn paperback and placed his hand over the cover.

But not before I recognized it. "Are you reading a paranormal romance?"

Mavis snorted. "I've read that one," she admitted, pushing Ferral's big hand off the book and picking it up. "They're tiger shifters, aren't they?" She waggled her brows at the cranky advocate. "Are you thinking of going feline?"

I barked out a laugh at the "I just sucked a lemon" look on Ferral's face.

"Don't be ridiculous. It was sitting here, and I just picked it up because I was bored. I barely finished two sentences and was about to throw it into the trash."

I put hands on hips and gave him the "look." "First of all, don't you dare throw out any of my books. Those books don't belong to you. Secondly, the only way you saw the book and picked it up was if you went into the living room and perused the shelves. Thirdly..." I looked at Mavis. "Is that correct grammar?"

She shrugged. "Works for me."

"Thirdly," I repeated, "There's no way you only read two sentences and were offended enough to throw it away. Just admit you liked it."

He stood up. "The girl's in her room. She's an emotional wreck and probably needs your dubious talents as a faux parent."

"Nice try," said a sleepy voice from the door. We all turned to find Wanda shuffling in, yawning. "I'm fine. It was fun watching you guys beat the bat-snot out of those snakes."

I arched a brow at Ferral.

His usual glower deepened. "I hope you have something useful for getting rid of the Trickster. Your usual methods of flying by the seat of your pants aren't going to cut it with this particular nemesis. Your dominion is a mess."

Guilt took a bite out of my chest, as he'd no doubt hoped it would. I shoved it back to deal with later. "You're particularly spicy today, advocate. Are you feeling snake bit?"

"Har," he said. Turning to Gren, he arched a brow in silent question.

"We do have the beginnings of a plan," my angel said. "I'll let Mavis tell you all about it."

I joined Wanda at the refrigerator, putting an arm around her skinny shoulders. "Did you have a nap?"

She nodded. "I've been studying the books the crone gave me for hours. My eyes got tired."

I was thinking about asking the teen for help trapping the Trickster and almost missed her words. "You mean the empty journal?"

She pulled a can of root beer from the fridge and headed to the pantry. "No. The other books."

"When did the crone give you more books?"

"Yesterday." Wanda shuffled back out with a large basket. A red and white checkered cloth covered whatever delectable treats filled the basket—Tilly's signature presentation. "I thought you knew she was coming."

I had not. And, I didn't like it. Not one bit. The ancient witch was too powerful to allow to traipse into my house willy-nilly. "Was I home at the time?"

Wanda shrugged. "Anyway, the crone told me to search for ways to trap the Trickster. She said you would need the information soon. So, that's what I've been doing."

Mavis heard the last part as she joined us. She slid a wide-eyed look my way. "The crone was here?"

I nodded, biting my lip. "Apparently, she knew what we were going to need before we did."

"That's...disconcerting," Mavis said.

Wanda set the basket on the table and uncovered a pile of cookies. The sugar and butter scent rose out of the basket and permeated my sinuses. I nearly moaned from the delicious aroma. I grabbed a cookie and was happy to discover that it was still warm. The centers were just the right amount of gooey. "I'm going to ask Tilly to live with us," I told the teen. "She can have your room."

"Hey!" Wanda said, laughing. "No fair."

I shrugged, letting a smile fill my gaze. "She bakes me cookies and muffins. What have you done for me lately?"

Wanda dropped into a chair with her goodies. Ferral was sitting there staring at us with his perpetually cranky face. "The brownie spoils you too much."

It wasn't clear who he was scolding, but none of us thought being spoiled was a bad thing, so it didn't matter. "Just have a cookie. I promise, it'll change your life."

Gren reached past me and took one. "Coffee?" he asked us.

"Yes!" Mavis and I said in unison.

"Did I hear you say you're looking for a way to trap the Trickster?" Ferral asked Wanda.

She had a mouth full of cookie, so she nodded.

"You might want to change tactics and look for ways to *attract* him instead. We don't actually need to trap him. We just need to know where he is at any given time so the witches can engage their spell."

Wanda swallowed. "Okay. That makes sense. Maybe I'll have better luck finding that. I haven't had any luck finding something that would trap him."

Ferral eyed the cookies. "I'm not surprised. Tricksters are nearly impossible to trap and, since they're even harder to kill, no one's put a lot of effort into trying."

Something flashed past the kitchen window, catching my eye. "Did anybody else see that?"

Gren was fixing coffees, but he straightened, immediately coming to attention. "What did you see?" he asked, his gaze finding mine.

"I'm not sure, I..." Light flared behind the glass, a pinpoint of illumination in the growing darkness beyond the window. "There it was again." I started toward the mudroom door, but Gren stepped in front of me. "Let me check it out first." He spoke softly, glancing toward where Wanda and Mavis were still chatting.

Ferral's silver gaze lifted to us and he stood, nodding at Gren.

I watched as Ferral moved to stand between us and the door as Gren stepped outside.

There was a shrill scream a beat later, followed by Gren's voice, deep and quiet. I started toward the door, but Ferral stopped me with a look. "Wait," he said.

"What's going on?" Wanda asked, turning in her chair.

The door opened again, and Gren stuck his head in. "Aggy, can you come out here, please?"

I hurried past Ferral, who followed me outside. I scoured the area with a wary gaze but saw nothing. "What is it? Is somebody here?"

"She won't talk to anyone but you." My protector pointed to the top of the flower-covered archway. I saw nothing at first, then a small form rose off the structure, glowing with white light. The tiny figure was barely larger than a dragonfly and had a distinctly female shape. I stared at the tiny pixie for a beat before recognizing her. So much had happened since we'd come back from Fairy. Too many things had drawn my thoughts away. "Mari! Did Trish send you? Is she okay?"

The pixie rose into the night in a fall of white pixie dust, her wings fluttering so quickly she sounded like a hummingbird. She shot toward me, a cloud of glowing white dust leaving a trail on the air behind her. The dark-haired pixie wore a tense expression, her tiny hands weaving nervously together as she hovered in front of me. "Madam Lares, I bring you bad news. Trish is in danger, and all is not well in Fairy."

20

THE QUEEN, HER SUBJECTS' LIVES ABORT

Curse, curse, swear, swear!

"What can I do?" I asked Mari.

The pixie buzzed around me, clearly too upset to settle. Softly spoken words followed in her wake. The conversation was not addressed to me or, apparently, anyone else on the patio. The pixie was talking to herself. I listened carefully and still caught only about every third word.

Promise...idiotic...killed...move...

"Mari," I urged. "Talk to me."

The pixie jolted to a stop in front of me. "Trish says you shouldn't come. She says it's too dangerous. The guard has revolted against the queen, and Das has lost her mind. She's killing anyone who crosses her path." Tears glimmered on Mari's pale cheeks. "Everyone has gone into hiding, but that doesn't save us from her wrath. She's destroying Fairy."

My stomach twisted at the report, and a deep well of frustration overflowed as my mind tried to wrap around what Mari was telling me.

"Why did the guard revolt?" Ferral asked.

The pixie's pretty green gaze shot to him and narrowed. Then she turned back to me. "Das has taken a child from a soldier's family. She insists the child is hers, to be raised like a princeling and showered with gifts and affection. But the family worries for the child's safety. Das is not a nurturing person, Madam Lares."

If I hadn't been so mired in worry over the pixie's words, I might have laughed at her enormous understatement. "Whose child is it?"

The pixie seemed to fold into herself. "His name is Arvin. The queen killed his wife, the child's mother, in a fit of pique last year. Das took a shine to the child. Her fawning attention to the boy set the mother on edge, and Das accused her of being disloyal. Killed her on the spot. Arvin took his son and hid him, but the queen recently found him."

"Arvin is a member of the guard?"

Mari nodded. Her hand wringing sped, her wings whirring louder. Fairy dust sifted downward, creating tiny dots of illumination on the paving stones.

"Why is Trish in trouble?" I asked. I could guess at the reason but needed it confirmed.

"She is sensitive to Arvin's pain, of course. But

there is a larger issue. Das is devolving quickly. Much faster than we'd expected. It seems that sending a Trickster to Rome has unraveled her mind."

It isn't doing my mind much good either, I thought.

Gren and Ferral both glanced my way, and I realized I'd broadcasted that thought to everyone. *Sorry*.

"Trish has been forced into the role of leading the rebellion. No one else had the will to do it, and she's learned a lot from working with you and the witches. Das swears she'll string Trish up by her entrails for her disloyalty." Mari's small face folded into a mask of rage.

I grimaced at the visual her words created. "Tell me what I can do to help."

Mari looked miserable. But she reached into a pocket of her dress and brought out a paper packet, holding it out to me. "Take this. Keep it close. When the time is right, use it to enter Fairy."

I took it but shook my head. "I don't understand. How will I know when the time is right? What does Trish want me to do when I get there?"

Mari shot skyward, seemingly eager to be away. "Trish knew you would doubt yourself. She asked me to tell you that she trusts you to know what needs to be done when the time arrives." The pixie dropped to look into my eyes, her expression earnest. She leaned forward and touched my hand, her touch cool and gentle. "Trish has no doubt you will do what is right, Madam Lares. Fairy is counting on you to help. Please, don't let us down."

I stared at her for a moment and then nodded, holding up a finger. "Wait. Just one minute."

I hurried into the house, coming back out with a small bakery bag containing the chocolate muffin I'd promised to Trish. But, it was more than a muffin. It was a pledge. Handing it to Mari, I said, "This is for Trish. It represents my oath to her that I'll do whatever it takes to help Fairy when the time arrives."

The pixie gave me a little curtsy on the air and shot away into the night before I could form a single word to stop her.

I stared at the little packet in my hand, my stomach churning with new worry. The contents throbbed warmly through the fabric enclosing them. As if they were infused with electricity. Or magic.

The back door opened, and Mavis stuck her head out. "Aggy, you need to come inside. Wanda thinks she's found a way to attract the Trickster."

———

We'd moved into the sanctuary turned living room when Tilly arrived to start her cooking for the next day.

Wanda had spread her research materials over the couch cushions, and we were all sitting on the floor going over her findings.

I read a specific passage for the third time in the book Wanda had given me. Like many of the books in the crone's library, the tome was ancient, the leather cover cracked and worn. The language was flowery and hard to read, let alone understand. I pointed to a section in the middle. "This feels like pertinent information here." I read it out loud since reading it silently hadn't worked. "Whatever pow'r hath set the Jester's diabolical energies to plunder, hath supremacy o'er the beast. If called to account by its master, the Jester must needs respond."

I sagged in my chair. "Any way I read that, it comes down to the same thing. Das set him on us. She's the only one who can call him back."

Wanda shook her head. "Don't be so literal, Aggy. I'm not sure that's what it's saying at all."

"What else could it be?" Bev asked. My sister's delicate features bore witness to the fact that she'd gone too long without a solid night's rest. Her gray eyes were dull with weariness, and her hair was pulled back in a messy ponytail. She was wearing yoga pants and flip-flops, an ancient tee-shirt with the name of our old high school topping it all off.

I took a moment to hate her for still being able to fit into that tee-shirt at the age of forty-six. Then I forced my mind back to business.

"Fae magic," Wanda said. "The Trickster was engaged by the fae. He could be summoned by the fae."

I shook my head. "Das isn't just any fae. She's very powerful. I doubt anybody else in Fairy could engage a Trickster."

Wanda nodded in agreement. "Engage one, no. But summoning doesn't take nearly the same amount of power." When I continued to frown, she said. "Do you think Das communicates with this thing herself? Queens don't do anything themselves. She probably sends a guard to talk to it. Guards aren't the most powerful fae, right?"

No, they weren't. "Trish could probably do it," I muttered to myself.

"That may be, but Trish has chosen to stay in Fairy for now," Ferral said.

"My point was that I think Wanda's on to something. All we need is a magically-talented member of fairy. Who do we know who might have enough fae magic...?"

My words dropped away as singing drifted to us from the kitchen. It was a beautiful sound. A magical sound.

My gaze flew to Wanda's and slid to my mom and sister. "Tilly!"

Tilly had been cutting perfect shapes out of dough to top what looked like a peach pie when we all entered the kitchen. Looking up from her work, she raised a perfect red-gold brow in question, pushing bangs out of her eyes with the back of one slender hand. "Hello."

I carried the book over to her and set it on the counter next to the pie. "We have to ask you something."

The brownie shifted a look over the assembled group and nodded. "You'd like to request more fudge caramel brownies?"

Goddess yes! Wait. More? I glared at Wanda, and she grinned. "No," I said. Then reconsidered. "I mean, do you have time to bake them?"

"Aggy!" Wanda scolded. "Focus."

I gave her a tight smile as my stomach growled. "Sorry."

Mavis threw up her hands. "We forgot to eat dinner. I'll call for pizzas."

No wonder I was having trouble focusing. "Salads too, please!" I called after my mom.

Mavis threw a hand up to let me know she'd heard.

"That's a definite yes on the brownies," I whispered to Tilly. Behind me, Wanda gave a long-suffering sigh. I ignored her. "But I was actually asking for help from you on something else. Something important."

Tilly's face fell. "I'm so sorry. I know I promised to look into reversing the Trickster spell, but my bakery business has exploded since I moved it here. I've been swamped."

I shook my head. "Actually, I think we've found a better way for you to help."

Tilly leaned against the counter. "Tell me."

I quickly filled her in on our plan to trap the Trickster. She listened carefully, frowning when I got to the part where we thought we needed fae magic to summon him. "That's why we're here. I would have asked Trish, but she's stuck in Fairy and things are apparently going very badly there."

Tilly nodded. "Yes. I'm aware. Trish is needed there."

"That's what Mari said. But that means I'm missing my ancient fae warrior. Your power is prodigious, I said with complete sincerity. "Your food is pure magic. Do you think you can help us draw the Trickster here so we can send him into the trap we're going to lay?"

Tilly frowned at me, her amber gaze filled with doubt. She picked up a towel and wiped her flour-covered hands on it, bending over the book to read the passage we'd marked. A moment later, her frown turned thoughtful. "You'll need something he created to form the summoning spell."

The first fingers of excitement slipped up my spine. "That shouldn't be hard. He's made a mess of the entire town. There has to be something...."

Tilly shook her head. "It's not going to be as easy as you think," she warned me. "My magic is food-based. Whatever you bring me, I must be able to turn it into something edible. Once that has been done, its essence will draw him to wherever the food is."

My excitement withered and died. How did one turn upside-down trees and missing cemeteries into food?

The kitchen was silent for several moments while we all thought about the problem. I was staring down at my still-purple arms when it hit me. "Wizrooms."

Tilly's eyes went wide. "Excuse me?"

"Do you still have the baked goods he poisoned with the wizrooms? Those would count, right?"

Tilly shook her head. "They were poisoned with wizroom dust after they were created. He didn't create the baked goods." Her eyes went wide. "But he did create the wizrooms. If I'm remembering right, my great, great, great, great...." she shook her head. "Never mind. Suffice it to say, she was really great. My Grans had a recipe for wizroom soup. I remember eating it as a kid."

"Ew!" Wanda said.

"It was surprisingly good," Tilly argued. "But more importantly, they were no longer toxic once they were cooked in her special way. They would, however, serve our purposes here."

"Great!" I said, giving her a hug. "Then, you'll help?"

"Of course. If it wasn't for that monster, I

wouldn't have lost my shop. I'd be thrilled to get him out of our hair."

"It's settled then. We'll get you the wizrooms and set everything into motion."

"Not so fast, Aggy," Gren said. "We destroyed all the wizrooms in Rome, remember?"

Swear!!

21

A WORM A WORM A WORM FOR YOU

My nose itched really badly. I scratched unsatisfactorily at the unforgiving bubble over my head, getting no relief. "Can't we make these things more flexible?" I whined at Mavis.

She'd given up responding to my whining a half-hour earlier and simply acted like her own bubble was making her deaf. "I know you can hear me."

Mavis flipped her hand in my direction, her gaze locked on the ground in front of her.

In addition to the stupid protective bubbles we all wore like space helmets, we were also wearing spelled gloves and boots to keep any residual wizroom dust from finding a handy orifice to infect.

Since I was already purple, I'd begged to be excluded from that particular protection and was told I could still be infected. My memory of poor Becca stilled my complaints. Being purple was weird enough. Wearing polka dots over my entire body for a year was decidedly less than optimal.

"How did all this grass grow after the ground was salted," I asked my mom.

"Once the wizrooms were dead, we used a healing spell for the earth." Apparently, Mavis's deafness had fled. Very selective thing, her deafness. "What if there were still wizroom spores in the ground?"

Mavis cast a narrowed gaze on me. "That's what we're hoping for, right?"

I opened my mouth to argue with her but decided against it. She was cranky. I was cranky. Everybody was cranky. We'd had a tough week, and we were all tired.

Unfortunately, the Trickster's tricks hadn't stopped long enough for us to focus on engaging our plan. Very inconsiderate of him. Luke, Niele, and Bev had gone to get rid of the fast-moving river currently replacing Rome's Main Street. Not only was the water rushing through town at an intimidating pace, but it had come complete with some type of water monster that had nearly eaten a family of four who'd been rushing along the sidewalk trying to get safely home. Luckily, Niele had been nearby, and he'd gotten the family to safety. But the river and its nasty inhabitant had to go.

Catching myself trying to be logical, I forced my thoughts back to the problem at hand. Mavis, Gren,

Wanda, and I had covered several acres of park land and hadn't found a single wizroom for our efforts.

"Figured we'd do too good a job extinguishing something when we need it," I grumbled.

Mavis grunted in agreement.

"Oh!" Wanda exclaimed, drawing all of our attention to her. She bent toward the ground as if she'd found something.

"Is it a wizroom?" Mavis called out.

The teen straightened back up, her face the picture of disappointment. "No. It was just a regular mushroom." She threw the unwanted fungus back to the ground and kept moving.

I took a step, and the ground beneath me seemed to roll away from my foot. I stumbled forward, nearly falling on my face.

Mavis moved closer. "You okay, honey?"

I fought dizziness and lifted a hand. "I'm fine. I think I'm just tired." Subsisting on two-hour naps was starting to catch up with me. I spotted a large, flat rock ahead. "I'm just going to sit for a minute."

Mavis nodded. "Let me know if it doesn't pass."

I licked my dry lips and wished I could drink some water. Unfortunately, the head bubbles wouldn't allow drinking any more than they allowed nose scratching.

I sighed.

Are you well, beautiful Aggy? Gren's voice in my

head was deep and warm, intimate in a way nobody else's voice ever was.

I smiled at the sound. I'm *fine. Just resting for a minute.* I waved at him in the distance, and he returned the wave. Then he went back to work.

The rock under my backside shifted just a tiny bit. My hands lifted out to the sides in an instinctual balancing movement. I waited. Nothing happened.

Sighing, I closed my eyes and let the last rays of the sun soothe me. My nose itched again. I stabbed the bubble with my finger trying to scratch it. "Curse, swear," I mumbled.

The ground rolled violently beneath me. I gave a little yelp as I was thrown backward off my rock, slamming into the grassy ground behind me.

I started to push to a sitting position just as the earth exploded upward, sending me shooting into the air. I gave a little scream as it rose up like a wave on a surfer's beach, followed by a heartfelt shriek as it suddenly disappeared, leaving me hanging in mid-air.

I plunged downward, trying to land on my feet, but another rolling wave caught me before I landed. I slammed into the dirt hard enough to knock all the air from my lungs. Assuming the fetal position, I wheezed and screeched, trying to pull air into my chest.

A distant scream forced me to my knees, holding on as the ground shook and rolled and generally tried to expel me. I searched frantically for Wanda, finding her clinging to a stout branch of a nearby tree. The tree didn't seem to be affected by whatever was happening. It stood tall and motionless in the midst of the chaos.

Another scream drew my frantic gaze as the sound of wings thrumming against the sky told me Gren was on his way. I spotted Mavis, arms high and flailing, just before the earth rolled over her, covering her up to her wrists.

The magic bubble over my head popped away. Mavis's spell had failed. There were very limited reasons for that to happen. None of them good. My stomach twisted in horror. "Mavis!" I screamed, trying to scramble to my feet. But, the rolling waves of dirt wouldn't let me up.

"Aggy!" Gren's voice was filled with fear.

I looked up and shook my head. "Help Mavis. Hurry!" He hesitated for a beat.

"I'm okay," I assured him. "But she's in trouble." The words hadn't even left my mouth before Mavis flew upward on a choking scream, the soil flinging her high enough that her landing would be deadly. "Gren!" I screamed.

He shot in her direction as I tried again to get to my feet. The earth stilled beneath me for a beat, and I managed to stand. Glancing toward the tree, I yelled at Wanda. "Stay there!"

She nodded, though she was deathly pale and

her worried gaze kept skimming over the roiling terrain.

I started working my way toward Mavis, no easy task since the ground hadn't flattened back out. Like a field filled with enormous cow bumps, it jutted upward in sharp peaks, with deep, uneven craters in the spaces between. I jumped from one peak to the next, occasionally having to jump down into a crater and climb back up. It was impossible and so slow I worried I wouldn't make it in time to help.

I watched the ground ahead of me, hoping for a glimpse of Gren or my mom. He hadn't flown past me with Mavis, making me wonder what was going on. "Gren?" I screamed. "What's happening?"

Nothing.

Then the ground around me exploded into action again.

A scream yanked my gaze toward Wanda. I frowned, not understanding what I was seeing at first.

Something thick and red and slimy rose out of the ground and wrapped itself around the teen. Wanda screamed again, struggling against what looked like a giant worm as it tightened around her in a grip that seemed to cut off her ability to breathe.

Beyond disgusted, I threw out a bolt of magic energy that sheared the worm thing off at the ground. It writhed in silent agony, momentarily loosening its grip on Wanda. But, a beat later, it somehow healed its severed end and renewed its attack on the teen.

Another worm rose from the ground where the first one had been severed. It wrapped around Wanda's legs at her ankles. Her dark eyes were wide in her too-pale face, and she seemed unable to scream with the nasty creature wrapped around her chest.

I called for my staff and snatched it out of the air as it arrived. Above me, the thrum of oversized wings warned me of Gren's return. I looked up and, to my relief, saw a filthy but alive Mavis in his arms.

I turned back to Wanda and shot a bolt of magic into the second worm, watching it disintegrate into a hundred pieces and splat wetly against the ground. I couldn't blast the one wrapped tightly around her chest for fear of hurting her too.

Gren lowered Mavis gently to the ground next to me and shot back into the air.

"Gren!" I yelled as he flew off.

"I see it," he called back.

I wrapped my arms around my mom and squeezed. "You scared the beans out of me?"

She nodded, then bent over and spat dirt out of her mouth. "Where's the gnome when you need him?"

I shook my head, pulling her into another hug. She smelled like fresh dirt and broken grass. "You scared the ship out of me."

Mavis gently pushed me away. "I need to create a spell before these worms take over the park."

I frowned. "There are only two of them."

Mavis's fingers danced on the air, a shimmery pale green web forming beneath them. "Look again, honey."

I did and gasped. Everywhere a piece of the worm I'd exploded had landed, another giant worm was rising from the dirt. "But..."

Mavis gave me a look. "Haven't you ever heard that worms regenerate?"

"I knew they could do it if you cut them close to the head...but." Shaking my head, I felt panic blossoming in my chest. "This is too much."

"Magical worms regenerate magically," Mavis said matter-of-factly

Gren landed on the branch near Wanda, his wings snapping closed. He grabbed hold of the worm where it was twined around her chest, tugging it away from her body.

My pulse pounded, blood rushing loudly in my ears as I watched, praying Gren would be in time to save her.

Wanda's eyes were too wide...her skin too pale... and she was clearly struggling to breathe. "How are you going to get that one off Wanda without hurting her?" I asked Mavis, my heart racing.

"I'm not. Gren will have to pull it off her before I release the spell."

He was trying, but the thing wasn't budging. Wanda's mouth gaped open as she fought for air. She wasn't going to last much longer. "Wanda!" I leaped to the next peak in the earth, trying to get to her. "Gren, we're losing her."

One of his hands was suddenly holding a blade. He slashed at the worm, and it reacted violently.

Uncoiling from Wanda in a flash of movement, the worm bunched its muscular form and sailed toward Gren. It wrapped around his arms, pinning them to his chest before he could use the blade in his hand. I fought my way across the uneven ground, but I kept stumbling, barely staying on my feet. Wanda was clinging to the tree, her chest heaving.

"Don't come down," I warned her.

Already the worms on the ground were starting to move, and all of them were moving toward Gren. He was airborne, hovering about twenty feet above the ground, fighting to keep the worm from pinning his wings.

"Gren?"

He writhed violently, managing to gain a little room to maneuver. "Stay back, Aggy. There are too many of them." His unspoken message was that he didn't want me to divide them again and create more. "You need help!" I argued, still moving forward.

"Aggy, watch out!" his cry made me jerk to a stop. The worm hit my back hard, taking me down to the ground under its prodigious weight. The soil beneath us seemed to melt away, and I was suddenly underneath it, still being borne downward by the heavy monster on my back. Pressure around my legs told me the thing was twining around me. I panicked, unable to use my magic as fear of suffocating under the earth ripped coherent thought away. I coughed and choked and struggled to get free, all the while knowing I was moments from death.

Nobody would get to me in time.

I tried to scream but couldn't, my mouth filling with dirt. My heart slammed against my ribs, pounding so hard and so fast I thought it would explode in my chest. I clawed at the dirt, my fingers tearing on rocks and roots...

Roots.

Forcing my mind to calm, I reached out with my magic, searching for the nearest collection of healthy roots. The seconds ticked painfully by as I continued to sink, my chest screaming from lack of air. The world starting to gray around the edges, my mind shutting down from lack of oxygen. Finally, I found a collection of roots that would work. I sent my energy into them, using my thoughts to draw them closer, while forming an imperative with my mind.

Obey.

I pictured the roots piercing the worm,

entwining it in their resilient grip. I felt the soil sifting around me, the soft scratch of pliable roots moving through the soil. And then the worm twitching violently as the roots found their target.

My downward plunge into the earth stopped. A heartbeat later, the worm was lifted away under a powerful shift of dirt and roots. I turned my spinning thoughts toward escaping the soil. I dug and twisted, trying to move toward the surface. But I'd lost my sense of which way was up. I might as easily have been digging myself deeper as digging my way out.

My chest hurt from too little air. My thoughts were growing muzzy.

Something hit the earth above me, magic burrowing closer. And I feared another worm had come to help its friend. But a moment later, as the world turned charcoal inside my mind, a warm, desperate grip found my ankles and yanked me from my early grave.

I came to in a fog of smoke. There was no crackling fire sound to accompany it, but the smoke haze still clung to the air, covering everything in its path with an acrid stench. I sat bolt upright as my memory returned. "Wanda!"

"I'm okay, Aggy," the teen said. She appeared in my line of sight, crouching down next to me.

I grabbed her hand, squeezing it. "Thank the goddess." My eyes went wide. "Gren?"

"He's okay too. He's watching out for more worms as Niele works on flattening out the land."

I lay back with a relieved sigh. Then sat bolt upright again. "Mavis?"

Wanda hesitated just long enough to turn panic into terror. "She's sleeping. The spell took a lot out of her."

The spell. "Was she able to get rid of the worms?" I grimaced as I thought of the huge, slimy things.

"I did," said a raspy voice behind me. I turned to see Mavis sliding out of the back of the Range Rover. She grimaced, stopping to bend double and stretch out her back. "You need to put a mattress in the back of that car, honey."

"I would have if I'd known you were going to take a nap in there."

She grinned.

"The spell?" I asked.

"Fire. I burned those nasty suckers into ash."

"It was awesome," Wanda told me, giving Mavis a double thumbs up. "The flames didn't touch us or the trees, only the worms."

I nodded, depression sliding in to replace my

earlier panic. "If only it had all been worth it. We still don't have any wizrooms."

Mavis's phone rang. She looked at the ID. "It's Bev. Hey, honey. Wait until I tell you about the giant worms."

Mavis grinned as she got the expected reaction from her daughter. "Yep. I'm never going fishing again."

I chuckled.

"Oh? Really? That's great." Mavis's smile faded. "You're right. I'm sorry. But it is good news for us." Her shoulders sagged, and she rolled her eyes. "Okay. Okay. Okay! We'll stop by there on the way home."

She disconnected and shook her head. "Remind me to hex some of your sister's sanctimoniousness out of her. She's getting more like Ferral every day."

I fought a smile. "What's up?"

"Huh?" She looked thoughtful.

"Why did she call?"

"Oh." Mavis perked up, her gaze dancing with sudden light. "Good news! One of the women in town just called. She and her husband have stripes."

22

THE SEARCH ALAS HAS SPAWNED ANEW

"Where's Trish when we need her," I mumbled.

Mavis nodded.

The young couple glowering at us from across the lawn seemed to blame me for their newly striped state. The thin black stripes ran from their hairlines into the necklines of their clothing and covered their exposed arms and hands. The good news, if there was any, was that they weren't non-magical, so at least we didn't need to deal with that.

"Tell me again what happened," I said. "From the beginning."

The man, whose name was Kurt, narrowed an accusing gaze on me. "Aren't you supposed to have control over all this stuff? Isn't it your job to protect us?"

I ground my teeth together on the myriad excuses I wanted to make. The couple wasn't in a reasonable state at the moment. I couldn't blame them. "We're working on it, sir," I said. "Tricksters are...well...tricky."

Two pairs of eyes narrowed to slits.

I sighed. "Where did you get the wizrooms that made you...um...." I shifted from one foot to the other. "Look, I understand how you're feeling. You might have noticed that I'm purple. But you're going to have to trust me on this. We're doing everything we can to fix things. You can help us by telling us where you got the wizrooms."

"I found them in the park," the man finally said, skimming a look toward his wife, Suzy. "A couple of days ago."

"You should have warned us," Suzy growled. "If we'd known they were magical mushrooms, we wouldn't have touched them."

There was no point in trying to explain that a large portion of the town was non-magical, creating a much more complex problem.

"Where exactly did you find them?" Mavis asked.

When he described where he'd found the wizrooms, hope died. He'd found them in precisely the spot where we'd just battled the giant worms. It was another dead end. I nodded. "Okay. Thanks for the information. We'll try to find someone who can do a glamour for you." I turned to go, feeling more depressed than I had in days. I was starting to feel like we were never going to make any progress.

"Wait," Kurt said. "Don't you want the evidence?"

I spun around, hope flickering in my chest. "Evidence?"

"Yeah," Suzy snarled. She held out an angry fist, turning her hand over and opening it to show us a mashed and mangled collection of...wizrooms!

I paced my yard like a caged animal, my stomach twisting with worry and fear. Behind me, Wanda and Niele stood quietly, seeming to have designated me the team worry mascot. The entire Rome coven, minus Trish, sat in a large circle, a fat, white candle on the grass in front of them. Above me, Bathilda fluttered to and fro, snapping at bugs and softly chirping as if there weren't an alternate realm being created mere yards from her small black form. Only the bat's glowing yellow gaze, which regularly skimmed in my direction, told me the magical creature was paying attention.

Before night had fallen, I'd heard the call of a raven from high in the trees, and had wondered if it was Ray. I hadn't clapped eyes on my friend since the Trickster showed up, impersonating him. That led me to another thought. Please goddess the Trickster wasn't in the trees watching us create our trap.

The coven chanted softly as they went around the circle, each witch taking a turn crafting a spell upon the air. The candle flames flared higher with every freshly woven spell.

A mass had begun to form at the center, its surface glossy black and roiling with power. As the witches chanted and wove their spells, the mass steadily grew until it fit the area they'd created on the grass. I wondered what they'd do as the mass continued to grow. Would they move back, widening the circle?

But the mass didn't grow past their boundary. Instead, the night above began to spin. It spun faster and faster in a space about the size of a dinner plate. I watched in fascination as the mass the witches created began to spin in the opposite direction, shrinking inward the more quickly it spun.

Then I realized that the mass wasn't just shrinking. It was being pulled into the tiny vortex spinning above it, like a balloon being pulled slowly inside out as it was sucked into a bottle.

By the time the last of the mass had been pulled through the vortex, the night seemed heavier than it was before. The witches' chanting grew louder, the candle flames rising six inches above the candle tops, and the night slowly smoothed out, the heaviness steadily dispersing.

Bev was the last witch in the circle to cast her spell into the wind. She sent it free with a final, firmly spoken word of power. "*Vigeo!*"

Thrive.

My sister turned to me, dark circles staining the skin under her eyes, and inclined her head.

It was done. The inter-planar space had been created. All that was left to do was get the monsters inserted into it, summon the Trickster to us, trick him into entering, and then lock him down.

Piece of cake.

One by one, the witches stood, gathered their candles, and trudged wearily in my direction.

The Rome coven was smaller than we'd like it to be, currently including only four witches and Trish, whose earth-based magic was similar enough to the witches' for them to work together. Since Trish was missing, we really only had four witches. Four powerful witches. That aside, creating something as big as an inter-planar space had taken them four hours, and every last one of them looked as if she was going to fall over from weariness.

"Coffee and cookies in the kitchen, ladies," I told them. "Care of Tilly." Who was currently concocting her wizroom soup in her old kitchen, so the fumes and dust of the magical fungus wouldn't poison the rest of us.

"I'll stay out here and watch for the others,"

Niele said, blushing when he looked upon the coven. Particularly two of them.

I patted his arm. "Do you want me to bring you anything out?"

"No. I'm good. But thanks, Just Aggy."

I punched the arm I'd patted. It was a running joke with us. He insisted on calling me Madam Lares and I kept telling him to just call me Aggy. So, when he was feeling mischievous, he'd call me "Just Aggy."

Wilhelmina Marks or Willy, as she preferred to be called, threw an arm around Mavis and kissed her cheek. "You da boss." A curvy woman with flames of fiery red curls springing from her head and piercing green eyes, Willy's pale skin was a solar system of freckles. She and Pietra, the last of the four witches present, were both in their early forties and took even the most difficult tasks in stride.

I gave her a grateful smile as Mavis laughed. My mom had never said anything about it, but I suspected she had moments when she felt the extra years between her and the rest of the coven and had moments of self-doubt because of it.

"We're all da bomb," Pietra—pronounced pie-tra—said. She dropped an arm around Bev's shoulders and gave her a squeeze. "That was the most fun I've had in years," she said, her brown eyes flashing. Pretty, with smooth brown skin and hair she liked to wear in an enormous fro, Pietra had a husky laugh that shook her entire body. The witch was only around five feet tall, but she seemed larger than life despite her diminutive size. Her lush form only added to that impression.

"If you think that was fun, you're going to love stuffing your creation with monsters," I said, laughing at the two women as they did a little dance. I didn't know how they could possibly have so much energy after the last few days. I reached out and hugged Pietra. "Thank you for all the help you've given me with this Trickster mess." I hugged Willy too. "You guys are the best."

"We're happy to help," Willy said. "The boys have been helping too," she added proudly.

Willa's twin boys were reluctant witches who hadn't spent much time practicing their craft. I'd figured since they were headed to college in the fall, that wouldn't change anytime soon. "That's great," I told her. "You've got them in training?"

"Does a frog give warts?"

"No," Pietra said, rolling her pretty brown eyes. "A frog doesn't give warts. That's an old wives tale."

"Really?" Willy asked, looking appalled. "Are you sure?"

"Yep."

"Dang! So, what about bears pooping in the woods? Is that a thing?"

Pietra threw back her head and laughed.

I pulled the back door open and they filed past me, arguing about warts and pooping bears and whether the pope is really Catholic.

"Ladies," Mavis said, handing them each a steaming mug of coffee. "We need to talk about getting those monsters into our new realm."

Willy dropped into a chair at the table. "Do we have them identified?"

I nodded. "Gren and Ferral have been working with Bathos to hunt them down for the last several hours. They have most of them tagged. The last one is still out there."

I thought of the fear-eater and shuddered. According to Bathos, it would stay close to the spot where it left the prison. Fear-eaters apparently tended to stick to ground they knew, which meant it wouldn't go far from Bathos' house or grounds.

"They're stalking it now," I finished.

Willy nodded.

"When they get here, we'll use the tags the guys have been marking them with to send them into the inter-planar space we created. Once they're inside, they can't come out until we call them back." Pietra took a huge bite of a chocolate-chip cookie and moaned. "I'm so jealous you have Tilly living with you now," she said. Crumbs spewed from her mouth, and she threw a hand over it. "Thorry."

"How do the tags work exactly?" I asked the witches.

Mavis sipped her coffee, sighing with pleasure. "Think of the tags as magical laser beams," she explained. "The beam is tied to the inter-planar space."

"It just kind of reels them in," Pietra added. She licked crumbs from her fingers and eyed the basket of cookies, reaching for another one. "I'm going to need my strength to get me through the rest of this," she said, winking at me.

The floorboards in the hallway creaked. I looked up to find Wanda shuffling in with her note-book in her hands. "I know you've been busy," she told me. "But I think we need to talk about this now."

I nodded. "Have a cookie."

I was a terrible mother figure, pushing sweets on my ward. But she was too skinny and we were always trying to fatten her up.

"You want a glass of milk, honey?" Mavis asked.

"Thanks," Wanda told her and smiled. "Have you guys tried the caramel fudge brownies yet?"

"No," we all said.

"We'd love to, but there don't appear to be any left in the basket," I told her, raising my brows. "Just crumbs."

"Again," Bev said.

Wanda giggled. "I'm a growing girl."

"You're growing on my nerves," my sister said, her lips twitching.

"Tilly will make more tomorrow," Wanda said, pulling a peanut butter cookie from the basket.

"Tell me about the notebook," I said.

Wanda opened the book, and we all looked at the blank pages. "I have a spell to help get the Trickster into the planar thingy."

We all looked at the empty pages, frowning.

Wanda blinked. "Oh. Sorry." She picked up a pencil and started writing on the first line. I watched her write, "Force a Trickster into something."

The teen lifted the pencil, and we waited as the words she'd written shimmered on the page and began to melt into the paper.

"Um," Pietra said.

"Just watch," Wanda said.

A moment later, words started appearing on the lines beneath where Wanda had written her question. They were in longhand, tidily written in letters, symbols, and numbers that flowed across the lines as if someone was actually writing them.

"Is that a spell?" Willy asked.

Wanda nodded. "That's the spell for trapping the Trickster into a prison of some kind." She pulled out her cell phone and snapped several pictures of the spell. Then looked at me. "It disappears again after fifteen minutes or so."

I nodded and opened my mouth to respond.

I never got the chance.

A roar sounded from the backyard. Followed by

a feral screech. The window over the sink rattled under the concussive force of footsteps from something really big.

We all jumped to our feet and ran outside, jolting to a stop at the sight in front of us.

23

COME FANG, COME CLAW, AND
DEADLY BEAK

"This is like Jurassic Park for monsters," Wanda breathed. "So cool."

I wasn't sure how cool it was. My torn grass and broken trees certainly weren't cool.

I eyed the enormous pterodactyl bird and the massive snakes moving inexorably toward the spot where the witches had created their new realm and then looked at the spinning, dinner-plate-sized hole in the air. "Are you sure they're going to fit?"

"They'll fit," Mavis said with confidence.

Another roar filled the night as a massive bear with fangs that curved down to its chin and glowing red eyes that told me it hadn't come from the human realm leaped off the ground and was grabbed by the magic of the inter-planar bubble. His massive paws flailed against the power, five-inch-long claws raking the air as it spun him like a corkscrew and tugged him through the too-small opening.

"Awesome!" Wanda said, her face alight with wonder.

The pterodactyl thing was next. It screeched mightily as it too was wrenched, spinning like a top, into the opening to the witch-made realm.

The snakes almost defied the magic. At the last minute, the first one wrapped its thick, muscular body around a nearby tree and held on, seemingly willing to be wrenched in half rather than being pulled into its new prison. The tree bent and creaked, its twelve-inch-diameter trunk finally cracking under the pressure and giving way. A beat later, both the tree and the snake were inside the realm. The second snake didn't even have time to anchor itself before it was yanked into the bubble with its friend.

Several more monsters I hadn't seen before followed in quick succession until, finally, Gren, Ferral, and Bathos were all that was left walking toward us across the yard.

"The fear-eater?" I asked them as they approached.

Bathos shook his head. "We set a trap for it in my closet. Hopefully, it will show up soon."

"Good." I hid a yawn behind my hand, but Gren noticed. "Have you gotten any sleep recently?"

"I had a couple of hours."

He narrowed his gaze on me. "When?"

"I think it was today." My mind blanked out on me. I was so tired I could barely hold a thought. "Maybe yesterday." He grabbed my hand. "Come on. You shouldn't try to trap the Trickster when you're this tired. It's not safe."

"I'll be fine," I argued. But I didn't put much behind it. I knew he was right. "I'll just drink more coffee."

Bathilda chittered at me from overhead, adding her scolding to Gren's. "Zip it, bat," I told her. "You don't get a vote on my naps since you won't even talk to me." Batty had said a few things in my mind when I hadn't been expecting it—real words. But she'd refused to talk when I wanted her to.

Behind me, I heard Bathos say, "Is she talking to that bat? The pressure's finally getting to her, isn't it?"

"You zip it too, demon!" I shouted into the darkness as Gren gently pushed me through the door.

"Maybe you shouldn't antagonize Hades' favorite lawyer," Gren suggested dryly.

I started to laugh. And kept laughing until I could barely breathe. Wiping tears from my eyes, I gasped in a few breaths, fighting more laughter. Gren walked me to my room, his touch gentle but firm.

I didn't fight him. I was officially slap-happy. It was time for a nap.

He stopped at my door and I turned around, leaning against the frame to stare hungrily into his eyes. He lifted a finger to skim gently along my jaw, his melted chocolate gaze settling on my face. The angel's hungry regard sent ribbons of pure need ambling through my body. "You are one of the strongest people I know," he said in a quiet voice. "I know you doubt yourself. You believe you aren't capable of serving as guardian to the people of Rome. You think you are untrained, inept, and not enough. In all of those things, you are simply wrong."

My heart did the rhumba against my ribs. I reached out and placed my hand against the tightly covered geography of his chest. "I'm wrong?"

"You are." His luscious lips curved upward in the corners, and I found myself joining him in the smile.

He leaned in so close his heat bathed me from my head to my tightly-curled toes. "I will always tell you when you are wrong, lovely Aggy. I will also tell you when you are right. What I won't do, is tell you a lie. So listen well and never doubt my sincerity in this. You are powerful and kind, dangerous and gentle. You are everything a woman should be, and more than one person has a right to expect. It is my endless pleasure to have known you at all." His lips touched mine, infusing me with heat even as they eased the tension from my muscles. Gren broke the kiss a moment later, and it took me a beat to open my eyes. When I did, I couldn't miss the twinkle in his dark gaze. "I fully intend to get to know you *much* better in the days and months to come."

Leaving me with that deliciously intriguing message, Gren turned away and strode down the hallway toward the kitchen. Watching him, I clutched the door frame so tightly my knuckles were white. It was all I could do to keep from following the almost irresistible impulse to tug him back for more.

I woke at the sound of the front door closing and voices. Monty was beside me on the bed, his warm, soft body stretched along my hip. I rolled over and hugged him, kissing his little nose. "Thanks for picking me," I whispered to my little hero. Since Wanda had come to live with us, I'd nearly lost my tiny companion. He'd seemed more interested in spending time with her. It was like he understood on some level that she needed the comfort after learning her mother was dead, and her father was...well...himself. I'd missed my constant companion. I missed the days when it had just been him and me.

I blinked at the thought, realizing it was selfish. The teen needed him. *More than I did?* was the traitorous follow-up thought. The answer was yes. For the moment. But not forever.

Glancing at the clock, I rolled out of bed and headed for the bathroom. I'd take a quick shower and change into battle gear.

We had a Trickster to trick, and he wasn't going to come easily into our trap.

When I came out of the bathroom fifteen minutes later, Monty descended his doggy stairs and padded after me down the hall. Tilly was in the kitchen with the others, a soup tureen sitting on the table in front of her.

Wanda and the witches had their heads together over by the sink, discussing the spell Wanda had uncovered. There was no sign of Gren or the others.

Tilly looked up from where she'd been staring at her hands. "Madam Lares."

I opened my mouth to tell her...again...to call me Aggy, but decided not to fight that battle at the moment. "How are you, Tilly?" I touched her shoulder, noting the weary gaze and lines between her eyes.

"I'm good. I've brought the soup." She frowned when she looked at the tureen. "It was a difficult recipe."

I could only imagine. "Thank you for making it."

She nodded. "Anything I can do to help us get rid of this monster."

I couldn't agree more.

I headed across the room. My sister looked up as I joined them.

"You look better," she told me.

Mavis nodded. "Much. Did you get some sleep?"

"I did." I'd been surprised by how deeply I'd slept. Though it had only been two hours, I felt as if I'd slept three times that many. "Where's everyone else?"

"The fear-eater showed up," Pietra said. "They shooed us all inside because it was getting inside our heads."

Alarm spiked as I remembered just what that had felt like. "What about them? They're in danger too." I started toward the door. Willy put a hand on my arm, stopping me. "Luke and Ferral are in their shifted forms. Their animals aren't susceptible. Gren is naturally immune to the creature's powers."

"And Niele?" I asked.

"He volunteered to keep an eye on things in town until we finish this," Mavis told me. "He'll be back before we do the spell to lure the Trickster."

I nodded. "Okay. Are we ready to perform the luring spell?"

"We're all set up outside," Bev said.

The fear-eater is in the pocket dimension, Gren said in my mind. *The witches can get started now.*

Bev and Mavis heard the communication. Their heads came up at the all-clear. "Showtime," Bev said, grinning at her coven. "Let's do this. For Trish."

"For Trish," they repeated as one voice.

I followed them out to the patio, where they'd pushed my little table and chairs back and made a large circle with salt.

They placed the soup tureen in the center of the circle and removed the lid.

I eyed the setup, frowning. "Shouldn't you be closer to the trap?" I asked.

Willy shook her head, bright curls dancing around her pale face. "If we're too close, we run the risk of the Trickster coming for us before we trap him. This way, he won't even see us. There will be nothing to distract him from entering that circle out there."

I squinted toward the dark backyard, seeing no tell-tale ring of salt in the grass.

"It's not salt," Pietra said as if reading my thoughts. "Salt was incompatible with the demon's warden magic. We cut the circle into the soil and filled it with elderberries."

"Elderberries?"

"Good for both summoning and banishing," Mavis clarified. "Bathos infused the berries with his magic to hold the Trickster once he steps inside. After we get him into the circle, we'll call on the berry's banishing properties to send him into the inter-planar trap."

"What about the tag?" I asked, frowning.

"We'll still tag him. The banishing magic will

only enhance the tag," Mavis clarified. "The Trickster is strong. We'll need all the help we can get to shove him inside."

I nodded.

The coven focused on preparing for the spell Wanda had given them. I always found their preparations and magic fascinating and tended to pester them with questions whenever I watched them work. "No candles?" I asked.

Bev shook her head. "Too visible. We don't want to draw the Trickster to us. We want him to step into the circle near the trap." She didn't bark it at me, though she certainly would have been within her rights. They had just told me they were trying to stay invisible.

"Got it."

I bit down on any further questions and watched as they instructed Tilly to sit in the center of the circle with the tureen.

Wanda, having not made a promise to herself about asking questions, asked one that was burning its way through my mind. "How will he smell the soup if it's way back here?"

"He won't," Bev said. "Not really. Its essence will pull him in because of Tilly's magic."

"It's not really a smell thing." Willy said. "Food is just the form Tilly's magic takes. It's the fae aspect of her magic combined with one of his own magical creations that will draw him to this spot."

"Will he be suspicious about the summons?" I asked. Okay, I broke the promise to myself not to ask any more questions. I could live with it.

"He shouldn't," Tilly said. "The magic won't feel like a summons. He'll think he's following his own impulse. In this case, to bedevil you." She gave me a smile.

"It's not like he hasn't done it before," Wanda mumbled.

"Okay, no more talk," my sister groused. "We're losing the night. We need to get started."

I made a zipping motion over my lips. Wanda and I stepped back, closer to the house. Behind us, Monty whined and scratched at the mudroom door, unhappy to be excluded from the fun. I ignored him, staring out into the darkness and wishing I could see Gren and the others out there. But the plan had called for them to hide in the trees and bushes, staying out of sight until the Trickster had been trapped and tagged.

The witches arrayed themselves around the circle and closed their eyes, their hands coming up to begin the spell. They chanted softly as their fingers danced on the air, forming iridescent webs comprised of numbers, symbols, and words written in Latin.

Each witch had her own style of crafting a spell. Each one's magic filled the air with the practitioner's unique magical scent.

The sweet scent of roses. The rich smell of fertile soil. The delicate essence of lavender petals. The spicy bite of cinnamon. The air was abundant with a chaos of aromas that fought against each other rather than merging into one. When Tilly's magic joined the other scents, a sweet and buttery aroma overrode them all, tumbling through the witches' magics in a spray of fine, glittering specks. Before I realized what was happening, the air around us took on a spicy, rich scent that made my mouth water.

"It smells like the soup," Wanda whispered, and I nodded.

We watched as the magics coalesced above the circle, twining together to become one thick strand of smoky magic that took a single turn around the circle and then rose into the sky and trailed across the yard toward the ring of elderberry magic. There, it spun several times before settling down into the grass in the center and, with a final spark of pale green light, fused with the edges of the circle and went dark.

"Now we wait," Mavis said, her tone weary.

And wait we did. An hour passed. Then two. Dawn was beginning to peek above the trees of the Mystical Wood, and I was starting to feel desperate. "He's not coming," I said, tears of frustration burning my eyes.

"He'll be here," Tilly said. She said it so matter-of-factly I had no choice but to believe her.

I glanced over at the brownie. She sat perfectly straight on the hard ground, unmoving and resolute in her certainty. The sight brought forth all those insecurities Gren told me I shouldn't have.

I fought them back. We would beat the Trickster. We would trap him and begin the healing my dominion needed after a long and ugly week.

I had just started to relax when the world exploded into chaos again.

The night congealed above Tilly, and an enormous raven dropped onto her head, screeching and clutching at her with enormous talons that drew easy blood from her soft flesh.

Shouts from the yard intermingled with the snarls of angry shifters as several more ravens joined the fray.

In the blink of an eye, Tilly was airborne, and she was being carried, screaming and flailing, away from us.

Willy shrieked and shot skyward next.

Pietra was in the middle of a spell when she was yanked off her feet.

Mavis threw a spell and barely missed being snagged. Before I could stop her, Wanda was running to help.

I threw out my hand and my staff smacked into it. Magic surged through the weapon and I let it go in a jagged stream that caught the massive raven carrying Pietra away, punching it in the beak. The bird dropped the witch with a husky caw, and I screamed, "Slow!" as I sent a dispersed wave of magic into the darkness. Pietra's body slowed in its plunge toward the ground.

"Aggy!"

I whipped around to see Wanda being yanked off her feet. "Bathilda!" I screamed. "To me!"

Wanda shrieked in terror, her skinny limbs flailing and punching in a failing attempt to get the oversized bird to release her. Its talons clutched the back of her hoodie, the fabric too strong to give out. I fought the need to blast the thing, knowing I was just as likely to hit my ward and hurt her as the bird.

"Ray!" I screamed, firing blindly into the night. I avoided the witches' more visible forms, but the ravens blended into the night, a nearly invisible thickening of the darkness that defied my attempts to see. Aiming above the witches' heads, I could only hope to hit the monstrous birds carrying them away.

Yellow eyes flared through the dark and I barely gave the bat a glance. "Get Wanda!" I screamed.

Bathilda shot away, much too fast for a real bat. But then a real bat wouldn't be the size of a flying dinosaur either.

Light, Aggy! Gren screamed into my mind. *We need light.*

Light. Yes. I could do that. I held my staff above my head, pointed it toward the sky, and yanked as much magic as I could grab from my core. "Illuminate!" I screamed. Throwing back my head, I released it all, feeling its power burn through my veins and flood into the staff. A beam of golden light as big around as my arm blasted from the orb at the end of the staff and pierced the darkness above.

And I gasped.

Like the worst kind of horror movie, the night sky was filled with the enormous ravens, their eyes catching the moonlight and giving back a bloody glow that made it hard for me to breathe.

They dove at my people, slashing and pecking with their enormous beaks. They aimed for their faces, trying to gouge out tender eyes and pierce vulnerable throats.

As I watched, Luke leaped off the ground and snagged a massive raven in his deadly jaws, dragging it to the ground. Another raven landed on his back, ripping at him as he twisted the head of the one beneath him and snapped its neck.

Gren was airborne, battling the flying killers with his two long blades and having mixed results.

Bathos stood near the entrance to the trap, his summoning magic pulling any ravens who came too close to him into the inter-planar space.

But there were so many of the things. They stained the lightening sky with evil, an unending force of death and destruction.

To my relief, Bathilda had Wanda in her grip.

The girl looked okay, but she clutched at the bat as if she was afraid Batty would drop her.

Another raven dove for them, beak wide and screeching. I opened my mouth to warn them just as the earth exploded upward, and Niele launched himself into the air, snagging the raven from the sky and wrenching its neck as it snapped at Batty's wings.

Batty settled Wanda to the ground near the patio and hovered nearby until the girl ran to me.

Flinging herself into my arms, Wanda sobbed out her fear. I hugged her close. "You're okay. It's okay. I've got you."

She shook her head. "No. It's not okay, Aggy. He's here."

Ice crawled over my skin at her words. "Who's here?"

She turned away and pointed into the yard. I sucked air in a gasp, shoving Wanda behind me. "Get into the house."

"No, I want to help."

I grabbed her face, staring into her tear-filled eyes. "You can help by going inside. Please, Wanda."

She finally nodded. "Be careful, Aggy."

I pulled her into a quick hug and then pushed her gently toward the door. "Go."

I spun to find Batty still hovering. "Where's Ray?" I strode past her, not expecting her to respond.

But words sifted across my mind. *He is out there, in the battle.*

I jolted to a stop, looking at the enormous bat. Then I shook my head. "Okay. Can you save the brownie?"

Yes.

I inclined my head. "Thank you."

The door slammed open behind me. "No, Monty!" Wanda screamed.

Barking and growling as he ran, my dog shot past me and headed into the fray, the fur along his back standing at attention.

"Curse, curse, swear!" Panic overwhelmed reason, and I started to run. "Monty, come!"

"Madam Lares," said a hated voice I unfortunately recognized.

I skidded to a stop, my gaze lifting away from my dog to the little man standing inside the circle the witches had made in the grass. He was small, probably only five feet tall, with tiny hands that were folded together in front of him and a small face with a long nose and dense red brows that slashed across eyes of a blue so bright they glowed in the low dawn light. He wore pinstriped slacks and a yellow sweater vest over a white shirt buttoned up to his skinny throat. The slash of a wide mouth was filled with gleaming, shark-like teeth. He wore a bowler-type hat on his head. Chin-length straight red hair flowed out from under it.

Monty hit the edge of the circle and lunged, smacking into an invisible barrier and falling to the ground on a yelp of pain.

Above the Trickster, a strident caw warned me Monty was in trouble. My gaze shot skyward. One of the enormous ravens was diving toward my dog, its bloody red eyes glowing with anticipation of the kill.

"No!" I screamed as I started to run.

But I would never get to him in time.

24

THE LARES' FUTURE MAY SEEM
BLEAK

nother smaller raven swooped down behind the first one, and blood roared in my ears. My vision hollowed out as panic made mincemeat of my reasoning processes.

Monty slammed his little body against the invisible barrier, determined to get to the Trickster. Inside his protective bubble, the Trickster gave me a manic grin, his inhuman teeth gleaming in the rising sun.

The enormous raven lifted its wings, talons bared for the attack.

With a monumental force of will, I made myself stop running and point my staff toward the attacking bird. Magic roared from me in a prodigious wave that would obliterate everything in its path. All the doubt, fear, and pain I'd endured over the last several days came together in my mind, and something snapped. My control obliterated, I fought the magic, knowing I wouldn't just hurt the attacking birds, but the force of it would create collateral damage that would affect my dog and maybe my council too.

The smaller raven gave off an angry caw and slammed into the larger one, and I yanked the staff upward at the last second, recognizing Ray as the smaller bird.

Magic roared from my staff, blasting into the sky in a wave of energy so potent it ripped holes in the overarching branches and annihilated the attacking ravens as far as the eye could see.

Too late, I realized there was still collateral damage. A large, winged form sailed backward toward the woods at the back of my property.

"Gren!" I screamed, my knees giving out under the horror of what I'd done.

"Nicely done, Madam Lares," the Trickster said, his tone smug. "Too bad about your angel, though. I'm certain you'll be able to get another one."

I settled my gaze on him and snarled. Rising to my feet, I strode toward the hated creature with murder filling my gaze. I didn't pull my magic forward, though. I didn't need to. "Niele!"

An arrow speared the protection of the circle and pierced the Trickster's flesh. It sliced into his neck, protruding from both sides like a bad Halloween novelty.

The Trickster jolted as the arrow slammed into him, his eyes going wide. He reached up and touched the arrow, and then he smiled. Without hesitation, he yanked the arrow free.

Blood poured from the wounds for a few seconds, then quickly slowed and stopped, the torn flesh healing before my eyes.

A moment of pure fear stopped my breath. Could he actually walk away from what we'd planned for him? Was he really untouchable?

"Woof!" Monty leaped into the circle and caught the Trickster's leg, digging in and tugging as he snarled and growled.

Out of the corner of my eye, I spotted a large form flying toward me, and the fear multiplied tenfold. The ravens were coming back.

The Trickster reached down and tried to grab Monty, but the little dog danced away before attacking again and again.

Ray dove at the Trickster and pierced his bowler hat with his beak, clawing at the little man's face with his smaller but still deadly talons.

The evil jokester back-handed Ray, sending him sailing toward a nearby tree.

With a growl, the Trickster bent down and scooped up my dog. Monty snarled and snapped, sinking his teeth into the Trickster's shoulder.

I took off running, painfully aware of the vortex spinning just beyond the evil prankster.

The Trickster gave me a cold smile and then threw Monty into the air. My little dog sailed away on a yelp of fear, high enough that the landing would be fatal.

"No!" I stumbled, horror turning my legs numb.

The winged creature above us caught my dog, and relief washed through me. Gren was okay. Monty was okay.

I settled a venom-filled gaze on the monstrosity before me. "You're going down, you evil pustule."

The Trickster started to laugh.

His body jerked violently.

The laughing stopped. His eyes went wide.

I strode closer, glaring down at him. "Enjoy the monsters you created."

He jerked again, "What's going on?"

It was my turn to smile. "Good job yanking out that arrow. That probably felt pretty good, didn't it? But you missed the summoning tag attached to the shaft."

His mouth fell open, and he started to claw at the spot where the arrow had gone in.

"Yeah, that's not gonna work," I said, feeling the weight of the last several days finally easing away.

The Trickster's body jolted and flew into the air. He started to spin. Bright red light burst from him and bathed the air around me, stinging my skin.

Gren landed beside me and handed me my dog. "Did you lose this?"

I laughed, hugging my small hero close. "I thought I'd lost you, buddy." Monty kissed my nose, his tail wagging. "Sorry about blasting you out of the sky," I told my angel sheepishly.

He shook his head, a glint of humor in his eyes.

Something smacked me in the back. Hard. "Umph!" Invisible fingers dug into my back, breaking the skin. My eyes went wide, but I couldn't scream. All the air had left my lungs. Fighting for breath, I wheezed and coughed.

"Aggy?" My protector's handsome face had gone pale.

An invisible band of magic wrapped around my waist, locking my arms to my sides. Caught inside the magic with me, Monty barked and started to struggle.

Gren moved closer. "Aggy, what's going on?"

I wheezed out a single word, "Tricked."

Before Gren could even move, Monty and I shot backward and started to spin.

I felt myself being pulled into the trap...into the small realm the witches had created. Into limited space filled with monsters and one very angry Trickster. I wanted to scream. I wanted to dig in and fight. But I couldn't do either.

All I could do was cling to my dog and pray something would stop us from being drawn inside. The vortex at the entrance to the realm yanked on whatever was binding me, and I knew it was too late to escape.

The world spun around me, colors swirled, the familiar scent of wizroom soup passed briefly by. Then the scent of flowers, rich earth, and cinnamon assailed me.

Just before I left my world behind, something grabbed my ankle, and then I was slamming into ground that felt much harder than it should have been.

A large body slammed into the ground next to me.

Gren groaned softly.

Monty whined, wriggling free of my grip, and kissed my angel on the face. The little dog's tail was wagging, and his eyes were bright. He was just happy to be on another adventure.

Sighing, I sat up and looked around, surprised to see an area that looked much like my backyard. Grass covered the mostly flat ground where we lay. In the near distance, a foreboding forest hulked, shadows lurking beneath its mature trees.

Several feet away, the broken tree the snake had carried inside lay abandoned. Deep tracks marred the perfection of the grass. Pawprints, talon marks, and flattened grass suggested the passage of a lot of things I never wanted to meet again.

"Are you hurt?" Gren asked as he stood and reached for my hand.

I realized I wasn't. "No. You?"

He rolled his shoulder. "I'm good."

He wasn't good. I'd seen the slight wince when he moved his shoulder.

"You hurt yourself grabbing onto me, didn't you?"

"Actually, I got hurt when my girlfriend blasted me into a tree."

I winced from the reminder but didn't miss the girlfriend thing. My entire body heated and flushed. "Am I?"

Gren gazed around, his expression tight. "Are you what?"

A distant roar came from the woods, and I tensed. It hadn't been nearly distant enough.

"We need to get moving," Gren said. "They'll be on us in minutes."

"Get moving where?" I asked, looking around. "There's nowhere to hide."

We fell silent as our predicament hit home. The Trickster had gotten the last laugh.

Monty was sniffing around the grass, particularly over the spots where the monsters had clearly passed through. His head came up a beat later and he started to bark, his tail whipping the air behind him.

I scooped him up before he could run off and confront the creatures who were hundreds of pounds heavier than he was—with much bigger teeth.

"We'll fly," Gren said. He flexed his shoulders and two massive wings snapped out, the charcoal gray feathers glistening in the early sunlight. He scooped me into his arms and said, "Hold on, this is going to be bumpy."

His wings pounded the air, and we shot up from the ground. Whining and frantic, Monty wriggled against my grip. I knew I was holding him too tightly, but I had no choice. If he escaped, he'd fall to his death.

Below us, the disconcerting noise of approaching feet, claws, and coils finally made him still, his bright gaze filled with curiosity.

A moment later, the giant bear thing thundered from the woods. Two enormous snakes followed. A blood-curdling screech had my heart beginning to pound. "Gren!"

He glanced over his shoulder at the pterodactyl creature whose thirty-foot wingspan and lighter weight carried it across the sky much faster than we could go.

I looked down at the ground, then back at the flying monster.

We were well and truly trapped.

"Hold on," I told him, and sent a wave of magic behind us, counting on the wind magic I'd infused in it to at least slow if not stop the prehistoric bird.

Right on cue, the bird's wings shot up, and its head speared forward in an attempt to regain its balance in the air. But my magic was a force much stronger than the creature was used to. It tumbled to one side as another gust of magical wind hit it, then flailed its talons in an attempt to right itself.

With another bone-melting screech, it finally lost control and plunged downward, crashing to the ground right in front of the bear.

I grimaced as the bear monster fell on the bird, and the sound of crunching bones drifted up to us.

"There," Gren said. "We'll find shelter on that mountaintop and come up with a plan."

A slash of sleek metal shot up from below, sliding through Gren's wing like a hot knife through butter.

He jerked and grunted from the pain, fighting to stay in the air. But his wing gave out, and his gaze found mine, filled with sorrow and pain. "I'm sorry, Aggy." His lips found mine and seared me with a kiss that felt too much like goodbye. Then we were plunging toward the ground.

We headed for a line of mature trees. Ripping through the trees' upper branches, our flesh was slashed and torn by the broken ends. I fought to keep from being impaled on a broken limb, and didn't see the ground until it was way too close. With no time to yank magic forward, I simply threw out the same power word I'd used before. Flinging my hand toward the ground, I yelled, "Slow!" We wrenched to a near stop ten feet from the ground and drifted downward from there.

Gren folded one wing away, but the other one wouldn't close. "We need to remove the arrow," he ground out, his face contorted with pain.

"We do," I told him, examining the spot where the arrow jutted. "But we have to keep moving too."

The dulcet tones of bells chiming brought my head up. I looked around, seeing nothing but trees and dirt interwoven with roots that bulged from the ground.

I grabbed Gren under the arm and pulled him to his feet. We tried to run, but his extended wing kept getting caught in the trees, the pain bringing him to his knees.

He tried to push to his feet again, but I stopped him with a hand on his shoulder. "I have to pull it out."

He shook his head. "I can keep going."

"No." I touched his cheek. "It's going to have to be fast, though. I'm sorry."

He glanced toward the trees, where hissing sounds told us the giant snakes were nearby. "Just rip it out," he said, his jaw tight.

I gripped it right behind the arrowhead, figuring the feathered end would pass more easily and cleanly than the tip through the tough membranes of his wing. I gritted my teeth.

A drawn-out, sibilant "hissssss" came to us on the breeze.

"Hurry, Aggy."

I took a deep breath and yanked.

Gren screamed, his muscular throat taut around the sound.

But the arrow had barely moved. "I'm going to have to put some power behind it."

"Just do it!" he ground out.

I sent magic into my grip and yanked, easily pulling it free.

Gren growled in pain but didn't scream again. He was no doubt worried about drawing the serpentine hunters our way.

The chimes sounded again. "Did you hear that?" I asked him.

Monty started to bark, a soft growl rumbling in his throat.

"No," Gren said as I helped him back to his feet. "Let's go."

"Well, well, well," said a hated voice from behind us.

I whipped around to find the Trickster, his bowler hat dented and aerated with a large, beak-sized hole thanks to Ray. To either side of him was a giant white snake, their arrow-shaped heads drifting eerily from side to side as he spoke.

I watched in hypnotized fascination as their tongues slipped out to taste the air and then retreated, their oversized fangs visible when they opened their blunt snouts.

"It's good that you've come along for the fun," the Trickster said, patting the top of each reptilian head. "My friends are hungry."

So much for our plan to feed him to his own monsters.

Chimes tickled my awareness. I glanced around. Nobody seemed to hear them but me. Warmth slipped over my hip and down my right thigh. I twitched in surprise, my eyes widening.

Then it came to me. What the chimes meant. I plunged my hand into my pocket and felt the parcel from Trish that Mari had given me. I'd forgotten it was there.

Gren moved in front of Monty and me. "You don't want to pick this fight, Trickster," he growled. It was a good bluff. But everyone knew that was exactly what it was. Injured and outnumbered, Gren and I didn't have a chance against the Trickster and his friends. "Tell us what you want."

I called my staff and yanked magic forward, but didn't do anything with it. My mind was spinning with questions. *What does the packet do? What does it mean that it's warming? What's with the chimes? How do I find and help Trish? How in the goddess's gilded garters do we get out of this realm?*

The Trickster laughed. "Isn't that obvious,

Angel?" The prankster lifted his chin. "I want out of this trap you've set for me. I want to be freed."

"That's not possible," Gren told him. "Maybe you could get the one who sent you to torture us to set you free."

"Maybe I can," the obnoxious little man said. He lifted his arm and snapped his fingers. "Good luck with my friends," he told us, a smug smile on his ugly little face. "I have an endless supply of them."

As if to prove his point, a strident cry sounded high above us. We looked up to find a sky filled with giant hawks.

Curse, swear, curse! We hadn't put any of those into the realm. He was making his own monsters again.

"Hssssss!"

Monty started barking as the snakes began to move. A distant roar brought the small hairs up along my arms and robbed me of breath. The packet in my hand heated to the point of nearly burning my skin. I forced myself to hold onto it. The chimes rang again, and I felt their pull.

The snakes slithered closer, covering the space of ten feet in a mere second.

"Run!" I yelled and took off. Fangs snapped at my leg, scoring a painful slice along my calf, but I didn't slow. Adrenaline had me tightly in its grip and I barely noticed the pain.

Chime. The sound yanked me to the right, and I

didn't hesitate.

The scream of a hawk sounded above our heads. Close. So close.

I stabbed my staff skyward and sent magic in a wave that caught several of the unnaturally large predators and sent them plummeting to the ground. I barely noticed the meaty sound of large bodies smacking down around us as the chimes rang again.

I adjusted my direction slightly, dodging around a large tree.

Fangs found my calf again, catching it in a piercing grip. My leg jerked to a stop and I fell, releasing Monty as I dropped so I wouldn't crush him.

Agony burned along my leg, sizzling pain that left behind an icy numbness. The snake's maw opened wider, enclosing my benumbed foot. The flesh surrounding my leg contracted painfully, pulling me into the creature's overextended jaws.

Gren grunted as the second snake hit him in the back, dropping him to the ground. His hands were already moving, slashing at the nasty creature with his two long knives.

Another hawk descended on us, tearing at the snake on top of Gren in a rabid effort to get to him.

Half of my leg was buried in the snake's body. The numbing poison had traveled past my knee.

A flash of black and tan flew past me and landed on the snake. Snarling and snapping, Monty bit into the massive reptile's body just behind its jaws. Growling and whipping his head from side to side, Monty tore off pieces of the snake as I tried desperately to pull my leg free.

The second snake reared up and snagged the hawk from the air, swallowing it whole. Gren didn't waste the opportunity to slash one of his blades across the snake's meaty throat, nearly severing its head with the strike.

The enormous reptile slammed to the ground, motionless.

The snake holding my leg suddenly released it, rearing straight into the air with Monty clinging to its neck. My little dog gave the thing one, last yank and a big piece of it tore free. He hit the ground with his prize, and the snake turned on him.

I sent a wave of adrenaline-fueled magic into the creature, exploding it into a thousand pieces. Gren helped me stand as hunks of snake rained down on us. "You might have overdone that last strike a bit," he told me, his lips twitching.

I shrugged, panting. "Maybe just a little.

"Let's go," I told him. "Monty, come!"

The little dog trotted after us with his nasty prize still in his mouth. I leaned heavily on Gren as we tried to shuffle faster. I could only hope we were close to safety. With my bum leg and his torn wing, we weren't going to win any three-legged races.

Another roar exploded behind us. It sounded

much closer than the last roar I'd heard. Something heavy crashed through the underbrush, its footfalls making the leaves in the trees shimmy from the concussive force.

Chime.

I jerked to the left. "This way," I told Gren.

"Where are you taking us?" he asked.

If he'd asked me that question a moment earlier, I wouldn't have known. But I had a moment of sudden clarity. "To Fairy."

We circled around a massive tree, and I finally saw it. A shimmering rectangle hung before us, seemingly not attached to anything.

Roaring angrily, an enormous shape slashed through the underbrush and spotted us, skidding to a stop as it took us in.

I lost the ability to breathe as I looked at it. My legs forgot to move.

Monty dropped his hunk of snake and his bright gaze flattened. Tail drooping, he whined softly and moved closer to me.

Gren swallowed loud enough for me to hear.

"The fear-eater." I choked out.

My angel didn't respond. I finally risked a glance his way and found him taut with pure, unadulterated terror.

He gave a short jerk of his head.

I risked moving to touch his arm. "Gren?" He gave me a look that was so haunted it sent shivers down my spine. I lowered my voice. "I thought you were immune?"

He gave a violent shudder. "It's this realm, I think. The rules of magic are different here."

Monty whined pitiably and sank down into a puddle between my feet, quivering from head to tail.

I stared into the creature's fathomless dark eyes and remembered its cold, burning touch. I recalled all too clearly falling helplessly toward a fiery pit far below. I remembered its hissing words, *Feel your death.* Fear turned my mind to mush and my muscles to rock. I was locked into immobility, unable to escape the icy threat of the creature whose very essence was an assault.

Somewhere in the distance, a soft chime sounded again. The seemingly innocuous tones inserted themselves into my terror-filled brain with more impetus than seemed reasonable. I tried to focus on the sound, knowing it was somehow important, even while my mind got lost beneath the paralyzing veil of fear.

Gren twitched beside me, his big body locked into a nightmare of his own. Something tickled over my shoulders, touching my cheek in a gentle warning.

The flesh of my palm burned, the heat growing with every second that I stood immobile.

Chime!

I blinked. The melodic summons was suddenly

louder, more insistent. It was enough to break through the haze of fear. I tore my gaze from the silver glow of the fear-eater's eyes. Something gripped my waist. I looked down to find Gren's wing wrapped around me. That had been the touch I'd felt.

Aggy...

His voice in my head was strained. His form was rigid with emotion. It became immediately clear that I would somehow need to break the monster's hold on his mind. I considered several things, discarding each one. Slapping him seemed wrong. Kissing him too cliched. Plus, if he sloughed off my kiss, I was gonna take that very personally.

Chime!

I had to do something. I bent down and scooped up Monty and did the simplest thing I could think of to do. I yanked my magic forward and threw everything I had at the fear-eater. It jerked off the ground and hung there for a moment, surprise lighting its shadowy, terrifying face, and then flew backward, slamming into the massive tree we'd passed.

Almost immediately, the fear-eater's shadow slipped into the tree and down to the ground. The earth began to bubble and crack, spreading apart to expose a river of molten rock. Flames danced along the boiling surface, flowing along the burgeoning crevice on an inexorable path to our feet.

I didn't know if it was real. But its effects

certainly would be. If we didn't move, we would die.

I grabbed Gren's arm and screamed into his ear. "Run!"

We ran.

The fear-eater's whispering promises of death and loss hissed in my ears as we stumbled toward the sound of those chimes.

A cold, burning touch slashed across my back, conveying promises of pain and death with the agony of its touch. I arched away from it and cried out, feeling Gren tense against a similar attack.

I couldn't shake the monster's hissing promises or outrun its searing touch. So I kept my gaze on the target ahead and prayed for the strength to get us there.

As we approached the shimmering door hanging in the air, I grabbed Gren's hand, the packet from Mari pressed between our palms. The fear-eater's horrifying touch wrapped around one ankle. I looked down to see the fiery crevice beneath us, widening too quickly to escape. At that moment, I knew we wouldn't make it.

"Gren!" I screamed, having no idea what I was asking him. But he didn't need the words to act. He threw himself at Monty and me, and his enormous wings throbbed against the air. We left the ground just before hitting the shimmering portal and slammed through it with molten rock still nipping at our heels.

25

ALL THINGS ARE RIGHT. ALL THINGS ARE GOOD. JUST GIVE THE PIXIE A LITTLE BLOOD

We landed inside the queen's pavilion in Fairy.

The stark change between the horror we'd left behind and the terrible sight before us was startling enough to turn both Gren and me mute.

Even Monty was struck momentarily dumb. Then he spotted his favorite fairy and gave a happy bark, his tail whacking my back in an exuberant greeting.

"Maybe you could have cut it a little closer," said fairy complained.

I raised my brows at Trish. "Maybe you could have given me more information."

Trish sighed. "As you can see, things have gotten a bit more difficult here."

I looked out over the crowd, which might have included every fairy in the queendom. To the last one, every face was hostile, every jaw tight. The fae who were dressed in the garb of the queen's soldiers all suddenly looked as if they were going to charge. Though I wasn't exactly sure who they were going to charge against.

The crowd was arrayed against the small group of fairies near the pavilion. Trish stood facing the queen, the blade of one of Das' soldiers against her throat. Several feet away and facing the crowd, the queen stood stiffly, her hands behind her back and clamped into what I could only assume were iron-infused cuffs since she hadn't blasted free of them yet. The soldiers around the queen, surprisingly, seemed more like jailers than loyal staff.

"What's going on?" I asked, feeling silly as soon as the question left my lips. It was pretty obvious what was happening. Except for the part where both sides of the tableau represented by Trish and Das seemed to be prisoners. If I could believe their antagonistic expressions and aggressive postures, they were hostile to each other. Was there a third party trying to take over fairy?

A pixie buzzed up from the crowd and flew toward me, leaving a pretty trail of pixie dust in her wake. Mari rose up to eye height in front of me and gave me a pretty curtsy. "Madam Lares."

"Mari. Can you tell me what's going on?"

"You have no business here!" the queen shouted. She tried to turn around to look at me, but the soldier closest to her lifted his sword in warning, and she stopped. "Fairy is outside your jurisdiction," she growled.

I didn't respond because I wanted to know what was happening first. "Mari?"

The pixie sighed. "Queen Das has been overthrown. She is a prisoner. But we have a problem because Fairy cannot be without a queen."

"Has no one stepped forward?" Gren asked.

"Trish has offered to serve as temporary queen until a more suitable candidate comes forward."

I winced, my gaze flying to my friend and council member. Trish's expression remained neutral. But her posture was stiff. She lifted her chin slightly, appearing to be braced against my reaction. I struggled for a beat with the facts of the situation, not sure what my reaction should be. If it was up to me, I'd ask Trish to come back to Rome. But it wasn't up to me. Das was wrong about many things. But she was right about Fairy. It wasn't within my jurisdiction.

"Okay. Then, what's the problem?" I asked.

Mari sighed again. "Since you are the Lares for the physical area where Fairy is currently located, you are the closest thing to a queen we have."

My back stiffened. I didn't like where Mari's words were taking me.

Mari didn't seem to notice. She went on. "There

are many in Fairy who won't accept a commoner for a queen, temporary or not."

I glanced at Trish again, realizing her stiffness had more than one cause. Anger swirled through me on her behalf.

Gren gently touched my back in warning. His unspoken message was clear. I shouldn't take the customs and eccentricities of Fairy personally. I wasn't fae and didn't understand the way they thought. That wasn't my job.

"I am not fae," I said loudly, stating something I was sure was already foremost in their thoughts. "What do you need from me?"

"They need you to sponsor me," Trish said.

I frowned. "Sponsor?"

"You must sign an agreement, secured by blood, that if Ancient Warrior Tricia of the Northern Fae fails Fairy in her endeavors or creates a hostile or unsuccessful environment, you will personally replace her as temporary queen of Fairy," Mari said without emotion.

"She has no right!" Das spat out. She wrenched away from the soldier holding her, his blade slicing neatly across her throat in a shallow wound. She turned to me, venom in her eyes. "You are an interloper. Your kind is as cattle to the fae — a subspecies without intelligence or value. How dare you presume to rule in a fae realm?"

Monty growled softly, his little body stiff in my arms.

The queen's magic tried to escape, rising up in an aura of sputtering light, and then died under the quelling influence of the cuffs.

I stared at her for a long moment, considering whether to bother with a response. In the end, I decided my time would be better spent elsewhere. I swung my gaze to Trish and saw many things in her expression. Regret. Determination. Fear.

At that moment, my respect for her blossomed into something that humbled me. "People of Fairy, you have chosen your new leader wisely. She is a woman of strength and honor. I consider her a friend and a valuable ally. During the time she sits upon this throne, you will have an ally in me as well." I turned back to Mari. "What do you need me to do?"

Twenty minutes later, as Gren and I drooped wearily against a pillar of the pavilion, listening to my stomach growl, Mari finally nodded for me to come forward. Trish stood near the throne, her gaze following me as I approached. On an impulse, I pulled her into a hug. "Are you sure about this?"

"I'm sure I need to do it. I'd be lying if I said I

wanted to be the queen of Fairy. But, if I don't do it..."

"They'll reinstate Das," I finished, finally understanding the imperatives Trish was working under.

"I prefer to live outside Fairy," Trish said, her vivid green eyes glistening with unshed tears. "But these are my people. I can't abandon them."

I nodded, trying not to think of all the renovations still needing to be done at my house. Those were selfish thoughts, and I wasn't proud of them.

"Don't worry," Trish told me, smiling. "Luke can finish the work at your church. He's good at almost everything still needing to be done. And what he can't do himself, he knows who to call to do it."

I nodded, relieved and a little embarrassed that she'd read my thoughts so easily. "I'm going to miss you," I told her.

"All of us will," Gren agreed.

Trish finally let the tears fall. "It won't be forever. And, unlike under Das, you'll be welcome in Fairy anytime."

I could live with that.

Trish gave me a sly grin. "By the way, thank you for the muffin. I savored every crumb. And I'll expect many more of those while I'm here. They will be the cost of an audience with the queen."

"Deal," I said, grinning back.

"Shall we get started?" Mari asked.

I nodded. "Where do you need me?"

She pointed to the throne. I tensed. "Um..."

"It's fine," Trish said. "You're only the sponsor. I promise."

I reluctantly lowered myself into the strange chair. Mari buzzed away and buzzed back with Das' coronet, placing it on Trish's head. The crown was a pretty affair, made of twisted vines covered in jewels and beads of gold. As it settled onto Trish's fine blonde hair, tiny white flowers burst from the vines, exuding a delightful scent.

I grinned at her. "You look good in a crown."

She shook her head, though I could tell she was secretly pleased.

"Queen Trish," Mari said. "Place your hand on the arm of the throne."

Trish did as requested.

"Sponsor Agnes Madam Lares of Rome, place your hand over Trish's."

I followed orders, giving Trish's cold, trembling hand a squeeze.

"I need a blade!" Mari suddenly screamed out to the crowd.

Gren stepped forward. "Madam Pixie," he said as he handed one of his knives over, hilt first.

The knife shrank as her tiny fingers touched it, fitting itself to her grip.

"Nice trick," I whispered to Gren. He dropped a warm hand on my shoulder and gave it an encouraging squeeze before stepping away.

"Now, repeat after me," Mari said, holding the blade over our hands. "I, Agnes Madam Lares of Rome, do solemnly swear to sponsor Ancient Warrior Tricia of the Northern Fae."

As I repeated the words, I gave Trish wide eyes and thought, *Are we getting married?*

Trish giggled softly.

Glaring at us, Mari turned to Trish. "Repeat after me. I, Ancient Warrior Tricia of the Northern Fae, do solemnly swear to accept the sponsorship of Agnes Madam Lares of Rome. I hereby also swear to do my utmost to keep the people of Fairy safe and to enhance the prospects of one and all to my best abilities until another queen is sworn."

Trish repeated Mari's words. As she spoke, a gossamer silver thread rose from between the floorboards and twined around our clasped hands, forming a magical bond.

"The pledge has been made," Mari said, avoiding our gazes. "We will seal the bond with a small amount of blood."

I took a deep breath. I could stand a tiny prick of pain in one finger. It was no big dea....

Mari stabbed the tiny blade downward into our clasped hands, connecting us like so much shish-kabob.

There was a shocked beat of silence as Trish and I shared a look, and then the shrieking started.

I held my hand against my chest and closed my eyes, so tired that I could barely keep them open. Unfortunately, every time I closed them, I relived the shock and agony of being speared like a club sandwich with an extra-large toothpick.

"Is your hand still aching?" Gren asked, handing me a glass of water.

We'd come home to a raucous welcoming party and lots of questions. By the time we'd satisfied everybody's curiosity, I was dead on my feet.

It could have had something to do with the massive portion of spaghetti and meatballs I'd downed like a person who'd been stranded on a desert island for a month without food.

My council filled me in on Rome and the surrounding area. It seemed that everything returned to normal as soon as the Trickster was yanked out of the human realm. All lingering evidence of the wizrooms was gone. I was happy to report that I was no longer the purple people eater, and Becca had no polka dots. Wanda checked on her personally.

Mrs. Twimblee was home with Rufus. And there were happily no pregnant men in Rome.

Thank the goddess.

Cats and dogs and squirrels no longer spoke languages that were foreign to them. Buildings were where they were supposed to be. And cemeteries had reappeared everywhere, including my own. According to Davis, there had been no more ghost sightings in town. Hopefully, that was the end of that too.

Alas, there'd been no sign of Reverend Dodson when I'd visited my little graveyard earlier in the evening. I really needed to do something about that soon.

Happily, Tilly was still using my kitchen and shop to do business. I wasn't in a hurry to cast her out. If the repairs on her shop took a year, I'd be fat and happy. Emphasis on fat, unfortunately.

I was not pleased about losing Trish for the near future, but I was confident she'd return to us eventually. And having an ally in Fairy would be a very good thing.

Everyone else on my council was healthy and, for the moment, safe. Monty was sprawled on the floor next to the couch, snoring softly.

For my crew and me, that was as good an ending as we could expect.

Except for one small thing. My angel and I had unfinished business that needed to be addressed. He'd promised he wanted to get to know me better after the Trickster thing was done. I planned to hold him to that promise. Starting immediately, since we were uncustomarily alone in the house.

Gren had shooed everyone out after dinner,

including Wanda, who'd been invited to a sleepover with one of her new girlfriends from school.

I smiled at the thought. My little girl was growing up.

"A penny for your thoughts?" Gren said, his hand warm against my thigh.

I sipped my water. "It's just nice being home."

He nodded. "I should get going. You need your rest."

"What I need is to get my head examined for not asking more questions about the *small amount of blood* thing."

Gren fought a grin.

I narrowed my eyes at him. "You think this is funny?" I held up my bandaged hand, which had been totally restored by the fae healer five minutes after the spearing, but which somehow still hurt.

"A good night's sleep will make it better," Gren said, taking my hand into his own and turning it over to kiss the palm. "Better?"

I took a deep breath and released it on a frown. "Almost. Maybe you should try again."

He nodded. "Where?"

I pointed to my wrist. "Higher."

He laid a soft, lingering kiss on the inside of my wrist. My body warmed delightfully at the touch. "Better?"

I forced myself to frown again. "Maybe a little higher."

He complied, happily moving to the crook of my arm, the most exquisitely sensitive of spots. "How's that?"

I sighed, shaking my head. Fighting a grin, I touched my shoulder. "I'm pretty sure it will be better if you kiss it here." He didn't hesitate. His warm lips branded me on the bare skin of my shoulder, and I thanked the goddess for the delightful invention of the spaghetti-strapped cami.

When he lifted his head, his lips were mere inches from mine. "Did I get it?"

I shook my head again, my entire body feeling like molten metal. I pointed to my lips.

His mouth covered mine, claiming it in a perfectly ravenous kiss. My angel had been holding back. What a delicious discovery.

I turned to him, wrapping my arms around his neck and showing him that I'd been holding back too.

The kiss heated. Passion that had been banked and restrained for too long broke its tether and slid over us in a heated, sensual wave. I didn't even notice when my back hit the cushions. But I did notice the delectable weight of his body over mine.

I noticed that my body was on fire in a delicious way that I never wanted to stop.

As if he'd heard my thoughts and was channeling the Trickster. Gren lifted his head. "I need to go."

I barely bit back a cry. "You don't have to."

He rested his forehead against mine. "You need to rest. You're dead on your feet."

I nodded regretfully. "I know. But every time I close my eyes, I remember getting brutally stabbed."

His lips twitched. "Brutally, huh?"

I nodded, placing a feather-soft kiss on his throat, right beneath a perfect ear. He shivered under the touch, his dark hair tickling my face.

"It would be cruel of me to make you relive that horrific stabbing."

I nodded. "Right? I really need a distraction."

A low sound of pure male satisfaction rumbled from his chest. "I think I have just the thing for that."

I let my pleasure sparkle in my gaze. "You do?"

Always a man of few words when action was required, Gren just smiled. The sight twisted delightfully in my belly as he lowered his lips to mine. Then he proceeded to distract me...thoroughly.

And what a delightful distraction it was.

The End

DON'T MISS OUT

Stay up on all Sam's news by joining her newsletter, and get a copy of a fun mystery just for signing up!

SIGN UP HERE!
https://samcheever.com/newsletter/

READ MORE MATURE MAGIC

If you enjoyed **What Trickery Is This?** you might want to check out the rest of the series: https://samcheever.com/books/#maturemagic

Enjoy this taste of Book 5 What Spookery Is That?:

I'm trying to find my missing Council member, which might involve visiting the spectral plane. Something that I'm strangely not looking forward to. (sarc) The last thing I need is this...this mess. Achieving my full powers feels like mega-menopause, hot flashes and all. Unfortunately, these flashes can actually burn.

Something's changing. Something big. I'm finally achieving the last stage of my Lares power. I realize the transformation is going to be hard. It's going to be painful and confusing. I know all of this because my advocate, the world's crankiest moon hound and consummate know-it-all was elated to inform me about it. What I didn't know was that I'd be trying to save one of my council members and beat off a demon invasion in the middle of the whole mess. Unfortunately, this is all starting to remind me of my initiation into the Lares gig. I barely survived that transition. I'm not so sure I'm going to survive this one.

WHAT SPOOKERY IS THAT?

The moon was blue. It hung over us like a threat, so big and so close I imagined I could feel the touch of its rays against my skin.

My hot, sweaty skin.

Ten feet away, Wanda and Caleigh, otherwise known as the crone, had their heads bent over a grimoire they'd opened in the thick, overlong grass of the graveyard. I'd been informed by my groundskeeper, the gnome, that the grass would go into shock and falter if he cut it so late in the season.

I didn't know about any of that. I just wished it wasn't drenching my sneakers. Blowing air through my lips, I felt instantly shamed. I was a sweaty, cranky mess. I knew my mood was bad, but didn't seem able to do anything about it. I was facing the last stage in becoming a full-fledged Lares, a guardian protector for Rome, Indiana. The process encompassed four levels of acclimation: Understanding, Acceptance, Outreach, and Response. I was working my way through *Response*, and, as far as I could tell, it seemed way too much like menopause.

Just delightful.

I tugged the damp t-shirt away from my chest and sighed as a wisp of cool air slipped beneath it. Impatience rippled under my skin. I bit it back, knowing its source. I'd been impossible to live with for a month. Maybe longer. Really, since my friend and council member, Trish had left us to manage the fairy realm.

With Reverend Dodson also missing, I was feeling out of sorts and scattered.

That was what I blamed it on, at least. But I had a notion that wasn't really the cause.

I had bigger problems.

Wanda broke away from the crone and ambled toward me, her long legs eating up the distance between us and her hands shoved into the pockets of her fashionably ratty jeans. I took a moment to enjoy watching her move. She'd grown a couple of inches since she'd moved in with me. Filled out a little. And her dark brown eyes sparkled with humor and pleasure more often than not. She reminded me of a colt whose legs had grown too fast and she wasn't always sure what to do with them.

I smiled at the thought.

A large black cat trotted after my kid, long tail

lazily fanning the air. Wraith fixed me with round, yellow eyes and licked his chops as if wondering if I'd taste like chicken.

The teen stopped in front of me, tucked a heavy strand of straight black hair behind one pierced ear, and frowned. "Aggy, it's sixty degrees out here. Are you sure you don't want your coat?"

I shook my head. The temperature of the air might be sixty degrees, but I might as well be standing on the crust of a volcano judging by my internal temperature. "I'm fine, sweetie. Did you figure it out?"

She narrowed her gaze for a beat. "Are you feeling all right?"

My entire body went rigid with irritation. I tried to hide it, hoping Wanda wouldn't notice. Everybody kept asking me that question and I was getting sick of answering it.

Taking a long slow breath, I forced a smile. "I'm okay." When she started to frown, I reached out and touched the sleeve of her coat. "I promise."

She expelled air. "Okay. Well. We think we know where he has to be." Her gaze slid toward the woods and her frown deepened.

At the back of the wide lawn, galloping from the woods at full speed, the White Mare thundered toward us. Normally, the sight would alarm me. It usually meant trouble. But I knew from my own experience that the magical horse was simply reacting to the magical influences caused by the thinning veil.

The blue moon. I'd been told by the white-haired woman crouched a few feet away that the veil was at its absolute thinnest during a blue moon. I could feel the truth in her statement. Magic danced along my skin, pulling up gooseflesh in its wake.

The crone was wearing faded stretch jeans, bright red sneakers, and a tee-shirt that read "Dachshunds Aren't Dogs. They're Necessities. Like Potato Chips and Wine."

That sentiment wasn't wrong. My own little necessity was in the house playing with the crone's two sweet girls. I could hear their happy yips all the way from the house.

"How much time do we have?" I asked the teen.

Wanda turned around and bellowed. "Caleigh? What's the timeline?"

I tensed every time the girl called the crone by her given name. Something told me the powerful witch slash magical historian didn't allow such intimacies easily or often. But the crone simply pushed herself out of a crouch and started toward us, her gnarled fingers wiggling as if she were mentally doing a math problem.

Or a spell. At five feet six inches tall, the crone was my height and slightly stooped from her unknown but decidedly advanced age. Her abundance of white hair blasted straight up from her scalp, rolled into a soft lift at the crown, and then plummeted straight down to skim the tops of her flat butt cheeks. Her eyes were her best feature. They were a beautiful ocean blue, touched with green and silver specks that made them always seem to dance with humor.

"Eight hours," she finally said. "In and out. If you're not out by then, you're stayin' there."

Ignoring Wanda's worried gaze, I asked, "Where exactly am I going?" I really didn't want to know... but I needed to.

To say I wasn't excited about ducking into the spirit realm to rescue my missing ghostly council member would be a massive understatement. I'd grown accustomed to the ghosts who haunted the little church graveyard and had considered Reverend Dodson a friend. But my advisor, the ever-snotty moon-hound shifter, Sir Ferral of the Guardian Assembly, a.k.a. my advocate, informed me that the spirits in the spiritual realm were generally a nasty bunch. It appeared the closer they got to the heart of spookdom, the meaner a spirit became. He'd also delighted in informing me that the kind and benevolent Reverend Dodson might not even know who I was if he'd gone too deep, which would make him a solid "them" in the "us vs them" column.

Swear.

Since it was Ferral's job to keep me informed and up-to-date on all the weird stuff my new role as

Lares guardian for the tiny town of Rome, Indiana threw at me, I trusted him.

He was generally an arrogant as...um...jerk, but he did know his stuff.

"I don't suppose you can tell by all that..." I swirled a finger in the general direction of the open grimoire. "...magic stuff, where the Rev is and if he's gone mutant on us?"

The crone glared at me from her mostly unlined face. The only signs of age on her face were a sunburst of "laugh lines" at the corners of her eyes, badly misnamed in her case, and the area around her mouth, which was heavily lined, probably because she had a bad habit of pursing her lips as she was currently doing, making her mouth resemble an anus. I squelched a smile at the thought. "I'm not a magical GPS, Lares. Nor am I a mystical mood ring."

Wanda snorted before catching a look from me that turned her expression neutral.

"What I *can* tell you is that you're going to be fighting for your life in there." She frowned, a smidgeon of warmth taking some of the coolness from her blue eyes. "Are you sure you want to go in there alone, girl? There's a reason you have a council, you know."

Wanda nodded enthusiastically. "Let me go with you," she said, her tight expression revealing the full extent of her concern.

I shook my head. "I need to go it alone," I said, my gut twisting at the thought.

"Who says?" barked the crone, sounding like an angry kid on the playground. "Is it written in the stars?"

I narrowed my eyes at her mockery. Even if I'd wanted to, I couldn't tell her why I felt an immutable need to enter the spiritual realm alone. I couldn't tell her because I didn't understand it myself. So, instead of responding to her question, I asked a new one of my own. "When do I need to go in?"

The crone held my gaze for a long moment. I got the sense she was considering pressing for a response to her question, but she broke eye contact before I did—go me—and shook her head. "Before the moon falls from the sky."

Then she turned on her heels and headed for the White Mare, who was waiting patiently for her near the house. The crone gave a shrill whistle and the door to my house swung open, seemingly without any help. Two little female dachshunds ran barking out of the house, my little darling, Monty, hot on their heels.

"Oh no you don't," I said, reaching out to snag him as he ran past. "The girls are going home, and you're staying here."

He barked enthusiastically in my arms, his happy brown gaze following them into the forest bordering my property. As they disappeared from sight, he sagged, whining unhappily.

I kissed him between his sad eyes. "Sorry, little man. We'll have another play date soon."

He lay his glossy head on my shoulder and sighed.

Wanda giggled. "You've broken him."

I grinned, bumping her shoulder as we fell into step, heading for the house. High above us, a dark shape fluttered against the night sky and yellow eyes shone through the darkness. I settled Monty's feet into the grass and he took off running toward the house, racing Wanda.

Watching them go, I smiled.

The spirit realm is restless.

I glanced up at the bat, which darted to and fro, chasing bugs that should have already been gone at that time of year. "I'm going in soon."

When?

"Early tomorrow morning."

The bat fluttered up to the belfry high above my head. I glanced up as moonlight painted a ribbon of light across its midnight-hued wings.

He's deep into the spiritual realm, Batty told me. *It's not going to be easy to get him out.*

I opened my mouth to respond as agony tightened through my middle, and I doubled over, a scream throbbing in my throat.

Wings fluttered overhead and a raven cawed

three times. A beat later, the door to the house slammed open and I heard Wanda calling my name.

Footsteps pounded toward me. Wanda's small hands, nails painted bright pink, grabbed my shoulders and eased me backward onto the grass. I sat down hard as another wave of misery clawed through me. Riding the wave were hundreds of voices, pleading for help, for advice, or just to be heard. It was overwhelming, impossible, and I fought to shut it down because it felt like the pleas were tearing me apart.

Soft hands pushed strands of silver-tipped black hair off my face and told me to take slow, careful breaths.

The jagged claws of pain eased slowly away and I was finally able to breathe.

A raven cawed again, closer than before. The big black bird dropped to the grass beside me and began to pace, its wings lifting and lowering with apparent stress. "Pee!" the raven announced enthusiastically.

I laughed, wincing as my stomach tightened around the pain. "Yeah, I almost peed myself too."

The raven ducked its head a few times and then, with a final caw, took to the air and flew away.

Wanda sat down next to me. "Is it getting better?"

I nodded, one hand rubbing my stomach where the pain had been.

"Aggy, you can't go into the spiritual realm by

yourself. What if you have an attack and nobody's there to help you?"

The "attack" she referred to was a side-effect of my body reaching for the final level of power inherent in my Lares magic. As my advocate, Ferral, had explained, the last phase included an elevated ability to mentally communicate as well as the ability to fix things without physically being present. The transformation required a full physiological overhaul that was extensive and painful.

I'd reached the third level several months earlier, but ascending to the last one had been slow in coming.

Judging by the pain of reaching it, I'd be okay if it took its sweet time. Or never came at all.

"I'm going to talk to Ferral about someone coming with you."

I shook my head. "No."

Wanda frowned, clearly annoyed that I wouldn't listen to reason...her reason, which, as a teen, she believed was the only reason there should be. I knew she didn't understand why I'd been digging in my heels. But I couldn't explain the feeling that I wouldn't need anybody to come with me. That I'd have everything I needed to accomplish my task when I crossed into spirit realm.

Besides, I had a burning need to prove myself worthy of attaining the fourth level of magic. Since taking over the Lares job, I'd been plagued by feelings of inadequacy and self-doubt. I couldn't shake the feeling that the magic had been given to the wrong person. Despite the fact that my own father, who for all intents and purposes had abandoned me when I was fifteen, was also a Lares, I couldn't get past the fact that I hadn't even known magic existed until I was already ankle deep in my seating, the hellish process I'd gone through to become Lares.

Andrew Lenore had left my mother and me behind to pursue his own guardianship. The scars of that rejection still stung, even thirty years later.

A new tightness began to build in my gut. Seconds before the wave of jagged pain hit me again, cold, oily sweat broke out on my forehead and trickled between my shoulder blades.

I took a deep breath and clenched my teeth against the building pain.

I had no idea how I was going to rescue Reverend Dodson from the spiritual realm in my current condition.

But somehow, I had to do it.

ABOUT THE AUTHOR

USA Today and Wall Street Journal Bestselling Author Sam Cheever writes mystery and suspense, creating stories that draw you in and keep you eagerly turning pages. Known for writing great characters, snappy dialogue, and unique and exhilarating stories, Sam is the award-winning author of 100+ books.

To learn more about Sam and her work, visit her at one of her online hotspots:
www.samcheever.com
samcheever@samcheever.com

ALSO BY SAM CHEEVER

If you enjoyed **What Trickery is This?**, you might also enjoy these other fun mystery series by Sam. To find out more, visit the **BOOKS** page at www.samcheever.com:

Mature Magic Paranormal Women's Fiction

(for more fun adventures with Aggy and Monty!)

Enchanting Inquiries Paranormal Cozy Mysteries

Yesterday's Paranormal Mysteries

Reluctant Familiar Paranormal Mysteries

Country Cousin Mysteries

Silver Hills Cozy Mysteries

Gainfully Employed Mysteries

Honeybun Heat Series